ELECTED

Rori Shay

Elected
Copyright © 2012, Rori Shay

Cover art by Suzannah Safi
Book design by Kelli Neier

Publisher's Note:
This book is a work of fiction. Names, characters, places, and incidents either are products of the author's imagination or are used fictitiously. Any resemblance to actual persons, living or dead, events, or locales is entirely coincidental.

First publication, 2014
ISBN-10: 0989676846
ISBN-13: 978-0-9896768-4-7

Silence in the Library Publishing, LLC
Washington, D.C., United States of America

www.silenceinthelibrarypublishing.com

Contents

To Mom and Dad, who read to me every night as I grew up.
To Jason, who knows how to read me.
And to my girls, who allow me the fun of reading to them.

1

ONE BLONDE CURL IS wrapped lusciously around my pointer finger. I gaze down at it and then force my eyes upward to drink in the image of my face. Long, blonde hair trails past my shoulders and onto my back. In the cracked mirror, my eyes squint, trying to capture this one fleeting picture of myself as a girl.

This is what I could look like if I weren't forced to masquerade as a boy.

I am staring so intently into the mirror I don't even hear my mother—my Ama—come into the room behind me.

"Take that off immediately!" Her voice is tight and stiff, like rubber being stretched too far, about to snap. "Can you imagine the controversy it would stir?" She whisks the blonde wig off my head and bunches it into a ball. Before I can say anything, she throws it into the fireplace in my room.

I look at my fingers, the ones that a moment ago delicately touched the wig like it was my own hair. "Sorry, Ama," I say, head bent downward. "I was just looking." My voice comes out gravelly like a dull knife coaxing butter across a dry piece of toast. I lick my lips and let a few beads of cold perspiration appear on my forehead without bothering to wipe them away.

My mother comes to stand behind me, peering into the shards of mirror in front of us both. She lays a hand on my fuzzy head. I try to imagine my dark blonde hair grown out, looking like the wig. But all I can see in front of me now are the short tufts my parents insist get trimmed every other week.

"My darling, your eighteenth birthday is coming so fast. Just two more weeks." I look up into her wistful, worried eyes as she tries to smile back at me. "You're going to be a powerful leader. I know it."

I'm not as sure as she pretends to be. I've been training to be the Elected all my life, but now that it's two weeks away, the worry makes me feel like I've eaten moldy bread.

I want to tell her my concerns. How I'm not sure I'll like Vienne, the girl I'm set to marry. How I don't think I'll be able to convince everyone Vienne is pregnant with my baby when it's utterly and physically impossible. How I wish the real future leader hadn't run away from the job, leaving it solely in my incapable hands. It's almost laughable how many ruses we'll have to pull over on our own people for me and my family to stay in power.

But I don't have time to voice any of these thoughts because there's a sharp knock at the bedroom door.

"Come," my mother commands. Her tone is authoritative, as it should be in her position as Madame Elected.

The door opens, and a maid with a bob of shoulder-length red hair steps inside the room. I can't help but stare at her, wishing my life was easy like hers—that I could be who I really am, instead of playing a part constructed for me. The girl is beautiful. I don't even know if I could be that beautiful, but one day I'd like to at least have the opportunity to see. For now, I shudder, remembering the ragged, short hair on my head and the men's clothing, which doesn't sit quite right on my curving waist.

"Ma'am, it's time for Aloy's lessons."

I stand up without having to be told. I actually like my lessons. Tomlin's been my tutor since before I can remember.

The maid leads me into the hallway, down a flight of stairs, and into a room once called the Oval Office. Tomlin is already sitting on the large, reddish couch near the fire. It's particularly chilly this time of year. I know August has grown colder since I was a child. Thoughtfully, someone has already laid a stack of blankets on the side of another couch, and I grab one for my shoulders before I sit. It smells like moth balls and bleach, but I wrap it around myself anyway.

"Are you well today, Aloy?" Tomlin asks, not even looking up from a book open on his lap.

"I'm fine. And you?"

"A bit cold lately, isn't it? I can't seem to shake the sniffles."

I look at Tomlin carefully and see the tint of blue shadows under his eyes.

"Have you called anyone to look at your cold?" My eyebrows rise with concern.

"No, I don't have time for the bother of it."

I know what he means. There's a serum stored in our house. The stuff will practically erase all traces of a malady the second you swallow one of the little pills infused with the serum. We have bottles upon bottles of it. However, because we don't have the ability to manufacture any more, the serum is guarded behind vaults, and only the Elected family is allowed to take any of it. No one is even worried I'll catch Tomlin's cold because I can easily be given one of these purple pills to cure myself. It's a waste really. But for Tomlin, a cold in August weather can mean months of coughing, sneezing, and sore throats. Unfortunately, there's nothing our doctors can do for him. So I understand why Tomlin doesn't want to bother seeing a doctor.

"We just have two more weeks until you're in office," he says, getting right to it.

"And just two more weeks till I'm married." My voice carries a distinct crack.

Tomlin looks me in the eyes for the first time, his brow furrowed. "Are you backing out?"

I purse my lips and smile, finally able to lose the formality I'd held around my mother. "No, don't worry. I'm still planning to be the Elected."

After all these years, I think they still worry I'll run away from my birthright, not wanting the responsibility and the farce, which goes along with it. But it's my duty to family and country. It's what I was born for. So while I may be reluctant, I'm still committed.

"Well, good." Tomlin relaxes a bit back into the couch. "Political history seems like a good starting point for today, given the upcoming events, don't you think?" He goes on, not expecting an answer from me. "So tell me, what was the year of the Elected Accords?"

I answer immediately. "Twenty-one fifteen. Too easy. Give me another."

He smiles. "All right, what countries signed the Elected Accord in twenty-one fifteen and why?"

This is a trick question, but I know this one too. "All of the ones still left."

"Go on. What kind of stability is provided by the Elected Accord?"

"Voters choose a whole family to take each country's Elected office

9

for a century at a time. Which means more stability and less chance of a new official negating any of the Accords."

"Very good. All right, what was the last Accord enacted by the countries?"

I stop for a second. "The Technology Accord?"

"No, you continually get that wrong. It was the Ship Accord." Tomlin doesn't look in my direction as he delivers this slight admonishment, like somehow my error signifies a foreboding, more significant ramification. He shifts in his seat with an uncomfortable tic of one shoulder.

I always get it wrong because I don't understand why the Technology Accord didn't fulfill its designated purpose. It was supposed to make all the fighting—all the world wars—stop. If people couldn't fire guns, fly missiles, or hurl bombs across oceans, then fighting should have ceased. My brow creases and Tomlin shakes his head.

"The Technology Accord banned creation of technology for two distinct reasons," Tomlin continues. "One, so we wouldn't keep destroying the environment, and two, so countries would become isolated from one another. It should have forced peace. Yet, people still rode ships through the oceans to reach distant lands and fight in hand-to-hand combat. The Ship Accord finally stopped world travel and communication as a whole."

I see my opportunity to ask the very thing that's been on the tip of my tongue for months. Something I know my parents won't answer but that Tomlin might—if for no other reason than to further my education. "The Ship Accord didn't stop everyone, though." I know I'm bringing up something painful.

"You're right." Tomlin looks down.

"My brother." I lean forward in my chair, expectant for some new tidbit of information from Tomlin. "What happened to him?" I am unwavering with my request for information on Evan.

"We don't know." Tomlin's sadness is apparent.

"You were his tutor, right? What was he like? Would he have made a better Elected than me?" I've always wondered if Evan would have been better suited for the role than I. I know the answer must be yes since he was the true Elected, the only male heir of the family. Only men are allowed to be the Elected since women must focus on repopulation. But my parents and Tomlin encourage me to have more confidence. They have to, I guess, since they have no other choice. I'm their only option left.

I know Tomlin doesn't enjoy talking about my brother. No one does. Evan was everyone's pride and joy until he ran away. But I never knew him at all. My parents had me as a hurried attempt for another child after Evan disappeared.

I keep pressing Tomlin for other information, knowing I won't get an answer about Evan's character. "How does everyone know Evan escaped via boat? How did he even find a ship to get away? I thought my grandfather destroyed all of them." I see Tomlin cringe at my word 'escaped', and I chide myself that I've yet again made the Elected role sound like a prison sentence.

"As far as anyone knew, they were all dismantled, the parts used for building materials." Tomlin rakes a hand through the thin wisps of his hair.

"So how'd Evan get one?" I am relentless. "And how'd he get it past Apa?" I can't imagine how Evan managed to plan such an elaborate departure under my father's tight scrutiny.

"Enough." Tomlin's tone is harsh but quiet. I know he can't be budged when he doesn't want to proceed. "We need to keep going with your studies. The public will expect you to be well-trained when you take office."

"Okay, just one more question?" I ask, looking at my fingernails. They are perfect half-moons except for the two pinkies on whose nails I obsessively gnaw. As I get nearer to the date of my inauguration, the two nails seem to get shorter and shorter.

"One more, then we go on. But it must do with the Accords."

"It does. Sort of. What do other countries do with people who make it through the sea to their lands?"

I can't look at Tomlin while I wait for the answer. It's something I already know in my heart, but I want to hear it out loud.

Finally, Tomlin answers, his voice a mere whisper. "What would we do?"

I stretch my palm out so I'm playing with my fingers instead of concentrating fully on my own words. I almost don't want to hear them—don't want to hear what might have happened to Evan.

"We use hemlock."

2

As IF IT WERE timed perfectly, there's a knock at the door. Before we can call out to approve the person's entrance, the door opens wide.

"Apa!" I exclaim.

"Tomlin. Aloy. A new day to you both."

My father nods his head in each of our directions and gives us the greeting of our time. "A new day" signifies the importance of each new sunrise. After the eco-crisis, any day the sun came up was seen as a gift.

"I've come to pick up Aloy."

My father, the Elected, has come to get me? Apa almost never summons me himself. A maid usually collects me and leads me to the next scheduled activity. I see Apa and Tomlin exchange a look, and I don't understand its meaning. I waste no time in asking, "Where are we going?"

"It's time for you to see, firsthand, what your new position will entail."

I get up from the couch, throwing the blanket onto the floor in a pile. I'm always excited to watch my father fulfill the duties of his office. I need all the practice I can get before my own time comes. There's a difference between hearing what Apa does and seeing, in person, how my father rules East Country.

I glance back at Tomlin, but his head is buried in the book, looking down. It's like he doesn't want to meet my eyes before I leave. I don't make it easy for him.

"Bye! I'm off to see Apa in action!" I slap Tomlin hard on the shoulder in a manly gesture before remembering he's sick. He winces and chokes out a few long coughs. Instinctively, my nurturing side takes

13

over, and I'm beside him again with an arm around his torso, propping him up while he wheezes.

"I'm so sorry!" I gasp.

Instead of granting me forgiveness, Tomlin launches into a reminder I've heard way too often.

"No, just walk away. Men don't come back and hug. Go."

He is short with me, as he's tried to teach me again and again how to appear masculine. He and my parents insist that I overcompensate just so there won't be any questions about my gender. I can see Tomlin's still in some pain, so I let it go.

"All right. I'll see you soon then." I get up quickly and follow my father who is already standing in the doorway, waiting.

"Tomlin is right," he says, as we shut the heavy door behind us. I can still hear Tomlin coughing inside, his wheezes sounding like wind crackling through dead trees. "You need to control your behavior. Especially now."

I refrain from commenting on my father's advice. I know he's right. I'm listening closely to what my parents say, more now than usual. In two short weeks, I'll have to remember everything they've taught me in the past eighteen years. I will never again get to hear the words from their own lips. This thought bothers me like none other. All other children get to keep their parents for their whole lives. Only I will lose mine, whether they're healthy or not, when I turn eighteen. It doesn't seem fair.

A tear threatens to well up in my eye, but I look toward the sky to gain composure. Men don't cry as much as women do. I've concealed many a tear over the years. In fact, any overt expression of emotion from me is simply not permitted. I must remain brusque and collected at all times.

We're outside now, and I wish I remembered to bring a jacket. The cold air causes the hairs on my arms to prickle. My father leads me out of our big, white house. The left side of it, which was once bordered by something called the Rose Garden, is still a black mass of charred wood. We've chosen not to repair that side of the house. My father says we leave it like that to remind our people how close we came to devastation, but how we triumphed in the end. The right side of the house, beautifully white, stands in stark contrast to the black, ashen left side. Sometimes I imagine I can smell smoke still billowing from the remnants.

I look wistfully back toward the lawn. I've heard from Tomlin that it used to be the richest color of green. It's now blotchy with black and brown. There are a few eager patches of grass, but even they struggle to hold on amidst the weeds, which we don't uproot. Anything green is allowed to prosper, as we cannot afford to be choosy with our plants. There are so few left.

We walk across the lawn over to a long, slate gray building adjacent to our house. I've never been inside this one, even though it's close by.

Before I can wonder what we're going to be doing together, my father says, "We keep prisoners here."

I stop in my tracks. Even though I started the conversation with Tomlin, it's like his session with me was manufactured for this exact moment. I think of my last words with my tutor. Hemlock.

My father stops and turns to look back at me. "Don't delay." His words are clipped, but there is the slightest bit of understanding in them. He is also reluctant to do this. I can see it in his eyes. "You know why this must happen, do you not?"

Unfortunately, I understand too well. It's a system I believe in. Just not one I want to witness.

I hurry forward to walk with my father. Who knows how many of these he's overseen? Soon they'll be mine, alone, to witness. The responsibility sits on my shoulders like a lead weight.

How have I not known the prisoners' building is so close to where I live? It was right next door all this time, in what used to be called the Old Executive Office Building. I realize my parents and Tomlin have sheltered me against the realities of my new role until the end. Taking the Elected position is technically my choice, but I don't get the full story until it's too late.

I'm angry at them, but when I stop to think about it, reluctantly thankful at the same time. I know I would have chosen the same route either way. How could I have abandoned my family and country like Evan did? If I declined the Elected role, my family would prematurely lose power before a hundred years' time, and East Country would be thrown into disarray. So, maybe it was better all along not to know the gory details of my leadership role. In two weeks, I will be the Elected, and nothing I see now will make a difference. My commitment to the generations of my family and East Country will not be deterred by seeing hemlock wreak its havoc.

We are both steadfast in our walk up the stone steps. Each of us is resolute. Both of us walk in the same manner. I've studied my father's manly gait for years. I can now recreate it so well, I walk more like him than I do like myself.

A few guards nod to us as we cross the door into the building. My father knows the way and thus no one leads us further. After a turn down one solitary corridor, we stop in front of a wooden door. Before we go in, my father turns to me.

When he doesn't speak and merely looks at me I say, "Apa?"

He touches my shoulder almost like he cares for my feelings. "Are you ready?"

"I am." I'm firm, even now that I realize exactly what we'll be doing.

"One day soon you will have to watch one of these by yourself." He stops squeezing my shoulder. "Do not close your eyes when it happens. The accused deserves for you to see them. Lock eyes with the prisoners. Give them your full attention. Think about their lives. How precious every life is. But remember our laws. If we did not have them, there would be no life at all."

I nod. I know why my father adheres to the four Accords so fervently. They're the only things keeping our world in check. Without them, there would be chaos, and we'd be thrown back into the old times. So, even though we might not like or agree with all of the Accords' policies, we have to follow them. At least, I might not like or agree with all of them. I'm pretty sure my mother and father are believers, one hundred percent.

We cross through the wooden doorway into the prisoner's quarters. It's a room sectioned into two parts. Our side holds a wooden bench and nothing else. A thick piece of glass separates our side from the one housing the prisoner. The accused seems to be in his forties, relatively old for our country. I look over at my father, who answers my question without being asked.

"His crime is invention. He was trying to manufacture a battery."

The accused sits on the small cot in his room. There's a large potted plant in the corner—a rarity for us. We try to provide a few luxuries in this small space. We try to make it nice for people's last days.

The prisoner's eyes are downcast, but then he suddenly leaps up. He moves toward the glass separating us. I can't hear what he's yelling, but I can make out what he's mouthing anyway. He screams over and over again, "We need technology!" He beats his fists against the glass, and I instinctively lean back.

"It won't break," my father assures me. "It's from the old days. Armor glass. A piece leftover."

Even when the atomic bombs went off, this glass didn't break. So I feel confident this man won't be able to get through. We aren't able to manufacture this glass anymore, so it's all the more precious to our country. However, I do see the irony in using the glass technology enabled years ago when we outlaw technology now.

I swallow hard when I see the prisoner eventually slump back onto his cot in defeat.

"How long until he drinks it?"

"Not long. They'll bring it in now that he's settled down."

A burly guard enters the prisoner's space and hands him a crystal glass containing approximately one hundred milligrams of clear liquid. It would seem like the prisoner was just given a cup of water if I didn't know better.

I'm reminded of the many chemistry and biology sessions with Tomlin where he taught me again and again what kind of plants survived the global eco-crisis, which ones we could eat, which ones leached in atomic radiation, and which one we now use for capital punishment. The prisoner's cup holds hemlock.

Withstanding the high and low temperatures brought on by global warming, the hemlock plant hung on, its lacy white flowers torturously beautiful, but deadly if eaten in large quantities.

The prisoner lifts the cup of hemlock to his nose, breathing in lightly. The toxic component, alkaloid coniine, will give off a small scent of anise, the same kind of smell one encounters biting into black licorice. It was my favorite treat as a child. I can imagine what it smells like even though it's impossible to detect the fragrance through the glass.

The man holds the cup out in front of himself, determining his next course of action. I watch him closely, as Apa told me to keep my eyes open for the duration. It's only right to give the accused the dignity of someone witnessing his final moments. But I turn to Apa anyway, fright and curiosity getting the better of me.

"What if he refuses to drink it?"

"He won't." My father's eyes never leave the man's face even as he answers my question. "It is honorable to drink the hemlock oneself instead of it being forced into his person by the guards."

I'm horrified by the thought of having to watch the guards perform the execution themselves. In our country, capital punishment is carried out only through assisted suicide. One person killing another is against the law. In fact, I've never heard of it happening. Murder is obsolete, but it's considered honorable for people to accept government-controlled suicide if an Accord is violated.

I pray silently that during this, my first execution, I won't have to witness a killing. I pray the prisoner will drink down the liquid by himself. As I watch him studying the crystal, I secretly wish the process would go faster, that he would just tilt his head back and pour down the hemlock as quickly as possible. But then I chide myself on being so callous. This execution is not meant to be easy for me to watch. These are the man's final moments, and if I cannot offer him anything else, I can at least grant my attention and time.

After what seems like an eternity, my father squeezes my hand and says, "It is happening now. He is starting."

The prisoner rocks back and forth on the heels of his feet, preparing himself mentally for the ordeal ahead. I can only imagine what resolve it must take to drink the liquid and know it will be the last thing you do.

The prisoner looks to us one more time through the armor glass, gives a nod, and then lifts the chalice to his lips, taking a large gulp. His eyes are tightly closed. Immediately, the glass shatters upon the ground as paralysis takes over. I know through study with Tomlin—the respiratory function is at first depressed and ultimately ceases altogether. The prisoner's death will result from asphyxia. However, the man's mind will remain unaffected to the end, allowing him one more fleeting thought of his loved ones and the life he's lived.

The man falls to the floor. I can see him trying to clutch his stomach, but his arm won't lift. Vomit erupts from his mouth, puddling next to him on the ground. Saliva bubbles around his lips, mixing with the vomit in a toxic pool. He gasps deeply, trying to take in air even though it's impossible.

My head aches as I watch the demise. Soon, I see the paralysis take its final toll as the man chokes again and again. Finally, when I think I can take it no more, the prisoner is stiff and no more mess exits his nostrils or mouth. He doesn't move.

The guards enter the room. It's finished.

My father finally turns his head to look at me. "Let's take a moment so you can compose yourself before we exit."

I'm sure my father sees my face and realizes it won't be wise to show my sick pallor to the public. Our countrymen won't want to think I'm ill or even squeamish watching a prisoner die. I try as hard as I can to block out thoughts of the execution I've just witnessed. I crush my fists into my eyes to block back tears. But it's no use. The face of the prisoner gasping for breath on the floor is burned into my retinas. I don't know how to compose myself.

"Let's try a little exercise," my father says. His face is composed, as serene as a thousand granules of sand all settled back down to the ocean floor after a tidal wave. "This always helps me focus. Let's think of a few facts we know to be true. Name one fact, and then we'll build upon it."

Thinking about something else may actually help, so I blurt out the first thing I can think of based on my latest history lesson with Tomlin.

"You're the ruler of the East Country."

My father laughs lightly. "Very well. Yes, that is true. My turn." He pauses for just a moment. "And you will be the ruler in a fortnight." He waits for me to go further.

"Great-grandfather was our first Elected."

Apa answers back with another fact along the same lines. "Our family is the only line that has held the Elected positions in East Country since the Eco-Crisis Accords were established in twenty-one fifteen."

"We've been in office for seventy years."

"Very good. You will marry Vienne and start your own family."

I shudder for a moment at the sound of Vienne's name. She's the one they've been training to be my match. But I don't love her. I don't even know her. I shake my head and close my eyes, trying to eject thoughts of her from my mind. It's too much to deal with at this precise moment. Then I look up again at my father, knowing he's waiting for me to go on.

"I will rule as the Elected until my oldest son turns eighteen."

"Then you and Vienne will leave just as your mother and I are leaving, so your son can act as an independent ruler."

I pause, thinking sadly about my parents' departure, which will take place the night before I turn eighteen. We'll have the entire evening together, alone, to say our goodbyes. And then they'll ride out on horses into the wilderness. I won't know where they've gone or if they're even okay. I won't have any more contact with them. It's a silly rule. Why must I lose my parents when all other children get to keep theirs? Sometimes the thought of being the Elected and having been born into this legacy is repugnant.

But this is what my grandfather did with my father when he turned eighteen. My grandfather left East Country so my father could make his own decisions—fully come into his own. It's always been this way since our family came into office. We need the current leader to stand on his own two feet, not rely on past generations to make decisions.

My generation is well aware responsibility lies with us. Our parents won't live forever. Radiation residue causes cancer to start in the thirties to forties. But I know people used to live past one hundred before the eco-crisis. Because the Elected family gets to take the serum in the form of neat, purple pills, we don't ever feel the effects of radiation. Cancer is one of the sicknesses the purple pill eradicates. Thus, my parents are in their fifties and thriving. Other children come into their own because their parents become feeble and die. I guess I should be thankful because, in my case, I come into my own since my parents leave and nothing more.

My father knows I've deviated from our exercise, lost in thought.

"Continue along a different topic," he says. "This exercise was meant to help you compose yourself, and I made you even more upset."

It's true. A solitary tear breaks free from my left eye and runs down my cheek. My father raises a hand and wipes my tear away with one of the most tender signs of affection I think I've ever received from him.

His gesture reminds me of the final day I was allowed to feel my parents' warmth. The day I learned I'd be the Elected, all nurturing abruptly stopped.

⊬⟨••⟩⊣

I was four years old, playing with a plastic necklace on the carpet of my bedroom floor. It was December then, so the air was warm and humid. My parents and Tomlin came into my room together and I was surprised, even at that young age. I knew something important was happening if the three of them were there together. Apa sat on the edge of my bed, while my mother bent over me and picked me up into her arms. Tomlin stayed rooted in the doorway, like he was uncomfortable with the ensuing events.

"Aloy," my mother said. "Your father and I have something we need you to do."

"Yes, Ama?" I asked, my face upturned and wide open with trust.

"We need you to give up your necklace and not wear it again."

I looked stricken, eyeing the floor where the colorful beads lay discarded.

"Why, Ama? Why must I give up my necklace?"

My father bent down and took the jewelry in his hands. At this, I

20

reached out toward him, away from my mother's arms, struggling to get the beads back, if only one last time.

"Because we are telling you to," my father retorted. He put the trinket away in the folds of his light coat.

I looked toward Tomlin for help, not having received an adequate answer from my parents. "Tomlin, why can't I have my necklace?"

Tomlin shifted on his feet, still standing by the door, looking out of place. But I was insistent. Tomlin was my teacher, and he explained everything. I fully expected him to explain this too.

Tomlin didn't speak at first, but I was used to this. He was thoughtful in his responses, so I'd learned to wait for him.

After a moment passed, he said, "Do you remember how I taught you girls learn how to get pregnant and care for children and how it's the most important thing in the entire world?"

I did. I remembered the conversation clearly.

"Yes. Girls are supposed to think about how to make a baby all the time."

"Right. Well, there is one job even more important than that."

Now I was curious. I leaned forward in my mother's arms, forgetting about my necklace now tucked away with my father.

Tomlin cleared his throat awkwardly and continued, "Your father's job is the most important. Being the leader of our country, making sure everyone abides by the Accords, making sure all of the women have resources to get pregnant. That is the most important."

"Ah," I said. I idolized my father, and this just gave me more evidence he was the biggest, strongest, most important man in the world.

Tomlin looked toward my parents. "May I?" he asked.

"Please, yes," my mother said. "Tell her."

Tomlin shifted on his feet again. "Aloy, one day you'll grow up and take your father's position. You will be the Elected and lead our country."

My eyes got big. "Me, Tomlin? But what about Apa?" I looked toward my father with worry.

"Umm..." Tomlin faltered, not wanting to scare me too much. "He will still be here." It was the only lie Tomlin ever told me.

"Oh, good," I said.

"Yes," said Ama. "But there is one thing you must do to take Apa's position."

One thing? That was it? I hugged her around her neck. One thing didn't sound hard.

My father stepped toward me. "You will have to pretend to be a boy," he said. "No more playing with dolls. No tea parties. No dresses."

I looked at my father like he just told me the sun didn't come out in the morning. "But why not, Apa?"

"Because you need to look and sound like a boy. No one must ever know you are a girl."

"Ever?" I asked.

"Ever," my mother replied. "We have indulged you, and in so doing, let you play with whatever you liked up until now. You've been hidden away in this house because we wanted to protect you, but now it's time for our countrymen to see you out in public."

I contemplated this for a minute. "Can I play with my toys when I'm alone?"

A sneak of a smile appeared on the corner of my mother's lips, but it was gone just as fast.

"No," my father said. "You must say goodbye to everything that seems female, even in private."

He started walking around my room, picking up my things and tucking the small items into his jacket pockets. My kaleidoscope, pink and pearly colored. My candy colored teapot, child size and perfect for recreating tea time in my own world of play. My favorite doll, which lay upon my pillow.

At this, I cried out. "No, Apa! No!" I tried to wrestle my way out of my mother's arms, pulling at her to get down. I needed to save my things, especially the baby doll, tattered from my four years of love.

My father was unyielding, loading toy after toy into a box that he brought forth from a nearby closet. When he was done, I was red faced and sobbing. All of the things I played with were gone.

I had no other friends except these dolls, stuffed animals, and trinkets. To my four-year-old self, this was my life.

"You will learn not to care for these things," my father said. "They are material. You must now focus on the immaterial. Learning to play fight. Knowing what it is to make a dying person feel strong. Learning to lead. There is no more time for dolls. Stop crying!"

I didn't understand any of my father's words as a four-year-old. What he said was cold, but over time I learned they were true. Over the next few years, my time was scheduled with Tomlin or some other trusted teacher every second of the day. Eventually, I learned not to miss the doll as I fell to sleep each night. I learned not to show emotion or cry when I was upset. It was a slow process, but I suppose, one that needed to happen.

❦

Now, fourteen years later, in this prison, I take the opportunity to lean into my father's chest and shake with an onslaught of sobs.

"All right," Apa says. "Take a moment and let it out. I'll give you two minutes. Get this episode out of your system now while no one is watching."

I choke on my tears, trying to hold them back. When I'm sure a minute's passed, I lift my face from my father's heavy brown jacket, wiping my eyes with the back of my hand.

"Come, now," says my father. "Tell me another fact. We were doing so well there for a while."

I think of the only fact I know to be utterly and unequivocally true and spit it out before I can change my mind.

"I am a girl."

23

3

MY FATHER TAKES A hard look at me. I match his stare for a few seconds but finally look down. I've said out loud the one thing my parents tried to cover up since I was four. My father clears his throat and abruptly stands. I catch his sleeve in my hand, trying to make it right and keep him here with me. In the two short weeks we have left, I shouldn't be callously throwing away even a moment. But Apa pulls away gently, prying my fingers from the fabric.

His back is to me. "I am aware of that. You should be wary of voicing it before more people become privy."

And then he's gone. I sigh, resigned to the fact I've pushed my father too far and can't take back my words now.

I peer into the prisoner's room again, trying to imagine what it would take to trade your life for your beliefs. To know the consequences of your actions but to do them anyway. East Country's laws and subsequent punishments are clear to everyone, but once in a while someone still breaks a law. The people who break the Technology Accord by inventing something man-made know the punishment is death, but they believe so strongly in technology as a way to advance society, they take the risk anyway. The rogue faction for technology is my father's biggest opponent. And soon they will be mine.

But is my family so different from these people? Am I not also breaking a law by pretending to be a boy? I am specifically breaking the Fertility Accord by playing the part of a male so I can take office. It's also punishable by death, but long ago my parents determined it was worth the risk.

As I was a baby at the time, I didn't have a say. My parents decided their lives and my own were worth the risk of death. I used to be angry but eventually came to terms with it. Either I take office by pretending to be a boy, or a new family must be chosen to lead. A new Elected family would open the floodgates to the Technology Faction and one of their own being put in a position of real power. We'd potentially be right back where we started when machinery, cars, fuel, and technology caused global warming and the eco-crisis over a century ago.

Twenty years ago when my brother ran away, my parents were devastated, as my mother was way past prime birthing age. It's hard enough having one child, let alone two. And hardly anyone can get pregnant anymore past the age of twenty-five. Not with all the side effects of widespread radiation.

Thus, when Ama got pregnant a second time, my parents were elated. And then I came out into the world. Yes, they were happy I was born a healthy child to add to our declining population. But I was a girl. And girls could not, by law, be the Elected.

They tried to have another boy after me, but my mother didn't get pregnant again. So, within days of my fourth birthday, my mother and father decided they would pretend I was a boy. I've trained to appear masculine ever since.

I don't cry in public. I don't learn about fertility as all of the other girls do. I don't let anyone hear my singing voice. Since I can't alter the soprano lilts of my voice when it's singing, I don't engage in that pastime at all. I don't show tenderness. My free-time is spent play fighting with a sword or a knife, something boys do to burn off extra testosterone. Obviously, I don't have too much to waste. But, in the East Country, all of the boys learn to play fight, so I continue the farce.

I keep up this constant act, even on days when my fully developed chest aches in its tight, cloth bindings. In these moments, I almost undo the bindings and throw them in the fire. But I always stop just in time, cinching the cloth tighter still.

Only Tomlin, Ama, Apa, and now Vienne are aware of my womanhood. It's a secret I will have to keep until Vienne's and my first born male is eighteen, and Vienne and I leave East Country for good. At that time, I plan to rip the bindings around my chest into a million shreds and never crush my lungs and rib cage again. I will wear skirts and grow my hair long. I will sing as loud as I can, knowing I've fulfilled the duties to my country and can now be true to myself.

Until then, however, I wait. And when I do get so angry about my predicament that I feel like testosterone is indeed eating away my insides, I practice swordplay with a tutor until his arm falls slack with fatigue.

A prison guard breaks my concentration with a loud swish of the door opening. "Oh, excuse me, Sir. I didn't know you were still here."

"It's okay. I was just leaving."

I walk out into the frigid air again, wishing Apa was still with me for the walk back to our house. I want to ask him more questions— like how many executions he's watched? Or if he talks to the person's family afterwards? And how they're absolutely sure the prisoner did the suspected offense? But those questions will have to wait until my parents and I are alone together for the ceremonial last night. I've already developed my list of discussion topics—things I mustn't forget to ask. It'll be the last time I get to ask their advice on how Vienne and I are supposed to conceive a child when I don't have the correct biological parts. Or how I'm supposed to hold off a revolution of the Technology Faction—a movement growing for more than fifty years.

I am so engrossed in my thoughts, looking down at the dirt by my shoes as I shuffle along the path, I miss, entirely, the sound of an arrow whizzing past my cheek. It's only when I see the arrow piercing the ground in front of me that I spin around to get on the defensive. A wave of adrenaline races through my bloodstream. My throat constricts in fear as I whip my head, looking in every direction to see from where the arrow might have originated. But when I spy no person furtively running away, and there are no more arrows threatening me, the adrenaline subsides, leaving me shaken and off balance. I stand in the same spot, my legs feeling like rocks.

I'm not the only one surprised. Three guards from the nearby prison run to my side, covering me in a protective triangle of their bodies, their eyes also whipping around to find the perpetrator.

My mother is running to my side too, having seen the incident from our front house windows. She's flying out the door, her skirts swirling up dust as she runs.

"Who did this?" she asks, pulling her way into the tight triangle so we're facing each other.

"I didn't see anyone!"

"Only one arrow? That was all?" We can't argue this wasn't an attempt on my life—only how much of an attempt. Out here, in the wide open, it couldn't be just any old target practice or play fighting.

"Only one. Do you think it was a warning? Or did they truly mean to kill me?" Everything I've assumed about murder no longer being part of human nature—that people are more civilized than generations past—comes crashing down. I am aghast, my eyes wide at the jumble of thoughts coursing through my head. No one ever tried to assassinate my father or my grandfather before him. Suddenly, all I can think is that I'd better get to shelter before any more arrows are aimed at my head.

"Come," my mother says, like she's thinking the same thing. "We will discuss this in the safety of the house." Before we leave, Ama pulls the arrow out of the ground and tucks it into her skirt.

The guards follow close behind, their faces and bodies pointed away from us to watch for any more arrows.

Once in the house, my mother leads me straight into a room where Tomlin and my father are talking. She closes the doors behind us so we're the only people inside.

"What is this about?" asks Apa. He glances over at me, probably thinking I've blubbered to my mother about witnessing my first execution. He can't help but give me a disapproving look.

"There's been an attempt on Aloy!" says Ama. I see her face in the mirror in front of us. It's white with fear. I'm about to say something to comfort her when I realize the face in the mirror is mine, not hers. I am the one whose pallor is dim, the one who is shaking like a leaf.

Tomlin rises out of his seat and makes his way to me. He inspects my face and body for injury while my mother explains what she saw.

"Up in the hills. I think the arrow came from there."

"Are you sure?" asks Apa.

"We will have no way of knowing," Ama says. "No recourse!"

"Of course there is recourse," says Apa. "For one, Aloy will have guards around him at all times. He will never be left alone. And I will go into town today to find out who trains in archery. Few arrows could have been shot so far."

Ama hands Tomlin the arrow, and he turns it over and over in his hands.

After a minute or so he gives us his report. "I'm afraid it is quite like a long arrow."

I come out of my stupor, able to wrap my head around something in the conversation. "A long arrow? Like the ones from before?"

Tomlin comes to stand near me, placing the arrow in my hands, always aiming to teach me something, even at a time like this. "No, not exactly the same. Look at the wood."

I peer at it closely. The wood shaft was whittled. It's not sleek and pristine like the long arrows from the past. It was not formed from machinery but from a person's meticulous handicraft. Before our Technology Accord was signed, people killed one another with small arrows, which could travel great distances, propelled by a digital signal. Countries carried out assassinations this way. It was a single shot, which could precisely target one person and kill without inflicting ancillary damage. No one else would be hurt, only the person for whom the arrow was intended.

But long arrows wouldn't work in our day and age. "This one is similar to the long arrow. It has the same design. The same tip. But there could be no signal to guide it," I say.

"Thus, the miss," says Tomlin.

"Where would they have found a piece of long arrow?" asks my mother.

"These were taken out of circulation years ago," says my father.

"They saved it all these years. For me." Though I don't have enough evidence to know this for certain, the idea washes over me like icy bathwater.

My mother notices the whiteness of my face and brushes a hand across my brow. "You need rest. First an execution and then an attempt. Too much for you in one day." She stands closer to me and then looks at my father and Tomlin, letting them know she's taking me away. We exit the room as the two men keep discussing how to find the assassin. Ama hurries me up the stairs and off to my bedroom, tucking me into bed with the express order to sleep. "I'm going to return to Tomlin and your father. See if we can devise a plan for determining the offender."

She pats my hand and almost leans in to give me a hug. My body unconsciously inches toward her outstretched arms, anticipating the touch, wanting it. I've seen other mothers embrace their sons, and I can't help feeling jealous every time. I know my mother's reserve is a show she puts on because of who I am. Not all boys in East Country are treated to this same harsh standard. I look up into Ama's face, almost begging her to hug me like when I was a toddler. But I hate myself for needing this. I squeeze my eyes shut, my mind chiding my body for its weakness. At the last second Ama thinks better of it and instead wraps my blankets more tightly around my shoulders, almost ensuring I can't sit up to embrace her.

The lack of intimacy has made me long for and yet abhor physical touching now. I don't know how I'll ever learn to touch my future wife without wincing.

I lie in bed thinking terrible thoughts of my upcoming role and who my new enemy might be. I've interacted with almost all of the townspeople through the years, and they've been extremely welcoming to me. Yes, there are people who disagree with my family's strict adherence to the Accords, even after all these years, but the majority favor my father and me, as well as the laws.

This leads me to think that their anger is not directed at my family's reign but at me specifically. But why? Have I not always followed my father's leadership style? Am I so different?

As my hands trace the flat, smooth skin of my stomach, I think yes. I am different. I'm a girl. And I shouldn't be in office at all. No one has said they suspect my gender, but perhaps they can just tell I have no business taking this leadership role. Maybe unconsciously, they know I'm not fit to rule the country. Even with all my training, I don't have my father's authority. Tomlin says it's something that can be learned, but I'm not so sure about that. I've tried to master it for years, and I still doubt myself.

I fall into a fitful sleep, but when I hear a noise in my room, it jars me awake. The mid-morning sun is high in the sky, which must mean I slept straight through to the next day. I don't make a movement, trying to assess the sound. It's footsteps coming from across my bedroom near the window. I expect to see my mother or a maid, but the figure is a man. It's too slender to be my father and too tall to be Tomlin.

My hand instinctively juts out from under my bed covers and finds the small whittling knife on my nightstand. I use it merely to carve wood, but it's the closest weapon I have. I close my fist around its small handle, ready to plunge it into my attacker should he step forward. I lie in wait, at the defense. But then I think, if he has a weapon, he could strike me from afar. So, I gently lift the sheets off my body and step out of bed, now on the offensive.

His back is to me, and since my footsteps are light as a feather, he doesn't turn.

I wonder why the guards at my door didn't stop him, but I have little time to ponder because I'm now inches from the man's back. He still doesn't move. He's got something in his hands at waist level. It must be an intricate weapon. One he's getting ready to use.

I lift the knife higher in the air, ready to advance on him, when the thing in the man's hand lets out a loud "Squawk!"

I falter for a second, the tip of my foot catching against a raised floorboard, and it's in that brief moment the man hears me and abruptly turns.

"Hey!" he says, stepping backward against my window when he sees me so close.

"Get back!" Still, I don't hear guards ready to storm in and rescue me. So I stand my ground, knife raised, ready to inflict damage against this man myself if I need to.

I look at him closer. He's not even a man. He's my age.

"Watch what you're doing with that thing!" The boy's voice sounds familiar, but I can't think where I've heard it before. I concentrate only on keeping my ground. Keeping him in place.

"Don't move," I say. "If you do, I'll advance. And show me your hands!"

"I'm not moving!" He raises both hands in the air, palms open so I can see they're empty. I want to trust this boy. I don't want to have to harm him with my knife. But it isn't until I see one of my pet parrots fly off the boy's shoulder and onto mine that I realize I know him.

I've never spent more than a second up close to the bird keeper, but over the years I've made a personal pastime of watching him from afar. The boy's name is Griffin. He's the son of my father's veterinarian. Griffin is the apprentice, administering to the smaller animals around our house. He's fixed the wing of my parrot before.

I step back but don't lower the knife.

"What are you doing in here?" My voice is gruff. I might know this boy, but he could still be here to do harm.

"I didn't know you were in here. If I'd known, obviously, I wouldn't have come in to look after your birds."

The parrot gives another shrill squawk. I study the boy for a moment. Close to me now, for only the second time in my life, I stare at him openly. The dark hair I've seen from afar falls forward over his brow but ends in sharp points around the sides of his ears, like he's cut it himself without a mirror. His eyes are a deep amber too. Like fresh gingerbread cookies straight out of the oven, glowing and bright. He's lean but relatively tall.

The one thing I know about him for sure is his gait. Since before I can remember, Griffin was the only male my age allowed into our house. He followed his father around, watching him work and then taking over some of the veterinary duties himself. I made an art of subtly watching Griffin to learn how a male my age moved and talked. It was one thing studying the masculine characteristics of my father, but it was altogether another to study someone my own age.

And then there's the one time I did see Griffin up close, just for a brief second when I was thirteen, but the memory stayed with me for years.

I realize we're staring each other down.

"Well, are you going to lower the knife, or do I have to knock it from your hand?"

"You wouldn't!" I'm disturbed he dares speak so brashly to me. My eyes squint into lines. "If you come one step closer, I swear I'll use this. What are you doing in here anyway?" My voice is rough from sleep, and I make no attempt to soften it. I want to appear hard right now—fearsome. Yet, Griffin doesn't seem to fear me at all. In fact, he's impertinent. It's not something I've dealt with much in my seventeen years.

"I didn't know you were in here. No one did, or they would have stopped me. You're supposed to be in training right now, like your usual schedule."

"Yeah, well, I'm not." I practically spit the words at him. "What do you know of my usual schedule?"

"You're not in your bedroom by mid-morning. That's when I come in to feed your birds."

I never thought who fed them each day. Knowing Griffin's been in my room daily gives me a strange shiver up the back of my legs. I feel a sheen of cold perspiration erupt on the back of my neck.

"Well, I'm in here now, so you shouldn't be."

"How come you're in your room anyway?"

"Not your concern," I say.

Griffin flicks a strand of unruly hair off his forehead and takes a step away from me to the right. He's getting altogether too casual.

"Get out!" I say again.

He ignores me. "May not be my concern, but your birds seem to care. No one's fed them yet today. They're hungry."

I watch as he dares to move from his spot by the window and walk over to my parrots' cage. He reaches in and softly smooths down the bird's back feathers. I see my parrot arch its back under Griffin's touch and bob its head in approval.

"Fine." I take a deep breath. "You can feed them and then leave."

Griffin scoops a handful of seeds out of his pants pocket and deposits it on the floor of the cage.

"Sleeping in?"

"Yeah, something like that," I mumble. I realize the hand holding the knife has fallen to my side, no longer on the offensive.

"I didn't realize you were allowed to do that."

Something in the way he says "allowed" irks me. I sneer back at Griffin. "Well, I guess my schedule is allowed to be modified if there's just been an attempted assassination against me."

Immediately, I know I've said too much. In the second he's looking at me, I see his eyes flash. But then Griffin's face points away from me again, shielded by the birdcage.

"Oh," he says, trying to act more casual with his voice than his eyes would convey. "Well, looks like they missed."

"Looks like." I saunter across my room to my writing desk, set the knife down with a *thunk*, and spin onto the chair so I'm still looking at him. "Aren't you done yet?"

"Just about." The coldness of his voice startles me. I'm used to everyone being overly nice to me, if not at the very least polite. Griffin's conversation leaves me feeling unnerved.

He brushes his hands against each other, letting a few leftover seeds fall to the floor. "Done." He starts to walk away from me toward the door, but halfway there he stops, his back still facing me. "You watch me."

It isn't a question. More of an accusation.

"No, I don't."

"Yes." He pauses. "You do. Have for years."

My eyes are wide. How has he seen me watching him? Has he been watching me in return? This thought unsettles me in ways I don't fully understand.

So who cares? So he's seen me staring at him. Why should it make a difference to me? But I can't fool myself. I do care. If he's seen me when I don't know it, what else has he seen me do? Have I done something genuinely feminine in front of him that he's guessed my secret?

As if he can read my thoughts, Griffin says, "I know what you are."

And before I can even think about the consequences of my actions, anger overtakes me. What I've hidden for so long and been so careful to keep secret is now in the hands of this impudent intruder?

I'm up out of my seat and running at him before I realize what I'm doing. I knock him forward, pushing with both my hands flat against his back.

He's surprised and falls forward, losing his balance.

In this moment, I look around the room for some more dangerous weapon than my two hands. My knife is too far. I find what I'm looking for on the wall to my right. One of my fencing swords. I grab it off its decorative shelf and get in an offensive stance, right foot forward at an angle.

As Griffin regains his balance and faces me, I hold my stance, looking him fiercely in the eyes. He doesn't say anything, but I see him scan the room fast. I lunge at him, but I'm a second too slow. He's already run to my left and grabbed a wooden cane I've been carving. It's now the wood cane against my steel sword. I've been fencing since I was seven, so I'm quick. I should be able to take him out easily.

I don't mean to really hurt him, just push him back out of my room, get my anger out. But Griffin is stronger than I expect. We're fighting, wood to steel, clashing in the air, the sword making gashes in the softer wood.

I jump back over furniture, toppling pieces as we both fly around the room. We're both spinning, checking each other's advances. Griffin surprises me, putting up a fight matching mine. I've received expert training, but who taught him to fight so well?

Griffin backs up against my door, but I can't let him escape. Unless I win the fight, he could run out that door and tell the world my secret. My family's future could come crashing down around me in an instant.

I push forward with more heat. We're up close now, our weapons right at each other's faces. I can hear his grunts through my own yells.

All at once his cane swings out at me, but not where I expect it to go. He doesn't aim for my sword. He aims for my feet, knocking me off balance onto my back. My sword clatters to the ground in the onslaught, and before I know it he's on top of me. I'm punching and pushing back at him, and we're in a fist fight, rolling on the ground. I don't easily give up, but he's got a few muscular pounds on me.

I'm furious, kicking and shouting at him. In between our wrestling, he spurts out, "It's your secret. Not mine." He's out of breath from our fight, so he has trouble getting the words out. "I'm not planning to tell anyone."

While he's trying to get the words out of his mouth, I take the opportunity to push harder. I end up on top of him and pin his arms above his head. He goes slack, letting me hold him there.

"You're a girl," he says, serious and amused at the same time.

"You have no evidence!"

He juts his chin out, pointing to my torso. His eyes are mischievous. I look down at what he's pointing to.

And then I realize.

The shirt I'd been sleeping in has lost a few buttons. It hangs open and ragged off my torso. Immediately, I let go of Griffin's arms and instinctively grasp around my chest for my bindings.

But I'm too late.

A milky white breast hangs out of the wrappings, announcing my secret loud and clear.

4

I JUMP BACK OFF Griffin, holding the binding cloth up to my chest. I'm furious. And ashamed. And angry at myself for this lapse.

"Don't worry. I won't tell," he says.

I'm numb, unable to say anything for fear I'll completely lose my cool and start pitifully begging him not to turn me in. If my gender is revealed, not only will my family lose power, but we could be executed too.

Griffin gets off the floor, brushing his pants and shirt sleeves. While I stand in a corner, staring at him, he quietly places the cane back against my nightstand.

"So," he says, "See you around, I guess."

I'm frozen in place, unable even to answer him in my shock. He thinks he's just going to leave my room? Walk out the door away from me, holding this nugget of information over my head?

And then he's gone.

I want to yell at him to get back here. Or yell for my guards and say Griffin assaulted me and needs to be taken away to the prison. I want to make sure he won't tell a soul my secret. But, if I turn him in, he might renege on his promise and tell everyone my true gender. I stand in the corner for another moment, trying to determine my best course of action while fumbling with the buttons on my shirt. Then, like lightning has finally infused my joints, I run forward. I can't let him just walk away.

I heave my doors open with so much force they bang against the inside of my bedroom walls with resounding vibrations. I don't even look back as I jolt into the hallway.

And... run straight into one of the maids. She and I both topple over, the tray she was carrying crashing to the floor.

"Oh!" she exclaims.

I don't even focus on her. My eyes are still darting around the hallway, searching for Griffin. I fixate on his lanky frame starting to descend the closest staircase. He turns back, his body aimed for the stairs but his head angled toward me. We lock eyes for a split second, long enough so I see him silently mouthing a sentence in my direction.

"You are a beautiful girl."

I shift on the floor with my arms thrown out in back of me, completely dumbfounded. He thinks I'm what? *Beautiful?* Griffin turns to run down the rest of the stairs, this time not slowing.

"Hey, come—" I start to yell after him, but I'm interrupted by the maid whom I just knocked down.

"I'm so sorry!" She's apologizing profusely. The girl starts to stand up, trying to collect few pieces of a broken dish. She kneels next to me, unsure whether to offer me a hand or not. I pick myself up and look over at her.

"No, my fault entirely." I try to make my voice steady. "Are you all right?"

"Yes, I'm okay. I was just coming to see if you were awake. You slept through breakfast."

I brush off my pants, keeping my head down, eyes centered on my legs. When I look up again, I see the girl's pale eyes are framed behind a sheath of long black hair. They're familiar, but they don't hold my attention for long. Griffin's mouth, moving to form his last sentence, lingers behind my eyes like looking into the sun and still seeing the white hot circle even when blinking.

"Thanks for thinking of me, but I don't need anything," I say, trying to get the girl to leave me alone. I take the overturned tray from her hands and step back into my bedroom letting the doors shut behind me. I hope she'll take the hint and go. After a few more seconds, I hear her footsteps walking away.

I fall to the floor against my wall. After seventeen years, in one single morning I've blown it all. I've watched Griffin before, but now I'll never be able to let him out of my sight. He'll be a constant worry in the back of my mind. The worst thing is, I've let this happen before. And with the same person, no less.

I should've told my parents about meeting Griffin four years ago, but because of my cowardice, I've inadvertently granted Griffin an immense amount of power over me now. In all fairness, I was somewhat distracted that long ago night with an even bigger threat. But that isn't a good enough excuse.

✦

Four years ago, at age thirteen, I sat in my bedroom after yet another argument with my parents. The fights were increasingly frequent as I grew into my teens and started stretching my wings. That particular night, I'd heard all teenagers in East Country, ages thirteen through seventeen, were attending the annual dance. The kids would mingle and hopefully start to find suitors, so a marriage could quickly be formed when they turned eighteen and became most fertile. I wanted to see what the dance entailed, even if I was forced to watch from the sidelines. My wife was already determined. Couldn't I at least be afforded the opportunity to see what I was giving up?

At dinner that evening, I'd asked my parents for permission to attend the dance. My father said no without even looking up from his plate.

"Of course that's impossible," said my mother, looking side-to-side to see if any servants were within hearing distance.

"But why, Ama? No one would even have to know it was me."

"Keep your voice down!" Her words scalded me like boiling water. "The future Elected gaping at all the young men! Can you imagine?"

My voice shook as I responded. "I wouldn't do that! I'd be discreet! I can handle myself!"

My father rose from his seat at the table, his body massive as he stood over me. "Enough of this foolishness! Why would you even want to go to the ceremony?"

I spluttered out my response before I could even think about the consequences. "I just want to see what normal kids do! The ones who don't have the Elected position hanging around their heads like a noose!"

My father looked at me, his eyes burning my now reddened cheeks. "Do not let me hear you say that again. You are to be the Elected!" He slammed his fist down on the table. "One that takes pride in his position and responsibility and does not seek out idle fantasies!"

"Shhhh," my mother said to my father. Her head pointed to the servants just arriving to bring us dessert.

"I've lost my appetite," he said, his feet pounding on the floor

39

boards as he exited.

I looked down at my plate, feeling forlorn. "It'll be fine again soon," said my mother. "Just give him a few hours. He won't be mad for long."

But she didn't understand me at all. I wasn't concerned about my father's anger. I was still upset they said I couldn't attend the dance. When I pressed my mother again, she just cocked her head to the side, like the conversation didn't warrant much feeling anymore. "It cannot be so."

I left the table, sullen and dark. Sitting in my bedroom with my hands clasped so hard my knuckles looked like individual marbles, I let self-pity flood over me. This was more than just a dance. This was about being able to make my own choices. Be my own person. For my whole life, I'd be beholden to the Elected position. It really did feel like a noose tightening.

When a knock sounded at my door, I knew it would be Tomlin. He often smoothed things over during those rebellious years.

"Come in," I said.

Tomlin opened the door gently, then let it click shut behind him. "You know, it doesn't serve any purpose to anger them so."

I looked up at him, my eyes awash with hopefulness and a few unshed tears. "Maybe they'll relent one of these times. Let me have an ounce of freedom."

Tomlin chuckled. "I don't think so. Your father is a... resolute man."

I stared at Tomlin morosely. "Why won't they let me explore our country at all? Shouldn't I see the people I'll one day be ruling? See the countryside? They hardly let me out of this house!"

"It is a dangerous thing you ask for. Freedom is always a tad dangerous."

"You want to know something?" I said, knowing my next words were heresy in this house. Tomlin was the only one with whom I could even think of sharing them. "I don't even believe in the Elected Accord!"

Tomlin stood over me, reproaching, but he let me go on.

"It's stupid that a woman can't be the Elected. I don't know why someone couldn't focus on having a baby and be a leader at the same time. I could maybe do both." I looked down at this last sentence.

I let my words hang in the air, growing cold. My "maybe" spoke for itself. Tomlin didn't respond, just let me think about what I'd just said. We both knew I was already having a hard time mastering everything I needed to know to be the East Country's leader. All the history, political and military. The science, the physics, the agricultural nuances of our planet. I needed to understand everything my townspeople knew and then some. Not to mention mastering the internal characteristics of the Elected—all the steadfastness I'd need to keep the country organized amid chaos. If I could barely do all that now, how could I focus on childbirth too? And even though I wasn't taught about reproduction, I knew bearing children was risky. The Elected couldn't very well die in childbirth, leaving the country without a leader. I didn't say any more on the subject. Instead, I narrowed in on my other complaint.

"When will I ever get to be my own person?"

"Soon. In just five years you'll be eighteen and in charge of yourself." He looked at me with one eyebrow raised. "And then you might think back and reminisce about the time you still had a chance to lean on your parents."

"I doubt it. I only wanted to see the dance. See what all the other kids were doing. That's all. Just see it." I whined out the last words.

He sat down next to me. Tomlin put a hand on my shoulder and said the magic words, which always seemed to settle me. "This too shall pass. One day at a time, Aloy."

He sat with me for a few more minutes, both of us silent in thought.

"Ah, well. It's getting late. I'd best be going." He patted my shoulder and used it as a crutch to help him stand. As he unclasped the door to exit, he turned his head back to me. "I'll send in a maid with some tea. Goodnight."

"Night," I mumbled.

I sat on my bed whittling a piece of wood, pulling the sharp knife over and over until I created a deep crease in the soft material. When the second knock sounded at the door, I barely registered it.

A new maid politely poked her head in. "I have tea. Shall I set it down near you?"

I hardly even looked up as I kept raking the knife over the wood. My voice was hoarse answering back, my self-pity still rampant. "That's fine."

She placed the cup on the nightstand next to my bed. The tea smelled of mint. I looked up at the maid for a moment, long enough to see she was a teenager. This just sent me into more of a depression as I imagined her getting ready for the dance soon. Every boy and girl in the whole country got to attend except me. I jumped up from the bed and faced the maid.

41

"Are you going to the dance tonight?" I asked.

She seemed surprised and instantly looked away from me. "Oh, me? I don't know."

"What do you mean, you don't know? You have to go. All eligible kids go to the dance. So you're going too, right?"

The maid looked down, locks of strange red hair falling out of the shawl around her head. Her voice was quiet. "I suppose."

"Well, have fun." I knew I was being obnoxious, taking out my pain on someone else.

She looked down and started to make her way for my door.

I turned, about to fall back onto my bed in a huff. But then I thought better of it. This was no way a future Elected should speak to his people. I'd never be a true leader if I treated my own servants cruelly. I felt the self-obsession and anger I'd been carrying all evening melt off my shoulders. I caught up to the maid as she placed one hand on the doorframe. "Look, I'm sorry." I reached for her arm. I breathed out slowly. "It's just... that..."

"You're lonely," she finished for me.

"Yes." I was surprised she understood so quickly.

The maid paused a moment, still looking away from me. She swallowed before speaking again. "Every day you get one step closer to marrying the Madame Elected. You won't be lonely then."

I looked down and loosened my hold on her arm. That's what everyone hoped.

My reply to the maid was thick in my throat. "Thank you for the tea. Goodnight."

"Goodnight." She started opening the door. The maid faced the outside hallway, her back still to me. "Everyone's a little preoccupied right now. There's some secret technology meeting going on tonight that all the guards are trying to find. I don't think anyone would notice if someone snuck out." She paused. "Sometimes it's kind of... exhilarating... to get away."

"What?" My head shot up, but as quick as the maid uttered her brazen dare, she was out into the hallway with the door slamming against her back. I ran forward, pulling the door back open. However, looking left and right, I could see no one in the hall. The maid was gone.

I slumped back onto my bed, continuing to whittle the piece of wood into a pipe for a water spigot. Leave the house alone? Without an entourage of guards? Without my parents' permission? It was a ludicrous notion. But as the minutes ticked by and the moon got higher in the sky, the maid's words sounded more and more enticing. Here was my chance. Possibly my only chance to get out, when everyone was preoccupied with the Faction's secret meeting and the teenagers' annual dance.

I couldn't sit still any longer. I grabbed a cloak and a bundle of other clothes out of my bedroom closet. I stuffed miscellaneous shirts and pants under my sheets to make my bed look plump with my supposedly sleeping body. Then I tossed the dark cloak over one arm. I would easily blend in with the night shadows once I put it on. I took one look at myself in the mirror, gathered my nerve, and then cautiously pulled open my bedroom door.

The maid was right. No one was patrolling the hallway tonight, so it was an easy escape down the wide staircase to the first floor. In fact, the house seemed uncharacteristically deserted. No guards sauntered back and forth across the lobby downstairs, and no servants were left cleaning up in the dining room. I was able to slink out the side kitchen door into the night shadows with none the wiser.

Once outside, I thrust the cloak around my shoulders and over my head. I started walking against the house until I was sure no one from the stables was milling around. In one more minute, I'd walked into the open yard, still staying low in case anyone lingered here. Two guards flanked our front door, but I was far enough away now they wouldn't see me unless I made a sound. My soft feet padding along the ground didn't bring their attention. Before I knew it, I was running across the open Ellipse field in the direction of the town hall pavilion. I catapulted forward, almost throwing myself down behind a stone bench for cover.

I felt lighthearted, sniffing the cool night air like a hunted animal who'd just escaped from a trap. I sidled next to dark, thatched houses on my way to the town center. I concealed myself well, running blithely from the shelter of one awning to the next.

In minutes, I saw lights ahead and heard the hum of excited voices. As I got closer, the sight was breathtaking. Four long, wooden poles surrounded a square dance floor. On each pole hundreds of candles sat on small shelves made of bits of metal attached to the wood. The flickering lights threw shadows across everyone's faces and seemed to make this small square of land stand out, floating in a sea of darkness. Girls were transformed into fairy tale princesses for the night, their hair pulled back into intricate swirls. And the boys were everything I'd imagined—gallant, offering their hands to the girls who blushed demurely back.

I snuck closer, one step at a time, until I was part of the crowd, my hood still loosely covering my head. All around me were the sights and smells of teenage desire. A girl brushed past me, brandishing some kind of meat on a stick.

"Excuse me!" she called out over her shoulder as she kept going.

"It's ok." I whispered, the words catching in my throat.

This was it! I was there! In the midst of my people, enjoying the festivities along with everyone else. For a few minutes, I watched from the sidelines as girls and boys linked arms together and spun in intricate patterns on the dance floor. I couldn't help blushing as I looked at the strong, lean boys of the country. If my hair were longer—if I didn't dress as a boy—if I weren't the Elected—would any of them want me? I blinked hard to empty my head of the ridiculous fantasy.

Instead of staring at the young couples, I turned my attention to the older villagers standing around the dance floor. Parents stood by the sidelines, taking notes and talking hurriedly amongst each other. I pulled my hood closer over my head but continued to stare at all the festivities with immense interest.

"Look! Margy is taking a liking to him for sure!" crooned one parent to another.

"Yes, it does look like she and Albine will make a good pair," said the father to my right. "We won't even have to push them together. They're already linking up!"

I kept standing by the candles, taking it all in, until I felt someone grab my arm.

"Hey, come on, let's dance! What's your name? Mine's Griffin!"

That's when I first met the boy with the birds. He pulled on my arm as he ran us both onto the dance floor. I couldn't think of what to do. Did he think I was a girl? All this time, was this the reason my parents always wanted me hidden? Because even when wearing a hooded cloak, I still gave off the impression of being female?

"No, I... shouldn't..." The heat of my words made cloudy white puffs in the air.

"Why? Are you already linked up to someone?" He kept pulling me behind him until we were standing dead center in between all of the other dancing couples.

I tried to keep my head down so he wouldn't see my face, but before I knew it, we were standing in front of each other. His left palm rested against mine the way I'd seen other couples start dancing. I tried

44

to say something, but I couldn't think. I just felt his fingers against mine, the tips extending over mine by at least two inches.

"Umm... yeah, I guess that's..." My voice broke off as I looked up at the boy for the first time. Of anyone I ran into that night, my luck it would be this boy—the one who was always trailing his father in our house. Now I finally had his name.

His eyes opened wide as he stared at my face, recognition seeming to sizzle in his brain. Then he looked down at the size of his hand against mine. My delicate fingers hinted at the secret my haircut and falsely gruff voice couldn't hide.

"Hey..." His mouth was an O of astonishment. I could see Griffin's mind trying to make sense of the situation. I inhaled sharply, my eyes skirting to the side, trying to figure out what to do.

Griffin dropped his hand from mine. "Wait... but... aren't you..." His voice trailed off, but he kept staring at me.

Before he could get out one word more, I tore myself off the dance floor and started running. I didn't look back. Just continued to run toward the dark houses I saw earlier. I hadn't expected anyone to pull me onto the dance floor, let alone realize who I was.

I flattened myself against an empty house when I heard a group of guards shuffling by. They came out of nowhere, descending from the shadows to walk single file down the nearby path. They peered left and right, seemingly looking for me. I was so caught. The boy must have alerted someone, and now there was a posse of guards trying to find me. I shouldn't be scared of my own guards, but watching them walk in the stark, straight line away from the town center, they looked fierce and determined. The lines of their mouths were more firm than I'd ever seen before. I feared what they would tell my parents when they found me.

Then, suddenly, they all stopped in front of another empty house a few hundred yards ahead of me. One by one, they entered until all the guards were off the path.

I crept on my hands and knees from the side of one house to the next, determined to get past the guards unnoticed. But in front of the house, I couldn't help pausing for a moment. It was altogether too quiet in there, even though about thirty guards just entered.

I knew I was being careless, but I wanted to see what they were doing. I got up on my knees in front of a cracked window and peered into the dim house. I couldn't see anything. So strange. I could have sworn I saw guards enter there just a moment ago. And then a candle was lit right on the other side of the window, and everything inside suddenly came into view.

I saw the group of people, men and women alike, standing against the opposite wall. They were shedding their clothes, and I wondered to myself if this were a place where dirty uniforms were laundered. But the clothes these people tossed to the floor weren't all pieces of the guards' normal attire. Some wore a guard's shirt but regular linen pants. Others wore the guards' traditional blue and yellow braided pants but only a white t-shirt on top. Now that I could see these people in some kind of light, they didn't seem like guards at all.

One by one, the people all sat on folding chairs against the farthest wall, waiting for someone or something. I stared, spellbound, my hands resting on the windowsill. Finally, a man started talking, and I could make out a few of his words through the cracked glass.

"Thank... for coming... know it is... great caution... made it here tonight."

A few people murmured agreement from the sidelines, and the main speaker continued. "Quiet, quiet. We must remain... as possible... many... to discuss tonight."

The man, whose back was still toward the window, leaned down. When he came back up holding a large metal object, I realized what I was witnessing in this deserted part of town.

The speaker held some sort of saw, but when he flicked a switch, the thing shuddered to life. His audience gave great sighs of appreciation, trying to keep their excitement contained behind hands over their own mouths.

"...so pleased to show you... fixed this machine... tinkering... assure you! But... not all we have to speak of tonight! Tonight... venture... more interesting topics... fall of the Elected family!"

At this, my fingers broke away from the window, pulling out a mass of the sill's rotten wood as I fell backward. I scampered like an insect on its back, pushing my feet against the dirt to scrunch along the ground.

From within the house I heard movement and then the speaker's voice again. "What... that? Did... hear something?"

I needed to get away from there, and fast! But the front door of the thatched house opened, and a big man looked all around. I couldn't get up for fear he'd see me.

"Come back in!" hissed the speaker. Now that the door was open I could hear his voice clear as day. It sounded slightly familiar. "Don't

46

show yourself; it isn't safe. Here, put this on. Then go out and see what the noise was. If it's a spy, maim the bastard!"

At once, the big man was out again in a flash, something dark wrapped around his head. I scrambled backward again, hoping he wouldn't spot me, but my foot caught on a branch and the noise instantly set the man toward me. I crawled to my feet in a flash. My hood was off my head too, but it didn't matter. I ran like my life depended on it, because most likely it did. If the man caught me, he'd hurt me as instructed by his leader. And if he saw I was the Elected, I'd be in even more danger. But no matter how fast I ran, the big Technologist was right behind me. And since he seemed to know the outdoors much better than me, he enjoyed a large advantage. I stumbled multiple times on roots and other brush, and the man pressed on, gaining the advantage.

I ran amidst houses in the dark and back out to the Ellipse. But, out in the open, the Technologist gained even more of an edge on me.

I looked over my shoulder frantically. One of his beefy arms reached out, and it was on my cloak in a second. I shed the material, but the man grabbed onto my ankle, drawing a knife with his free hand. We both fell down onto the ground in a fit of grunts. We struggled together in the dark, me reaching down to try to unclasp the man's fist from my legs, his knife slashing my shin. This was it, I told myself. The Faction had me now. How pleased would they be to have found a member of the Elected family defenseless?

I could already feel my own hot blood leaking out of the wound on my leg. The Technologist was pulling me farther down toward him. In a second, his hands would circle around my neck. The man would destroy me here on the spot.

Right when I thought I couldn't fend him off anymore, a high pitched whistle came from the pavilion in front of us. The man hesitated just long enough that I was able to extricate my leg. Bleeding profusely, I didn't care to look back. I scrambled up and ran as fast as I could. When I reached the entrance of our stable doors, I finally stopped and looked behind me. I couldn't see the man anymore, but I didn't see anyone else either. Neither the Technologist, nor the person who'd startled him.

I clutched my leg, knowing I needed to wrap the wound so I wouldn't keep bleeding. At the same time, I knew my family deserved to know the Faction's plans as soon as possible, even if it meant I was forced to tell them about sneaking out. Tomlin was right; freedom was dangerous. Maybe I just didn't need to tell my parents exactly how dangerous it had become for me.

So instead of confessing everything that night, I held back. I limped my way into the dark house and up to my room without being noticed. I wrapped my leg tight with the bindings from my chest and made the resolution to tell my parents only about seeing the Technologists. I wouldn't tell them about making it all the way to the dance.

I'd sought independence, but I'd come away with a few other realities that night. Having seen the Faction up close, I finally understood my family's relentless dedication to maintaining stability. There were people who wanted to overthrow us and put our country in harm's way once again. My father was the only man with enough clout and power to keep the Technology Faction at bay. My family needed to stay in power. I should show pride in my Elected role, not lament how unfair my life was compared to all the other kids. It was time I embraced the responsibility.

That night, though, as I continued to stave off the bleeding from my leg, I'd taken one last moment to revel in the excitement of my escape. I'd run out on my own. Intermingled with my people. Caught up with the Technology Faction. And... the boy. Griffin, the one I sometimes saw helping his father around our house. He touched my arm. I looked down at my palm, tracing a pattern over where his fingers grazed mine.

Right there was my downfall. If I weren't infatuated with the excitement of being at the dance, I might have told my parents the whole story. I might not have merely centered my admission on seeing the Technology Faction, but also told them how someone may have guessed my gender. If I'd been brave back then, maybe I wouldn't be in this predicament now.

I SIT AGAINST MY bedroom wall, trying to think of something to set myself right again. What has Tomlin always told me when things are rough? After my parents took all the toys from my room? When my first "play" fight session ended with a black eye and a broken rib? And, of course, when I asked my parents if I could go to the annual dance and they said absolutely not?

He said, "This too shall pass. One step at a time, Aloy."

I do as he instructed. I get up off the floor and walk to my water basin. I splash a cold handful of the liquid onto my face. When I think I'm presentable, I open my bedroom door and step into the hallway again. This time the corridor is empty. My guards must still think I'm going about my usual schedule. By the daylight, I think it's noon. The sun is high in the sky. What do I usually do at noon each day? I eat lunch with my parents. So with this in mind, I walk stiffly in the direction of our dining room.

Once outside the room, I pull the heavyset oak doors open and see the comforting sight of both my parents at the table. My father holds a mug in his right hand and a piece of paper in his left. My mother sits adjacent to him, leaning against his arm to see the page.

When they hear me, they both look up.

"Ahh, Aloy," my mother says, smiling. "You're up! We wanted to let you sleep as much as possible after your ordeal yesterday."

I nod, not offering up the fact I encountered an even bigger ordeal this morning. I sit down at the table next to them and bite into a thick piece of wheat bread. It tastes bitter on my tongue, but I force myself to swallow anyway.

"Since you're up," my father says, "you should come with us to the town meeting today."

Every month there's a town hall where my father tells our people the latest news and they converse back to him with questions and comments.

"Of course," I say.

My mother notices I'm quieter than usual. "Don't worry. We'll keep a larger number of guards around you. No one will be able to reach you with an assault."

They should only know about the assault that just occurred in my own private bedroom.

"I'm not worried, Ama."

My father smiles. "That's the next Elected right there! Brave. Courageous. Not afraid to look the people in the eyes even a day after an attempt. This," he points to me, "is the Elected we raised."

I'm glad he's proud of me. I smile slightly at my parents. My anxious expression is in sharp contrast to their open faces, but they don't notice it. They wear huge smiles from relief that I'll be a strong, brave leader after they leave.

We ride out on horses to the Ellipse. It's close to our house, so we could walk, but my father wants us up high and able to travel fast in case there's another long arrow with my name on it. The horses' hooves thump softly upon the dirt fields between our house and the stone benches. Any pavement we used to have in East Country was either destroyed in the wars or ground up to use as building material. In the distance behind the meeting area, I see remnants of what used to be grand statues leftover from an era when our town used to be the capital of a larger country. We've repurposed the smooth white stone of those bombed monuments, but a few stumps lie scattered across the horizon. Tomlin's shown me pictures of something called a Washington Monument towering high over the town. In its place now is just a thin, stone square. I once asked Tomlin why a country would waste resources to build such a tall structure that didn't house anyone or offer any other sustenance. He'd just shrugged.

As we keep riding, I see the torso of a horse still standing tall on a pillar far off to my right. Its head is lopped off, and it stands on just two remaining legs. Perhaps once a rider sat astride its back, but the horse is now alone. We leave that one half-destroyed structure in place, calling it "Animal Remembrance," a memorial to all the species we lost in the eco-crisis.

We're the only family in the country with horses. Thus, the need for our own specialized veterinarian—Griffin's father. Horses are expensive to keep, and they're rare. Most horses died from the initial nuclear radiation, tumors growing rampant in their knees and legs, rendering them lame. Ours are the only ones left in the country, and we've taken great pains to keep them healthy and reproductive.

Since we don't create electricity, our world no longer keeps cars or airrides either. Most of East Country's population of four thousand people who come for our meeting today walked the great distance, camping for the few days it took to travel here. Or people came on bicycles. All of the bikes remaining after the eco-crisis were scavenged and distributed around our population.

Rust is a constant worry, since it can disintegrate the bikes' metal. All families are issued a bike and given strict instructions to wipe down the frames with a preserving liquid called nirogene ensuring these national treasures last for years to come. We harvest nirogene compound from hills bordering our country, and our chemists turn it into this miracle liquid by boiling the sooty, silver mineral. The resulting liquid smells like a mixture of urine and sweat, but we deal with the stench since it's such a valuable resource.

The bikes' tires are another concern altogether. Rubber tires went out of production years before the eco-crisis. In many cases our ancestors were just starting to adopt greener, more ecologically friendly materials when the planet went into destruction-mode. Unfortunately for them, it was too little, too late. Fortunately for us, the discovered alternative to rubber is actually something plentiful in the barren post eco-crisis era: dandelion root. Its gummy paste can be heated and congealed to make a substance akin to rubber when hardened. The root tires don't last long, but East Country planters grow dandelion crops with fervor, and thus, the bikes' tires are replaced constantly.

When we ride up to the pavilion, I see hundreds of shiny bikes laid out in lines before I even see the people. It's a magnificent sight and makes me smile. The metallic blues, reds, and greens shine in the afternoon sun like a rainbow.

My parents and I slide off our horses and descend into the amphitheater. We make our way down the rows of benches, security guards flanking me on both sides.

I wait behind my parents as they shake hands with random townspeople and stop to say hello to people by name. Our community is small, and my parents have an amazing mastery for names.

Once at the bottom, my father takes over the operation, while my mother and I sit down.

"A new day to you all!" my father says, his voice a firm bellow. It takes a moment for people to respond. But there's a growing roar of welcome cascading back to him.

The only way to amplify my father's voice and ensure all of our townspeople can participate in the town hall is by staging "talkers" every few hundred yards. We've perfected the system so the message at the end is always the same as the one spoken up front.

As soon as my father says his welcome, the first talker yells his words backward to the crowd. There's a pause of a few seconds before I hear the second talker take the words back to his group. While my father begins the discussion with talk of the crops we'll be growing this month and how the seeds will be distributed, I take a moment to look around.

I'm searching for one face in particular. My eyes scan the rows of people at the top, looking for him. It's not a matter of whether Griffin is here. It's where. I need to see his eyes to tell if he's planning to out my secret in this public venue. I realize my palms are sweating as I keep searching, and I thrust them in frustration against my pant legs.

Everyone is here today. I learned from Tomlin that not everyone participated in government before the eco-crisis. That there was widespread apathy. I can't believe that would be true. Why wouldn't people want to cast a vote or have their say? In East Country, everyone takes part. We have no government representatives. My mother and father talk to everyone personally. The Elected has no advisors except for the people themselves. And everyone in our country turns out for our monthly town meetings.

So I know he's here.

My father is now onto the subject of our water supply. There are a few questions from the crowd, and I tune out the meeting as I keep searching.

And then I see him.

Griffin is sitting in the front row, directly in front of me. When I realize how close he is, I jump in my chair. I'm unnerved by his proximity. Does he always sit up here? I never noticed before today. Why pick a spot in the front now?

He locks eyes with me, like he's been waiting for me to find him in the crowd. And when I do, he gives me a wink. I scowl back at him.

A big woman toward the back asks a question to her talker, and the words are sent down to the front. When her question finally reaches us, the rest of the crowd has already heard it, and there are murmurs spreading.

I straighten up in my seat, wondering what the woman has asked.

"Elected," says the closest talker, "Why can't the doctors use artificial insemination to help aid the process of increasing our population?"

This is a complicated question. I already know what my father is going to say because this question is raised at least once a year.

Apa looks back at me and then at my mother. She gives a slight nod.

"I'm going to let our son, Aloy, answer this." Apa nods encouragingly at me, but I'm completely shocked. They've never asked me to speak at the town halls until now. However, I realize I shouldn't be too surprised. My parents believe in trial by fire. I'm sure they've discussed this beforehand and were planning to have me answer one of the questions for the crowd.

I slowly get up from my seat and stand at the front of the stage. I know what I'll say, but I still feel swirls of anxiety rippling through my stomach. Without much food in there, the acid seems like it'll burn a hole through my insides.

I need to sound strong. I need to sound like I'm ready to take over my father's position in two weeks' time. And most of all, I need to sound like a man. I clear my throat and start talking with as low and gruff a voice as I can muster.

"Did that question come from Zet in the back?" Like my parents, I know the names of most of our people too.

The talker nods affirmation and then passes my question backward so everyone can hear what I've asked.

"Zet. Countrymen. We've discussed this many times before. While the creation of human life is our country's number one objective, and we will do almost anything to aid in this endeavor, we cannot bend the Accords even for this noble goal. To conduct artificial insemination would require us to not only use machinery but electricity and refrigeration as well. The use of machinery and technology is a slippery slope. If we started here, where else might we find ways to use tools to help our daily lives? Have we learned nothing from our past?"

I pause and let the crowd digest what I've said. A moment passes, and then the talker in the middle of the people returns with a follow-up question.

"Xavier agrees and requests you remind others in the audience, such as the hidden Technology Faction members, how our people were almost wiped out by such uses of technology."

I wipe my brow, which is now dripping miniscule beads of sweat. I pray no one notices, but as I look down into the crowd, I see Griffin's face. He's looking straight back at me and grimacing. No matter, I think. If he doesn't think I'm strong enough to answer the question, he's wrong. I am more than just a girl pretending to be a man. I am this country's next leader.

I stand straighter at the thought and gather my words.

"Xavier, yes, I can. You all know the story of our almost-extinction. However, it's necessary to repeat it as much as possible so we don't forget what caused the demise of so many people and the devastation of our planet."

I clear my throat and proceed.

"Because of human pollution and carbon dioxide emissions from our many machines, climate change crept up on our world a degree at a time. At first, the warmest areas of our planet became almost too hot to sustain life. Temperatures of one hundred thirty degrees Fahrenheit were reported on a daily basis. The arctics partially melted, sending massive floods. The lands of East Country, for example, which used to be inland, became coastal. After the floods came planet-wide earthquakes. The tremors damaged our extensive network of undersea oil pipelines, spewing black tar through the water. Sea life across the world was annihilated in a mere two months. Countries utilizing the sea's natural resources for the basis of their economy were ruined. Starvation was rampant."

I look out into the crowd and back at my parents. They give me another nod of approval, so I continue.

"Countries depending on oil for their economies were vanquished. People rioted. Not one country offered to clean up the oil. Resources were slim everywhere. Unmanned airrides landed, trying to steal other countries' natural resources. No one knows which country inflicted the first nuclear air strike. But, in a matter of days, warfare broke out worldwide, reducing our already thinning population by millions. And then the leaders of all countries congregated somewhere in an area called Europe. This was the start of the Accords. The Elected Accord. The Fertility Accord. The Ship Accord. And the Technology Accord.

If it were not for these four Accords and the ensuing isolation of our countries, human life would have been completely extinguished."

I pause for effect. My people are listening to the story, mesmerized.

"Even one small deviation from these Accords would begin a cycle that, without check, would lead us right back into the eco-crisis and demise of our civilization!"

Cheers erupt. I nod my head vehemently, empowered now by the widespread agreement.

It's so loud I don't hear the slight whoosh of air as it passes by my leg. But suddenly, there's an arrow embedded in the floor in back of me. The crowd has seen it too now, and there are screams and cries of surprise.

I don't even have time to react as I see another long arrow slicing through the air toward me. Its aim is perfect. Even as I see the shine of its metallic tip coming swiftly onward, I know I won't have time to move. My guards, who were on opposite sides of the stage won't have time to get to me now. I squeeze my eyes closed in fright since this motion is the only thing I can do fast enough.

My muscles tense and I know the arrow will find its mark in the next half second.

And then I'm on the ground. It's like a boulder just crashed into me. My eyes are still squeezed shut. I'm mentally screaming, trying to register the spot on my body that's hurting. Am I dying? Is this what it feels like to go? Not to be able to move? No longer having feeling in my arms or legs?

Through the screaming and pandemonium, I slowly let myself open my eyes. I tell myself I need to see the sun streaming through the clouds one more time before I die.

But instead of seeing blue sky and creamy white clouds above me, I see a different sight.

Griffin.

HE'S ON TOP OF me, encasing my body with his own. He's what knocked me over onto my back. Not the arrow at all. He's pinned me down with his own weight, shielding me, as I see a few more arrows fly over our heads onto the floor in back of us.

"Stop struggling and stay down," he says in frustration.

I obey, but only because I'm stunned and don't know what else to do. All I can do is move my head, so I look left and right, seeing my guards surrounding both me and Griffin. There's pandemonium in the amphitheater as people either run from the ensuing arrows or try to find the source.

I hear my father command the guards. "Take him out of here!"

Does he mean me? Or is the "him" Griffin? For a split second I wonder—did Griffin just save me or is he part of the onslaught? Are they taking him away because he's a threat to me?

Before I can ponder this or look fully into Griffin's face to glean an answer, his body is roughly pushed off mine, and I'm hustled away up the stairs of the amphitheater.

My foggy head suddenly becomes clear. My people can't see me like this—weak with shock and running away.

"Stop!" I yell. But the guard doesn't hear. I resort to digging my hands into the collar of his jacket, scratching the skin of his neck. "Now!"

He finally looks down at me in disbelief and then does what I command without a word.

I take the last few steps to the top of the pavilion, and for the first time I see how my people are reacting. They're running in all directions. They've never witnessed violence before, and they're like chickens with their heads cut off. The bikes, once in neat beautiful lines, are thrown out of the way in disarrayed piles.

"Stop!" I shout at the top of my lungs.

A few people turn at my voice and do stop.

"Hey!" I yell again. "Look! I'm fine. I'm not running. Do you see? I am not running!"

More people look toward me. Soon I have an audience of a couple hundred townspeople. Some come toward me slowly, sizing up my frame to see if I've been injured. When they see I'm fine, they come closer still.

Finally, a baker named Marjorie walks boldly up to me and gives me a bear hug around the shoulders. I quickly shift out of her embrace, extricating myself from her touch. I cough, feeling unsure about someone hugging me, in public no less.

But despite this awkwardness and the situation, I laugh out loud. "See, I'm fine," I say aloud to the crowd again. More people look relieved and a few laugh along with me.

This is my role. To lead and soothe my people no matter what. No matter what has happened to me personally. No matter how worried or confused I might be, it's essential I appear calm and in control in front of my people.

And I find, strangely enough, it suits me.

An hour later, my parents and I are sitting in our dining room, digesting the events. There's a knock at the door, and Tomlin ventures into the room. Ama looks up at him, giving a slight acknowledgement he's here. He nods back to her and then turns toward me.

"You look surprisingly calm," he says.

"I am," I say. "Really, I'm fine." I'm sure this won't be the last time I reassure people of this fact today.

I rake a hand across my beardless chin—a gesture I've seen Apa do many times. "Do you remember there ever being attempts on my father, grandfather, or great-grandfather?"

Tomlin stops to think a moment, but it's a short pause. He's already been thinking about this and has the answer ready.

"No. There's never been an attempt before. Not since the countries went into isolation."

"I thought not." My brow furrows. "Why now? Why would they

58

hate me?"

Tomlin hunches over, his shoulders growing closer to his ears. "They don't hate you. It's not you at all. It's just a matter of timing."

"What do you mean?"

"The Technology Faction is growing strong. It's been increasing in numbers for the last twenty years. And now there's a change in guard occurring. They think they'll find a chink in the system."

"And I'm the chink," I say. I place my head into the palm of my hand.

"I did not mean it like that. Your father remained in office for longer than was expected. Thirty-two years instead of the normal eighteen. It's hard for the Technology Faction to rise up against him when he's been the Elected for so long. But now, there's a break. Any change in leadership allows undercurrents to rise to the surface amongst the people. Remember, that is why the Elected Accord was created in the first place."

I finish his thought. "To discourage as much change as possible."

"Right."

"So why doesn't my father just stay in office?"

Tomlin looks at me like I'm younger than I am. He raises an eyebrow. Since he's silent I answer the question myself.

I roll my eyes but say, "Because most people don't live past their fifties in our country, and it's better for everyone if my father hands the office over to me in a polite and orderly fashion than if he dies and I have to take it in that chaos."

Tomlin's answer is quiet. "Right."

A little while later, I'm about to retire upstairs to my room when Tomlin, who's been sitting by the fire, says, "Aloy, they might be done with him if you want to say thank you."

For a moment, I'm not sure who he means. And then I realize who the "him" is.

"Who might be done with him?" I ask. I'd completely forgotten about Griffin.

"The guards. They took him to the prisoner's building to question him. Should be finished now, if you want to go over."

Suddenly, I realize it's exactly what I want to do. The thought of Griffin being pressured by the guards into saying who knows what scares me more than all the flying long arrows did this afternoon.

Tomlin continues, "They think he might have seen something and that's why he was so quick to your side. Certainly was faster than anyone else."

Now I definitely want to find out what he saw or said.

I grab a posse of four guards and march out directly for the prisoner's quarters. When I arrive at the gray front doors, I see Griffin's already being led out of the lobby. They're letting him go. For some reason this settles me. I should be hoping they'll keep him longer so I can sit in on the questioning, but I'm happy they're freeing him. I don't know why, but I don't like the thought of Griffin in this building at all. It gives me the chills.

"Griffin!" I say as our two parties meet on the front steps.

He bows his head politely at me. "Come to thank me?"

"Ha!" I'm smiling broadly, relieved he's okay. "Can I have a minute in private with him?" I ask the guards.

One of the men answers me. "Sure thing, Sir. We were just sending him home."

Griffin and I walk out together, and my guards stand a discreet distance away from us.

When everyone else is out of earshot I ask, "So what'd you tell them... about... you know?" I look down toward my chest.

Griffin laughs out loud. "Seriously? I just saved your life, and you're still worried I'm going to tell them you secretly wear skirts and play house?"

"Shhh!" I glance left and right.

Griffin's looking up at the sky. It's dark now, and a million small stars flicker overhead.

"You know, I heard back in the day, people couldn't even see the stars because of something called light pollution."

I look up to see what he's staring at. It really is gorgeous. "We take it for granted now, don't we?" We stand still for a few moments, long enough for me to register how close Griffin's arm is to mine. We're not touching, but he stands so near my heart skips faster. And I can't help remembering what he mouthed to me at the top of my stairs. He thinks I'm beautiful. Me? Was he trying to play me? Could he have really meant the romantic undertones? It's so impossible, I wonder if I just read his lips wrong. I'm even contemplating what word he might have actually been saying that could have looked like the word beautiful, when his next sentence breaks me out of the trance.

"If we manufactured light now, we wouldn't ever use it to block out the stars."

In that second I realize he's waxing poetic about using technology. He sees my sharp eyes, starts walking again, and interjects, "Not that I'm saying we should have electricity now or anything." Griffin clears his throat and looks away.

He's a little too quick with the response, and it reminds me why I'm here. Not to look at stars but to find out what he knows.

"You don't usually sit that close to the stage at the town halls."

Griffin looks down at me again but doesn't say anything.

I continue. "Why today?"

"Can't I want to be involved in politics? Listen closely to the Elected's speech?"

"Sure, but you've never been interested enough to sit in the front row before."

Griffin sighs. "Can't you just let well enough alone? You weren't hurt."

"Yes, but how'd you get there so fast? Were you in on it and wanted a chance to rip my head off yourself instead of letting an arrow take me out?"

He looks at me hard and, after a moment, sighs. "Well, that's a very nice outlook, isn't it?"

I shake my head. "Fine, obviously that's not what you were doing."

His voice is quieter now. "No, it wasn't." Griffin stands tall against the backdrop of the night sky, and I'm taken again by the way his body so easily fits into his environment. I can't help watching how he moves, even now. I wish I could look so comfortable and yet so commanding at the same time. I realize I'm staring at him and snap out of it.

"So... I guess I should... thank you."

Griffin's face lights up. "I'll take that!"

I face him, the moonlight throwing shadows off his cheeks. "So why'd you save me anyway?" I whisper the next sentence. "You know what I am. You don't think I'm fit for the Elected position."

Griffin looks at me, his lips turned down into a grimace. "Did I say that?"

I'm confused. "No... but... you know I'm... a—"

He cuts me off so I won't have to say it. "So what? That doesn't make you a bad leader."

Now this is unordinary talk. "Of course it does. I'm breaking the law."

Griffin pauses to think. "True. But it still doesn't mean you'll be a bad Elected. In fact, it shows you know sometimes you have to bend the rules to do the right thing."

I look at Griffin more closely. "But why'd you do it? You could have gotten killed."

We're stopped now in front of a large oak tree, one of the only ones we have in between my house and the outer village. The guards are over two hundred feet back, and between the darkness and the distance, I know they can't fully see us behind this tree. Griffin rests a hand against the trunk, pressing his thumb against the ancient ridged bark. I run the toe of my shoe through the dirt at the tree's base.

"Because even though you might not truly see it yourself yet, I know," he says.

"Know what?"

"Know you'll be the leader we've all been waiting for."

And in the moment it takes for him to say these words and for me to look up from the dirt I've been absentmindedly kicking, Griffin's thumb leaves the tree and brushes against my cheek in a decidedly romantic way.

7

I STEP BACK FAST, but not before I've felt the heat from his fingertip trail across my face. My eyes are huge as I watch him fold his arms back against his own torso. It happened so fast it's almost like he didn't touch me at all.

"You can't do that," I say. Although, at the moment, I would give my entire reign as Elected to feel his finger graze my cheek again. I am so confused. I thought I hated to be touched, but just the feel of Griffin's finger across my face is like electricity shooting through my cells. I want to experience it again in the worst way.

Griffin looks at me fully, trying to assess my true feelings, but I don't give him any indication of my desire. I let my words be my final direction.

He shakes his head and backs up. "Sorry." The apology is the first humble thing he's said in my presence. It sits in the air like a bubble aching to burst.

I want to tell him not to be sorry—that I'd enjoy it if he touched me again. Instead, I stand there quietly. I lick my lips, feeling the awkwardness growing inside my stomach. Before he can say anything else, I change the subject. "Why do you think I'll make a great leader? You've never seen me do anything before." I run my hand through the short spikes of my hair. "I haven't done anything before today."

Griffin takes my cue to forget what just happened and focuses on something else. "But you have."

"Yeah? Name one thing." I dare him, knowing when prodded he won't be able to give an example of my leadership skills. I haven't been given an opportunity before today, so he'll have nothing to report.

"It was three years ago, when you were fourteen."

I try to remember what he's talking about, but I come up blank.

"You were out with your parents in the village, visiting our people," Griffin continues.

"So? I do that all the time. That's not showing leadership."

"It's not the fact you were visiting people, it's what you did that one time."

He pauses to let me remember. And then I do. Suddenly, the memory floods my head. But how did he see it? How could he have known?

"I was there. My father let me ride double on his bike so we'd be sure not to miss seeing you."

"I remember that day. It was one of our trips to visit the chemists. To see their latest mixture of nirogene and chlorophyll."

"There was a sick girl. Aurora. The daughter of one of the chemists. We all knew her because she was three years old and already showing all the signs of radiation poisoning."

My chest aches at the memory of how sick the girl looked. How the circles under her little eyes were blue and how her silky blonde ponytail was losing strands of hair in handfuls as she pulled at it.

"The chemist tried everything he knew to help cure her. To stop the radiation from taking her so young. But nothing was working," Griffin continues.

I'm quiet. I know what Griffin is going to say next, but I wonder how he figured it out.

"And then you gave her a cupcake with frosting and rainbow sprinkles. It was a treat we hardly ever see in East Country. Aurora couldn't turn it down. Even sick to her stomach, she devoured the whole thing."

I smile, remembering. "She licked off that frosting like it was the best thing she'd ever tasted."

"Probably was," Griffin says. "But there was something else in the cupcake."

I look at Griffin in awe. "How'd you know?"

"Because she got better that same night. No more signs of radiation poisoning. Her father said it was a miracle. That maybe her young age helped her bounce back."

"But you knew that wasn't true."

"Right. Of course not."

I remember when I first decided what I'd do. I'd seen Aurora before and knew if she weren't helped soon, she'd die in the next several weeks. It was always hard watching my people suffer, but achingly so when the afflicted was young. It seemed cruel to do nothing when the method to cure Aurora was within my grasp. So I'd faked a cold and temperature, bathing my face in a hot, wet cloth every morning, for three days in a row. Finally, when Ama could see I wasn't getting better on my own, she opened the vault and gave me a perfect purple little pill filled with the miraculous serum.

"You sneaked a pill into the cupcake, didn't you?" Griffin asks.

"Yes."

"You really care about the people."

"I do."

"That's why you'll make a great leader." He takes a breath like he has more to say, but stops abruptly, deciding against it.

I gulp a deep breath of air, watching Griffin in front of me. My eyes grow bigger as the realization hits. He's right. I will make a great leader because I do care about my people. Their existence. Their survival. I will do anything for them. Pretending to be a boy, essentially giving up my childhood, having to say goodbye to my parents in a week. All of a sudden, it doesn't seem quite so hard. It seems possible. I'm up to the challenge because I have to be. It's what I was born for. To lead these people.

"You're staring at me," he says, and I blink my eyes, snapping out of my trance.

"Sorry." Embarrassed, I look down at the ground.

"Don't be sorry." He voices the very thing I wanted to say to him moments ago.

His dark eyes are chasms in this twilight. If I don't look away now, I think I may be lost in them forever. No one's ever gazed at me so intently. It leaves me feeling warm but exposed. But being exposed is dangerous. I need to stop this now.

I sigh. "I've got to go."

Griffin stares at me hard, his eyes boring into mine so it feels like he could see all the way back into my head. "Friends, right?"

I hold out my hand to Griffin. He shakes with me, our hands lingering on the sweep. "Friends," I agree.

And it feels nice to have a friend. I've never been allowed to have one before.

"I'd better get back to my father before he gets worried," Griffin says. "I'll see you around, Friend."

"See you." And I mean it. I'm already looking forward to the next time we'll bump into each other.

He's off, running into the dirt fields in the direction of his village. I'm left by the tree, grasping onto its trunk to stop my head from spinning.

A friend. I can't stop the smile from lingering on my face. I stare up into the sky, letting myself take it all in.

But a shiver goes down my spine, like the stars above have turned into liquid and are sliding, freezing, down my back. I never did get an answer from Griffin as to why he sat in the front row, today of all days. How he got to me so fast this afternoon.

I've opened myself up and immediately forgotten my duty, my agenda. It's dangerous for me to let my guard down, to waste time having friends. My smile falters.

Is Griffin really a friend? Or an enemy? My father always says, "Keep your friends close and your enemies closer." Well, whatever Griffin is, I vow to keep him close. And it's with this thought I make my way back by the house, head up.

FOR THE NEXT FEW days I'm completely beholden to my schedule, following my father to see as many townspeople as possible before he leaves. I have little time to think about Griffin, his so-called friendship, or the light touch of his fingertip.

Many of the townspeople bestow presents upon Apa. There will be an official goodbye ceremony, but people take the opportunity now to say something personal, wish him well, one-on-one. He receives a sheepskin water satchel from Neiall, the herder. A pair of bamboo shoes from Henricka, the shoe maker. A salted soft pretzel from Marjorie, the baker.

Apa shares the pretzel with me on the way home, each of us wishing we had a flagon of Ama's sweet lemonade to counteract the salt. We're passing by the chemists' corner of town, when Imogene, the head chemist, comes running out of her shop.

She flags us down, her white apron flicking behind her in the wind.

"Imogene," my father says, "what is it?"

"Elected, I was hoping to catch you. We're low on nirogene. Will you permit us to go into the hills to collect more element?"

"Of course, but why are your supplies low? You should have plenty."

"We don't know exactly." Imogene's brow furrows . "More than the usual number of people have come to see us for a bottle in the last month or so. It seems they are running out."

My father turns to me. "Aloy, at the next town meeting make sure to ask people to regulate their usage. There's only so much element we can harvest from the hills. People must conserve."

I jot this point down with a charcoal pencil and a small notebook I've been keeping with me for exactly such reminders.

We bid farewell to Imogene and keep up our meetings on horseback. We near the animal-rescue area. I'm looking forward to seeing the animal sanctuary Griffin's father mans, not only to see the exotic animals but for the off-chance we'll run into Griffin too.

As we turn into the sanctuary, Maran, Griffin's father, greets us at the gates.

"Nice to have you stop by, Elected," he says. "Would you like to come inside, see the animals one last time before your departure?"

"I wouldn't mind it at all!" my father agrees, his wind-burned cheeks rising into a smile. We dismount from the horses and follow Maran in through the wire fences.

"Shame they have to be cooped up," I say, referring to the animals in the compound.

Maran, who's walking in front of us as our guide, turns his head to look back at me. "May be a shame, but it's a necessity. These are some of the last animals of their kind. We need to focus on breeding them."

I nod absently, not really looking at Maran. I'm focused instead on the cage to our right. A furry rat with a bushy tail looks in our direction and gives us a "nit, nit, nit" before scampering up his fake tree.

"That," says Maran, "is a squirrel. There used to be a plethora of them before the climate change, but they've all mostly died out. This is one of just three."

I breathe out a gust of air, thinking it's a good thing we've managed to save this specimen. It's so small, it's a wonder the squirrel survived at all.

"Ahh," gestures Apa at a cage to our left. In it is a white bird with a long red flab of skin hanging from its neck, "I remember this one. Roster?" he asks.

"Close," says Maran. "Rooster. This is a rare animal in our collection. Named for the word roost. Birds called 'chickens' used to congregate together to rest. And the male bird, the rooster, would take advantage of their gathering to impregnate the chickens. One rooster would father multiple babies from many chickens at once."

"Ah, increasing the population. Something we understand, isn't it, Maran," my father jokes.

"Don't we all wish it was so easy," Maran says. There's hardness in his voice.

Griffin's mother, Maran's first wife, hoped to have more children

68

than just the one. However, she proved fruitless as miscarriage after miscarriage deformed her uterus and eventually killed her.

I remember my mother asking our cook, Dorine, to wrap up a basket of food for Maran. I'd clung to Ama's skirts in the kitchen that day, watching her help wrap basket upon basket for our villagers.

"Are these all for Maran?" I'd asked, hunger overtaking my stomach as I looked at a crisp, red apple being placed into the folds of a cloth.

"No, Aloy," my mother said. I remember her voice was soft like an old blanket. Comfortable, but worn out. "These baskets are for all the men who lost wives this week."

There were eight baskets.

I shuddered at the memory and then looked back at the haughty rooster strutting through his cage.

"It's not easy for him anymore, either," I say, pointing to the rooster. "There aren't any more chickens for him to mate with."

"Correct," says Maran, looking over my shoulder. "He's the last one. Even his parents died out a few years ago."

We walk along the dirt pathway of the sanctuary, my father and I pointing out the strange animals we haven't seen since we were here the last time. There's a parrot almost identical to the one I own. And a wolf. It looks like one of the dogs my parents keep with the horses, but this animal has grey fur and razor sharp teeth. It's agitated at our passage, so we walk by quickly.

I can't help but look for Griffin, thinking he'll be here helping his father. Finally, when I don't see him at all, I ask Maran.

"He's not around today," Maran says, avoiding my gaze. "Got a black eye play-fencing in one of the neighborhood matches. He's at the doctor's getting it looked at."

This seems strange to me. I can picture Griffin getting cut from fencing but not receiving a black eye from it.

We wave goodbye to Maran and start on the path back to our house. Along the way, I can't help peering into the windows of the doctor's house to catch a glimpse of Griffin, but I see nothing behind the drawn shades.

❦

Then, like time is proceeding faster than usual, my eighteenth birthday is upon us.

Three short days later, my parents and I arrive at the day we've

69

been planning as long as I can remember. I almost want to get it over with, as waiting for this night has worried me for too long already. But then again, I'm hoping the day will go as slowly, so I can linger with my parents for as long as possible.

We're sequestered together in an inner room of our house. We spend the entire night together with the rest of the village and our maids in repose. As is ritual, we are to have an evening devoid of distraction. No matter what else is happening in our country, tonight no one will come to us with their problems.

I lie with my head in my mother's lap as she lightly circles her fingers through my hair. I cannot believe she is allowing this comforting exchange, but I figure she doesn't have to worry about pretenses anymore. I know she's often wanted to nurture me but held herself back, thinking it would make me more girlish than I already am. Now it's her last chance to treat me like her daughter. My father sits across the room at a table, drinking a clear liquid. He looks less ferocious tonight than usual.

We've already gone through almost the entire list of questions I'd saved for this evening:

How do you know if an accused is truly guilty?

What do you do with the bodies of these people? Do they get buried along with our other townspeople or are they separated?

How do you apportion out the most highly demanded resources?

How are Vienne and I supposed to bear a child together?

My parents seem exhausted at my litany of questions, but still they answer each one in intricate detail, giving me everything they know. The only thing they don't answer adequately is the question about bearing children. When I ask, Apa puts his hand to his mouth and Ama looks away. I don't think they know the answer. "Vienne will think of something," my mother says.

Then she passes me the key to our vault—the one holding the last of the past's miraculous medicines. I take the ring and thread it onto a cord around my neck, pulling the key underneath my shirt.

"Aloy," she says, "I know you have sympathy for the people, but do keep the medicine for your family." It's like she knows I've given one of the purple pills away. "We don't horde the pills to be cruel. We do it because the Elected Accord states only the reigning family may take the cure. There's a finite amount of pills left. If those run out and the Elected dies before a full term, anarchy will ensue. The Accords will no longer apply. We need the pills to last until the planet's environment is strong once again and the Accords are not as necessary." In all the years I've heard my parents' advice, this is the first time Ama's mentioned anything about a future that didn't include the Accords. I just nod my head, too stunned to say a word.

My father clears his throat like he's about to add something but is having a hard time with it.

"What, Apa?" I say, sitting up from my mother's touch.

"Aloy. We... I... am sorry." He stops and looks down at his hands. "This wasn't ever supposed to be your burden."

He's never before apologized for forcing me into the Elected role. He's always been steadfast to a fault. Even when I once asked him why he doesn't even hear out the Technology Faction's thoughts, my father merely scoffed and said, "Listening to idiocy is futile." He looks down at the floor now, a rare moment of regret passing over his face.

"Don't be sorry," I say. "It wasn't your choice. It was Evan's."

His name is like a bell ringing. It drowns out everything else in the room. Evan. The real Elected. The one who was supposed to take this post years ago. We all wonder where he is. If he's still alive.

"Let's not think about that right now, shall we?" my mother says. My father and I both look away, wanting to say more but knowing it'll upset Ama. Neither of us wants to do that tonight. So there will be words left unsaid. I resign myself to that fact.

"Where will you go?" I ask. If I cannot talk about Evan, I will at least broach this next controversial topic.

My mother says, "What does it matter? We will never come back. And you will never come to find us."

"I know," I whisper. "But at least tell me what your plans are."

"Aloy, no," starts my mother again, but my father breaks in.

"Mid Country."

What used to be the United States of America, is now divided into three countries. I picture the old United States map with the top and bottom shaved off. The coldest and hottest regions became uninhabitable long before the full eco-crisis struck. Then I picture the country with its outermost states peeled away—land closest to the oceans that got flooded. I imagine what's left dissected into three small pieces.

East Country is what remains of the states Maryland, West Virginia, Virginia, and the former capital, Washington, DC. Of the three countries dividing our continent, ours is the only one with land bordering water. Because of the Chesapeake Bay's unique shape, we still have a small coast unmarred by oil spillage.

Then there's Mid Country, encompassing part of Maryland and what used to be Virginia to Kansas. The bottom of their land is Arkansas and the top is Iowa. Our most tenacious and previously disputed border with Mid Country is a small mountain about seventeen miles away from the White House. The Appalachians make up the rest of the border.

Last, there's West Country, which was almost unbearably hot even back when former leaders split up the country. That land consisted of Colorado, Utah, and Wyoming. I'm not sure if that country is even in existence anymore.

That's it for the North American continent. What used to be Mexico and Canada are no more. The land remains, but it grew respectively too hot and too cold to sustain life comfortably.

I shake my head of these images and try to focus on the fact my parents are heading for the great unknown Mid Country. I turn suddenly to Apa, surprised he's given me any hint of their plans at all.

"Are they expecting you?" I ask, incredulous. I always thought my mother and father would ride out quietly into the middle of nowhere, living on their own for the rest of their lives in the outskirts of East Country. I never thought they'd try to reach another country.

"Of course not," says my father.

My mother sighs. "We will ride through the hills, let the horses go when we're close to Mid, and walk the rest of the way in. Mid's people won't know who we are."

No one in East Country has ever climbed the border hill to its peak. It's only a mile up, so it's easily scalable. But climbing the hill, even to sneak a glimpse at Mid Country, is punishable by death. It violates the Accords' intent for isolation. So, our people stay firmly rooted at the foot of the hill on our side of the border. What my parents speak of now isn't only risky, it signifies their abandonment of East Country's laws.

"But what will you say?" I ask with alarm. "Won't Mid question who you are?"

"We don't know," says Apa. "Maybe their society is different from ours. Maybe they don't keep track of their people. Maybe there are so many people, we'll just blend in."

"And if we can't blend in," Ama continues, "we will say we've lost our memory because of the radiation poisoning. Don't worry, Aloy. We won't say anything about East Country. We will keep the isolation intact."

"I'm not worried about that!" My voice is panicked. "I'm worried they'll harm you. They won't know who you are. You'll be intruders!"

"Nonsense," says my father. "We'll be fine. Last thing you need is to worry about us!"

"You shouldn't have told her," Ama says. "Now she'll be thinking of it!" Her voice is high.

They're starting to fight, and that's the last thing I need to worry about. I don't want to look back on my last night with them and picture them arguing. So I raise my hands up in defeat, hoping to quell the situation.

"Fine, fine," I say. "I won't think about it. You're right. You'll be fine."

But before I can truly let the words settle over me, I realize I'm crying. Tears are streaming down my face, and for the first time I do absolutely nothing to stop them. My mother comes to my side, wrapping an arm around my shoulder and up to my face. She leans into me, trying to soothe but for once not trying to stop my actual tears. My parents let them flow.

I splutter, "You can't leave, you just... can't!"

Finally, my father walks to where Ama and I are sitting. He squats down in front of me so we're eye to eye.

He looks at me squarely, "We can. You're ready. My father left me when I was your age too. I survived. You will too."

I know he's right, so I don't try to argue. His words are solemn but assured. I sniff, trying to be as strong as he thinks I am.

He gets up again and fetches something from the corner of the room.

I look up to see he's holding a ratty looking toy out to me. It's my old baby doll they took from me when I was four.

"I was hard on you," he says.

I grasp the doll by the arms and hug it close to my stomach, hoping to feel an echo of the comfort it gave me in childhood.

His voice grows quieter. "Perhaps too hard."

My mother says, "We did what we thought was best. For you. For this family. For the country."

"I know," I say. "I understood."

My mother and father both grasp my hands in theirs. "We always hoped you did."

We stay like that, hands clutched together and silent for what seems like hours. I don't know if they've fallen asleep, my mother next

73

to me, her body leaning heavily upon mine. Or my father in front of me, seated on a high-backed chair with his eyes closed. But I haven't slept. I've looked at them closely, trying to memorize the rise of my mother's forehead, wrinkling now that I see it up close. And my father's white hair, thinning on the top, a symptom of age I know our people wish they could all achieve.

When I finally see the sun starting to rise, I gently touch each of my parents. They stir and stare at me kindly, thinking they've only fallen asleep for a few minutes. I let them keep this illusion and stare back at them. When the knock comes at our door, it still seems too soon. But my father gets up to answer the door.

It's Tomlin. "You have just five more minutes. The people are lined up," he says. His eyes are downcast, sorry for interrupting our last moments.

"Thank you. We will be out shortly," says my father, his voice thick with emotion. The "thank you" seems to be for more than just this reminder of time.

The door closes again, and my mother is still attached to my side, hugging me hard. "You will make such a good leader," she says, wiping tears from her lashes.

"We are proud of you," my father says. "Lead with a kind heart. But lead. Don't forget that, my child."

I nod, not able to get any words out of my throat. It's closing up.

I watch as my father grabs up a small bag. In it I know are the essentials: a water pouch, food to sustain them for a few days, and a blanket. One thing left out are the purple pills. They don't need them anymore. They will no longer be part of the Elected family.

My mother wraps a traveling cloak around her shoulders. It's lined with wool. They'll need the warmth, heading out into the unknown.

We walk out of the room together, holding hands in a small line, me in the middle. The maids and other help line the corridors. This is custom. People will line my parents' walk to the front of the house and will form a tight line all along my parents' path into the hills. For as many people as we have in our country, that is how long the line will extend on either side of my parents' path. Arms will be linked together, in solidarity with my parents but also as a sort of fence, knotted together to prevent my parents from veering back into our country. The linked arms signify my parents must leave. As much as this custom is for my parents, it's a pact of solidarity for me too. It signifies the people's recognition that my parents' time is over. That I am the next Elected.

We mount horses and ride forward together, my parents in front of me, side by side, with me behind. My parents stop in front of Tomlin and bow their heads. He returns the gesture, locking eyes with my father.

Without my father saying anything, Tomlin promises, "I will take care of him."

My father doesn't utter a word. I wonder if this is custom too or if he's trying to control his own sadness—if he fears the moment he tries to talk, his voice will crack. He gives Tomlin a small smile and another nod.

We ride for approximately an hour at a ceremoniously slow pace. That is all it takes to ride past the entirety of our people. As we go, I think I see Griffin in the crowd, but I can't look at him now. I fear my resolve will break at seeing a friend, and I'll fall apart. So, I keep my eyes forward and formal.

Finally, at the end of the line of people, it's just me and my parents left. The people are all in back of us now. The linkages of arms won't break until I've said goodbye to my parents.

Ama and Apa turn their horses around and look at me.

My mother juts her chin up, in a sign I know is meant for me. I've seen it many times when I'm about to cry. It's her reminder to me to keep my head up. This time the gesture seems softer, affectionate. I jut my chin up to her in response, and she smiles. I look over at my father and squeeze my eyes shut, trying to capture this last picture of my parents before they go. Then I put both my mother and father in my line of sight and mouth the words, "I love you."

They mouth it silently back to me.

I lean forward on my horse to say my last official words to them. Words that will be marked down in history as being my first act as Elected.

I raise both of my arms out in front of my face at forty-five degree angles. Elbows close to my sides and palms facing up like I'm offering a present. The physical salutation of our country.

And then in a booming voice reverberating off the mountains in front of us, I give them my final goodbye.

"A new day to you both!"

9

I WATCH AS MY parents become dots on the horizon. Even as their forms grow distant, I don't turn around. I can't seem to let them go. I stay face-forward for another reason too—I don't want my people to see the anguish carved into my eyes. I'm trying to collect myself.

I feel a tingling on my cheek. I brush it away, frustrated, thinking my emotions have taken over and I've ended up crying after all. But then I hear nervous murmuring behind me. I turn the horse around to look at my people. They're still linking arms, waiting for me as is customary, but they're growing restless. I wonder why until I feel another needle prick on my forehead.

I look up at the sky and see dark green clouds.

I need to lead. Now!

"Everyone find shelter!" I yell. As sharp drops of acidic rain fall down on us, everyone lets go of their neighbor's arms and starts running. I only hope my parents are able to find a cave or some brush to hide under until the onslaught passes.

Greenish clouds mean rain tinged with radiation-born chemicals. I should have seen the clouds earlier, but a wind must have blown them in quickly. The drops on bare skin will leave tiny blisters. Not enough to really hurt a person, but how would I truly know? We've never before stood out in the open as buckets of this rain fall down on our heads.

I reach down and grab up two small children onto my saddle. I look down at their parents and see their nods of agreement. I ride fast, heading straight for my house. Once under an awning, I drop off the children and ride out again to grab more kids onto my horse. I think I see Griffin helping more children to shelter on the back of a bike, but we don't have time to stop and talk to each other.

After a half hour everyone's indoors, and my skin is itchy and red. I return the horse to the stable, brushing it down because it also felt the acidic rain. Maran is already in the stable, ready to assist. He helps me walk the horse over to a fountain so it can get washed off. The horse thrashes its head around impatiently.

Maran doesn't make eye contact with me. He's too busy tending to the horse. But he says, "Elected, you should get inside and wash up as well."

He's the first person to call me "Elected." It sounds strange the way it rolls out like the word is too big to fit in his mouth.

I nod and exit the stables, careful to stay under the awning.

It's been a long time since we've been caught off guard by acid rain. I chide myself that it was under my watch on my first day as Elected. Now I'm not only reeling from my parents' departure, I'm also frustrated at my inability to protect my people.

I make my way up to my bedroom and immediately splash water from a basin onto my skin. Thankfully, not much of me was exposed since it was cold outside and I was pretty bundled up. But my face is blistered. I can tell as I look into the cracked mirror over the basin.

As I run a hand over my broken skin, I can't help feeling hopeless. I have a rebellion bubbling up, assassination attempts against me, and an environment slowly killing my people. And I'm alone. So utterly alone.

I give a tortured moan.

"Your face doesn't look that bad," comes a soft voice from behind me.

I wheel around, surprised someone is sitting on my bed.

The someone is a girl, and she's radiant. The rain outside must have stopped because this girl is bathed in light from the window. She looks serene in a white, somewhat sheer gown. Her long blonde hair flows down her back and a string of pale pink flowers circle her head.

It's Vienne. I've never seen her before today, but I know I'm right. I slowly walk across the room, taking in her presence. She sits with folded hands in her lap.

At once a rush of feelings envelops me. I'm jealous of her. She's everything I desire to be. Alluring. Poised. And most of all feminine. But at the same time, I'm proud she's mine. I feel a wave of possessiveness well up from my stomach to my throat. I've never seen any girl who looks like Vienne. I have a strong desire to protect her—to keep her all to myself. She seems delicate, like a gossamer-winged butterfly, but upon closer inspection, I can see the strength she exudes as well. It's obvious in the firm tilt of her chin and the way she doesn't break eye contact with me. Hers is a quiet but strong presence. Vienne is utterly enchanting. Every man will want her, but she's to be my wife.

When I'm almost in front of her, she turns her face to the nightstand near my bed and picks up a teacup and saucer. Offering it to me, Vienne says, "I thought you might like some mint tea."

Vienne's been raised for this position her whole life. She knows exactly what to say and do politically. It's a powerful feeling knowing someone was crafted just for you.

I look down at the delicate china cup in her palm and see three small mint leaves floating in the liquid. I take the tea from her hands, our fingers touching slightly. "Thank you." My voice still cracks from my fears of a few minutes ago. I sip the liquid, tasting a hint of bitter liquor balancing out the sugar. Vienne prepared it the way I most desire.

I try to gather myself so I can talk to this girl, my future wife. "I didn't expect to see you today," I say.

"I know it's customary for us not to meet until our wedding day. "However..." She pauses. "I thought you might need someone to talk to."

She doesn't apologize for breaking the rules. She is more my match than my parents and Tomlin may even have realized.

"You couldn't have known about the rain," she continues. It's like she's read my earlier thoughts. "I was watching from up here. The clouds swept in with the wind. No one noticed because it was already so cold."

"I need to notice."

She doesn't negate me. Doesn't placate me. "Well, now I'll be here to help you notice."

And with her words, I know Vienne won't just be a figurehead by my side. She is like the female leaders from long ago—the ones who, ironically enough, wrote the very Elected and Fertility Accords ruling out the option of women in office.

I watch her looking at me and eventually, because I don't know what else to do, I say, "Your hair. It's like spun gold. Like a princess in the old fairy tales."

"You were allowed to read fairy tales? I thought your parents discouraged your reading of fantasies."

At the mention of my parents, my eyes grow solemn. I stare past Vienne's face, concentrating instead on one of my birds in the background.

"I'm sorry," she says. It's not just an apology for bringing up my parents. Her "sorry" holds much more. From her years of instruction on me, she knows all about my parents' refusal of anything feminine in my childhood.

I look back at Vienne. "It's okay. I kept one book hidden under my bed for a while. When I was nine, I burned it in the fireplace."

"You burned it yourself?"

"Yes, I needed to grow up."

"What a hard childhood." She shakes her head.

"My parents spent their lives getting me to this spot. They were hard on me for a reason. I always knew that. And I always knew I'd miss them come today."

"It's okay to miss them." The way she whispers her words makes me sit down next to her. I realize I don't know her story like she knows mine. She's moving out of her parents' home now that she's to be married. It may not be the same as completely losing them, but I'm sure it's a shock. I realize I'm being callous by not asking her.

I stand again with my hands on my hips. "When can I meet your parents?" I am resolute, trying to pin a cheerful smile on my face.

But Vienne doesn't jump up with the same enthusiasm to match mine. "You can't. I've never even met them."

I look down and purse my lips. Was Vienne taken away from her parents long ago to get ready for the Madame Elected role?

Before I can ponder this for too long she says, "They died right after I was born."

"Oh, I'm sorry to hear that. We must go honor their grave site together on the day of our wedding."

"I know it's the custom, but it won't be necessary."

I stare at Vienne with shock. I know she'll have to be tough for this role, but not even wanting to honor her parents' grave site? This is too much.

Then she laughs slightly. "Don't look at me that way. I'm not unfeeling. They're not buried in East Country. I don't know where they're buried."

This is odd. All our people are buried in formal ceremonies. Even people who broke the Accords and took hemlock are prayed over in specific rituals by the Madame Elected—buried away from the regular graveyard—but still buried in East Country.

"What happened to them?" I ask.

"Supposedly, they started showing signs of radiation poisoning when I was young and left."

"Where did they go?"

"No one knows. But they never came back. So I figure they're deceased."

She is so formal in her tone when speaking of them. I want to push the issue. Ask her for more specifics. But then I look at her eyes and realize she's told me everything she knows. I make a mental note to ask Tomlin more about Vienne's parents.

"Where have you lived?"

Vienne perks up and turns her body so she's facing me fully. "You don't know?"

I shake my head.

Her answer is simple. "Here."

Vienne has lived in this house? Close by me for practically my whole life? And I've never known it?

"What better way to study you than from up close?" She seems amused I hadn't guessed. "What better way to learn about your family's ideals and the policies I'll be upholding now as Madame Elected?"

"Have I ever seen you before?"

"Of course! Although I did try to keep a low profile. I've been disguised as different maids around your house through the years. You've even borrowed some of my disguises. I have quite a few wigs."

I'm embarrassed until I realize if Vienne truly knows me, then she already understands my desire to be more feminine. I don't have to hide from her the fact I've often daydreamed about being a girl with long flowing hair.

I think back to the new maids I've seen flit in and out of my house over the past years. The ones who always looked sort of the same but with different colored hair—red, black, and yellow blonde—sometimes so straight it seemed like pieces of plastic. I realize my subconscious was smarter than my eyes. They were all the same girl.

"Sorry," I say, my hand now on my brow. "I didn't know the wigs I found in one of the rooms were yours. When I was younger, before I mastered this charade," I explain, my hand gesturing to my masculine attire, "I wasn't really allowed out. So I used to explore the house. I shouldn't have trespassed into the maids' bedrooms."

"It's nothing. Don't apologize. I never did get the blonde one back, though, since your mother tossed it into the fire." Her eyebrows rise in amusement.

I choke out a tortured laugh, remembering my mother's scolding just two weeks earlier. I want to say more. Ask Vienne about the many other times we've seen each other. Talk to her more about the night I snuck out. How, as the red headed maid, her dare to sneak out had gone wildly wrong. Did she know the danger I'd been in? And I want to talk to her about my parents. I miss them now, and I want desperately to tell her about it.

But the moment is interrupted by an urgent knock at the door, and at once it's pulled open.

A surprised guard stands in the frame, looking back and forth from Vienne to me.

I snap him out of the trance. "What is it?"

He coughs, remembering himself and that he shouldn't be staring so fervently at this vision of an angel that is Vienne. I have a premonition that, for the rest of our lives, Vienne's beauty will render people speechless, and I will be an accessory on the fringe. But I shake off the feeling, instead focusing on the guard's worried face.

"Elected," he says, "we have another accused."

At once, I am at attention, poised behind the guard, exiting the room after him. I look back quickly at Vienne. Her face is grave. She gives me one steadfast nod, and I raise my chin back at her in a goodbye.

"Is it the assassin?" I'm almost hopeful as we round the corner.

"Unfortunately, no, Elected. The scoundrel is still on the run. This accused is in possession of a unique technology."

"Unique? They're all unique."

The guard leads me out of the house. I keep pace with his brisk walk to the prisoner's quarters, almost running to keep up with him. I wonder why we're hurrying so fast. A prisoner just caught isn't going anywhere. What must this technology be?

At the entrance to the prison, I already see Tomlin standing outside. He gestures me in, his fingers tapping fast on his temple. I stare into his eyes intently. And then I see it.

He's excited.

It's unmistakable. Whatever's been found has rendered Tomlin giddy.

"Tomlin, is it dangerous? A bomb?"

Tomlin's eyes dart back and forth to see if anyone is close enough to hear us. He leads me to a corner of the room, away from the guards who are watching us like hawks.

Tomlin's actions are so odd, so out of character for him, suddenly I'm worried. The guards are watching us differently than usual. A wash of fear overtakes me. Is Tomlin the accused? Is he the one in possession of the technology? Is he the prisoner?

Before I can delve too deeply into that nightmare, Tomlin grasps my wrists. "Elected, it's a Mind Multiplier. I've never seen one before. Only read about these. You must come see it."

I breathe a sigh. So it's not a deadly bomb or a weapon threatening to destroy my people.

I follow Tomlin down a long corridor, past the set of wooden prisoner doors. I vaguely think about the fact that behind one of these doors sits our accused right now, awaiting his fate. All of the doors start to look alike until Tomlin eventually stops in front of one. A guard moves aside as the door is opened for us.

The room is empty except for a wooden table in the center. On it sits a helmet with wires crisscrossing all around. I pick it up, turning it over in my hands.

"Careful," Tomlin warns. But his voice is still giddy.

I look for a battery pack or some sort of solar panel, but I don't find one. "How is it powered?"

"By the pulsing of blood in the wearer's temples. Utterly amazing."

I look over at him with my eyebrows furrowed. "If I didn't know better, I'd think you were actually happy to see this technology."

Tomlin finally checks himself, aware now that it appears he's pleased to see the helmet.

"I apologize." His voice is an octave lower. "It is still technology, yes. Something we cannot have. But it is one of the most remarkable pieces I have ever heard about. So rare. Only a few were made over two hundred years ago before the Accords. I never imagined one would still exist."

"What does it do?"

"It is just what the name states. It multiplies your mind."

"I still don't understand."

Tomlin smiles. "It lets you see things your mind has locked away. Things you didn't remember you'd seen or heard. And sometimes on rare instances, it taps into a certain clairvoyance to give you pictures of the future or past you weren't physically present to see when they happened. Let me show you. May I?" He walks toward me with the helmet outstretched, ready to attach the various plugs onto my skin.

"Is it safe?" I know putting on the helmet constitutes technology use, but it's better we know what the thing is and if it'll be a danger to our country.

"As safe as increased knowledge ever is," Tomlin says.

I nod, letting Tomlin secure the helmet on my head. At once I'm tired of his riddles. Tired of his excitement over this piece of metal. I just want to sleep. I realize I still haven't slept since spending all night with my parents. I feel the urge to sink down onto the floor right now and collapse onto a warm pillow.

But, before I can fully let myself melt into a puddle, the helmet is fastened firmly on my head. It stings as the metal knobs pinch into the sides of my scalp.

"It's too tight," I complain.

"It's supposed to be tight." For the first time, he's not worried about my well-being. He's engrossed in this technology, and it makes me mad. I want to fling the contraption off my head. I'm starting to reach up to my chin to do just that, when Tomlin pushes a button on the helmet and the whole thing starts humming.

It's not a hum exactly. It overtakes my ears with singing. It's the voice of my mother, humming softly to me as I fall asleep the previous night. I can hear it so clearly. At once I'm awake and asleep at the same time. I'm utterly relaxed.

And I'm thinking. My mind is so open and malleable. I think of Vienne back in my room and how much I want to keep her safe from any assaults by the Technology Faction. I think of my parents and where they're heading in Mid Country. I almost see them right now in front of me, walking alongside their horses through the freezing countryside. They are close enough to be touched. I reach out.

And then a different image comes across my mind. I'm at the town hall meeting. The one where the assassin tried to kill me with the barrage of long arrows. I see Griffin looking at me. I take in his image, free now to drink in the sight of him without anyone noticing. His cheekbones are high and his hair is strewn across one eye. I want to reach out and push it off his forehead for him. More than anything, I want to touch him. But then he's looking backward. Fearful. He is watching. So keenly watching. I see an arrow coming for me in slow motion. And I watch Griffin. He sees the arrow too.

But instead of watching me, Griffin's face is pointed toward the back of the amphitheater.

He sees who launched the arrow.

10

ALL OF A SUDDEN, the helmet is off. I've ripped it from my head without knowing I was even touching it. I smash it onto the floor, screaming.

Tomlin is there, holding my arms back, trying to grab the helmet from me.

"Elected!" he screeches, imploring. "Aloy! Aloy!"

It is his use of my given name that finally breaks through my haze.

"I saw... I saw..." The words won't come.

"You thought clearly. Of multiple thought threads all at the same time. Things locked in your head. And now they're out."

I calm, knowing Tomlin understands. "Yes. I saw... saw..."

I can't seem to form words now. It's like my brain capacity increased for the period the helmet was on my head. Who knows how long that even was? And now that the helmet is off, my thoughts are back down to their normal size. Their normal capacity. Which isn't big at all, I realize, dejected.

And I want that helmet back on my head. Now.

I grasp for it like a blind man finding his spectacles, but Tomlin holds my hands back behind me. I cry out, exasperated.

"You must wait. Too many increased brain threads aren't good. It will overload you. You can't put the helmet back on right now."

I fall onto the floor, into the puddle I desired earlier. Tomlin sits on the ground by me.

"It's amazing, isn't it?" he says in awe.

"Yes. But my head aches." I find I can only make small sentences.

"It will ache for just a few minutes more as your brain capacity returns to normal."

"Where did this thing come from?"

"Only the prisoner knows," Tomlin says. "Unfortunately, it seems the information is locked in the accused's head. Too much use of the helmet, I'm afraid."

"With great technology comes great burden." I am quoting my father.

"Are you ready to stand up now?" I try my feet. They're gelatinous, but at least they support me. "What did you see or hear?" Tomlin asks.

"My mother's singing. Does everyone hear that?"

Tomlin laughs. "No. It's different for each person. It's based on your own brain waves. Did you see anything?"

My hand runs the length of my brow, massaging my temples in frustration. "It's hard to remember."

"It's ok, don't push too hard."

"I saw my parents," I say suddenly. "They're somewhere cold."

Tomlin nods. "Anything else?"

I concentrate hard. There was something else. I can almost taste the feeling of it. The anger. The betrayal. I yell without thinking. "Get me Griffin, now! NOW!"

Tomlin is off running, and I hear the pounding steps of multiple guards following after him.

I lie on the cold concrete of the room floor, trying to collect my thoughts. I want to find the helmet, but Tomlin took it with him. This helmet could be used for torture, I think. My brain aches. I want to use it. But I want to destroy it. No. I want to use it on Griffin, I realize. I want to bash his head in until it hurts like mine does now. I cry, rocking back and forth on the floor, with my head in my hands.

I vow never to put the helmet back on my head. What must this have done to people in the past? How many times did people use it? Did it make them crazy too? Or is it just the mix of radiation in our systems that now turns it so vile?

I throw up in a pool on the concrete floor, and it makes me feel better.

When the guards fail to return quickly, I finally stand back up and open the door into the corridor. The place is deserted. All of the guards are out doing my bidding—bringing Griffin to me.

I try all of the doors in the corridor, most of which are locked until they're needed for prisoners. When one finally budges, the force I use throws open the door. Inside, armor glass dissects the space in two.

As usual, my side contains just one long wooden bench. The other side behind the glass, contains the prisoner. A plant. A cot. And a cup of clear liquid.

As I walk in, the door slamming in back of me, the prisoner looks up. The accused can't hear me. But the reverberation of the door is jarring.

We lock eyes with each other. I'd expected to see a man. A man who had used the helmet and now knows too much.

But I was mistaken.

It's a woman. Imogene, the chemist.

She stands immediately, pushing both palms up to the glass. Her cheek crushes up against the barrier, squishing out into a blob of pale skin. It looks odd and almost makes me want to throw up again. She moves her cheek away and this time plants her lips against the glass. She kisses the armor glass. Over and over again.

She's gone crazy. Imogene, the smart, collected chemist has come unglued. I can almost hear my father's words in my head. *This is what happens when technology is used. Humans don't have the capacity to use it wisely. We must not use it at all.*

Imogene is trying to talk to me through the glass. I can't hear her, and even when I try to read her lips, I can't understand what she's trying to communicate.

I hold up one finger to her, to indicate I'll be back in a minute. She just opens her mouth in a big O. Screaming.

I run out of the room and down into the lobby. One guard is still there.

"I need to question the accused," I burst out.

He turns, sees the fierceness on my face, and instantly starts leading me to the back of the accused's room.

"Elected, you don't want to go into that side. The prisoner is unstable." I know he's warning me with my best interests in mind, but I don't want to be told what to do right now.

"Oh, but I do," I say, my voice uncharacteristically cold.

"Your father, he never..."

I get up in the guard's face, eye to eye, daring him to defy me when I'm feeling so vicious.. "I am not my father. I am the Elected now!" The guard needs to realize I'm no longer a child to be protected. Today I've become their leader. I try to compose myself, the headache coming back twofold. I attempt to contain my voice. "Let me in." I say my words with more restraint this time.

He immediately unlocks the door. I walk past him with a curt nod.

Imogene is still standing against the armor glass, waiting for me there. Her lips are again stuck to the partition.

The door closes behind me, the deadbolt flicking in a final thud.

"Imogene," I whisper.

She doesn't turn, just keeps making fish faces against the glass. I cautiously walk up behind her and put a finger on her shoulder. She wheels around, seeing me there for the first time. She throws her arms around my neck. At first, I'm worried she'll try to choke me and I look back at the guard's door. But then, Imogene starts crying, hugging me and mumbling incoherent words.

"Shhh," I console. "It'll be okay. I'll get you out of here. Don't worry. You... aren't of right mind. We don't make people drink the hemlock if they don't have control of their... wits," I say. I think back to my father saying people with mental problems are forgiven any trespasses against the Accords.

"You... you... never...," she blubbers.

"It's okay. Don't try to talk."

"No! No! I must... tell... you!" she cries.

I lead her over to the cot along the wall at the far corner of the room. I sit her down on it gently and then ease onto the bed next to her. We're facing each other, and she has her hands cupping my face.

"Need to tell!" she says.

"Okay, go ahead. I'm listening."

"No, baby... not for you!" Imogene bellows loud, choking on her own tears. "They'll take it!"

I smooth her matted hair, seeing the bare spots where she's pulled it out in tufts.

"It's okay. I know. I won't ever have a baby of my own. I already know. Is that what you saw with the helmet on?"

She nods, her eyes blank.

"What else did you see?"

"Niro... nirogene. No more. No more!" She's so distressed, she's shaking. "No more bikes. Rust. Everywhere rust!"

"You must be wrong about that. We still have stores of it. And we're harvesting more nirogene from the hills. There's plenty of it. Don't worry."

"Taking... taking it!"

"No, no. I won't take it," I say. "I'll make sure everyone gets some."

She grabs my cheeks, pulling at the skin. "Not you! Them! Them! Taking it! Save us!"

"The harvesters? They're taking it?"

Imogene looks confused, like I've posed a question too hard for her. I try soothing her again. "Okay, don't worry. We'll fix it. I'll fix it."

This quiets her, and she puts her head down on my shoulder.

"Where did you get the helmet?" I ask.

She looks up at me, searching my eyes. She says nothing, and I'm about to let the question drop when she moans, "Sky." She points up at the ceiling.

"It fell from the sky?"

She nods and then puts her head back down on my shoulder, exhausted.

I look in front of me, over Imogene's back, out toward the armor glass. Great. So the only person who can tell me where this strange helmet came from thinks it fell from the sky. Perfect.

When Imogene's breath is steadier, and she's panting less, I place a hand on her shoulder. "Let's go, Imogene. I'll get you out of here. You can stay with me in the White House."

"Black house." Her words come out in a quiet mumble. "Black like ash."

I shiver at her description. "Fine. Black house. You can stay with me there."

Imogene looks up at me, tears glistening in her eyes. I pull her bent fingers, one by one, from the fabric around my neck.

When I've finally extricated myself, I stand up, ready to knock on the door to get the guard.

"Imogene, let's go."

She stares at me blankly and then puts her fingers to her lips. I can't tell exactly what she's doing, but when her fingers come away from the kiss, I realize she's saying goodbye.

And before I can reach her, Imogene skids across the floor. She's upon the glass of clear liquid, more quickly than I would have expected.

"No! Imogene, no!" I scream.

She flails out at me, pushing me back. I scramble toward her again, but the liquid is already bubbling out of her mouth. She's thrown it on her eyes, down her throat, and over her head. She licks her cheeks where the liquid dribbles out of her mouth.

I crouch next to her, yelling for the guards. One of them flings open the door, and they're upon us, trying to help me.

But it's too late. Imogene is already convulsing, gurgling with the onset of hemlock paralysis. All I can do is hold her head, as it bucks and threatens to split in two on the concrete floor. There's blood pouring out of her nose and down her lips. I can hardly see anything as unshed tears obscure my vision.

When Imogene's body falls still, and I think she's gone, her eyes bolt open. There's no more choking. Imogene's at once clear and calm as she gazes at me, her pupils exploring my face like she sees something majestic. Then she lets out one long, shuddering sigh. Her body tenses, and I prepare myself for more violent thrashing. I stay on my knees with her, waiting, but after the quiet sets in I know it's finally over.

11

I HOLD HER, ROCKING back and forth, until the guards gently extract Imogene from my grasp and carry her body away. I know where they're taking her. To Vienne, as is custom. Vienne will dress the accused in proper burial clothing. She'll prepare Imogene for the special graveyard where prisoners have their final resting place.

It isn't a job I would wish on Vienne for her first day. We're not even married yet. Technically, she's not the Madame Elected. But in the absence of another, Vienne will take on this task.

I put my hands on my head, the ache from the helmet pulsing and then subsiding again. I don't rise up from the floor or lift my head until I hear Tomlin's voice at the door.

"Elected, we've brought Griffin to you."

There are indeed two guards hauling Griffin into the room. His arms are chained behind him, and the guards each hold him under one armpit, dragging him forward. He's fighting it, but when he sees me, surprise flashes across his face, and his legs go slack. He sees the droplets of Imogene's blood still on the floor, and his eyes widen.

"Leave him here," I say.

Tomlin looks at me with his eyebrows raised. "Are you sure, Elected? You don't look well. The helmet, it can do strange things..."

"Yes, I'm sure." I look toward the guards. "I want to see him alone. But keep the chains on his arms. And close the window's shutter on the door. Come back in only if I call you." My tone is sharper than usual.

They nod and leave the room, Tomlin glancing back at me, still worried. Griffin did nothing wrong that they know of. Yet, on just the strength of my word, my orders were followed explicitly. The surge of power I felt earlier at knowing Vienne was all mine, comes again.

I walk up to face Griffin, who is now standing squarely in front of me. He looks at me with a mixture of anger and confusion etched around his clenched jaw.

"Are you all right?" he asks.

Here he is in chains before me, and he's asking how I am? I want to laugh at the absurdity of it all. Part of me wants to finally tell him the strange feelings I'm having for him. Now that we're alone, in the privacy of this room, I'm free to say anything I want. I want to believe he might actually care about me. But another part of me can't connect those dots. I know what I saw in the helmet, and it doesn't fit with everything Griffin's told me to my face. I have to remember that. This boy could be my undoing, yet too often I'm fantasizing about him instead of doing my duty as a leader. That's got to change right now.

"It's you who's not all right." I brush off his concern like it's a disease I don't want to catch. I make a circle around him, inspecting the chains expertly tied around his elbows.

"Ahh, I see." Griffin glances down at his shoes and nods his head, starting to understand the extent of my anger toward him. "So now that you have me here, what are you going to do with me, *Madame* Elected?"

I face him, so we're almost eye to eye. He still doesn't get it. He thinks this is all a joke. He knows who the assassin is, and he thinks I'll just let it go. He says I'll make a strong leader, but he's about to find out just how strong my father taught me to be. Griffin's a few inches taller than me, but it doesn't matter. I don't blink as I stare at him, my fury building.

And then I hit him hard across the face.

His chin jolts to the side as the impact of my hand smashes against the side of his cheek.

Griffin staggers back, surprised at my sudden assault. "Hey! What are you doing?"

"What I should have done right away, when you 'saved' me at the town hall. You knew, Griffin. You know now. You're hiding the assassin!"

He's looking down, pushing his hurt cheek up against his shoulder and cracking his jaw. But then he looks up at me again, the initial surprise at my blow now leaving his eyes. "Aloy, you're safe, are you not? Isn't that good enough?"

"Elected." My mouth forms a hard line. "You're to call me Elected! Not Madame Elected. Elected!"

He doesn't say anything, just stares me down, refusing to say the word.

We stay like that a moment, two lions circling each other in a tight cage.

Finally, I sit down on the cot, leaning back with my elbows against the crisp, scratchy sheet. I give a clipped laugh, already knowing I've won. It doesn't matter what he says or what he can't bring himself to say. I'm the Elected. Power courses through me like oxygen in my bloodstream. Adrenaline pumps in my temples, accentuating the harsh effects of the Multiplier. I ball my hands into fists, fitting them against my eyes.

"It's not good enough. You have to hand over the assassin," I say.

Griffin responds almost so quietly I don't hear him. I stand up to get closer.

"What did you say?" I ask.

His voice rises so when I'm finally inches from his face, it takes me aback. "You don't understand. I cannot hand over the assassin!"

"So you'd rather sacrifice your country and your Elected than give up a traitor?"

"No! I won't sacrifice you or this country! I'll protect you until my dying breath, but I can't give you a name!"

He slumps to his knees, losing the roguish confidence he usually displays around me. The chains around his elbows hit the concrete in back of him in a thick thud.

I'm taken aback by his promise to protect me and his sudden, uncharacteristic anguish. "What do you mean 'protect you until my dying breath'?"

"Don't you know? Haven't I kept your secret for you? Haven't I given up almost everything to keep you safe? Risked my own life. And almost even my..." He is suddenly silent, looking down, but then speaks again, his voice a whisper. "Ever since I saw you at the dance... I... I couldn't..."

I desperately want to know what he's thought about since the night of the dance, but another part of me can't let him say it. His words will jeopardize everything. Instead, I interrupt, questioning him again. "Then why not give up the traitor?"

He no longer seems mischievous, playing a game with me. He's too serious. "Don't ask more from me than what I can give."

We stay like that for a few heartbeats, neither of us knowing what to do next.

95

Griffin finally breaks the silence. "So here I am, on my knees. Chained. Will you keep me here as a prisoner now? Am I to drink the hemlock just because I saved you but won't give you a name?"

I'm quiet, so he continues. "No?"

Of course I won't make him drink hemlock. But I stride up confidently to him, bending to the floor, fully prepared to tell Griffin if he won't give me a name, I don't need his further protection or so-called friendship either. But, right up in front of his bent figure, I hesitate. I remember the night of the dance, his hand touching mine. And then, more recently, his finger brushing against my cheek under the tree.

When he looks up at me and our eyes lock, I find I can't speak at all. Instead, I sink down onto the ground, the fight finally leaving my body for good.

This boy—no, this man—brings me to do things I don't understand. All of a sudden, I'm horrified that I hit him.

Appalled, I watch Griffin as he stares back at me, his face expectant with a bluish bruise already forming across one cheekbone.

I lower my head in shame. "I'm sorry. I can't believe I hit you."

He shrugs. "It's nothing. Don't worry about it."

"It is something. I've never raised a hand to anyone before. Let alone a prisoner in chains." I put my head in my hands, all my energy seeping out. "What's wrong with me lately?"

I can't believe I'm opening myself up to this man who sits shackled next to me on the floor. But, after using the helmet and feeling the rush of its mesmerizing power, now all of a sudden, I'm spent. My body sags.

Griffin sighs and moves closer to me so that I find I'm leaning on him by default. I shift away from him gradually, still not quite willing to trust him. But the feel of his body against mine as our arms touch, even for a brief moment, is like my own personal drug. I look away so he can't see the blush drifting its way up my neck into my cheeks.

"Wrong with you? In one day you've lost your parents, claimed your birthright, and met the woman you're supposed to marry. That's a lot for anyone to take on. I can't say I like the chains, but this new, tough you is sort of sexy."

I can't help myself. I look up at him and give a small laugh. But then I shudder. "How do you know that I met Vienne today?"

Griffin shrugs again, his shoulder rising with the gesture.

"I know a lot of stuff. I told you. I'm watching out for you."

"Watching out for me? Or just plain watching me?" I glance at him, but when Griffin doesn't answer, I say, "That's a little creepy."

"Look, I've never met anyone who's quite as... alone... as you are. I want to help so you'll be the leader we're all hoping for." He pauses and his assured smile comes back two-fold. "Think of me as your catalyst to greatness."

I snicker, unable to control myself. "My catalyst to greatness? Wow, don't you think highly of yourself?"

This time he laughs too. "No, I think highly of you."

I look him in the eyes, in awe once again of his unwavering confidence in me. But before I can become enamored of the picture he's painted of me and forget my purpose, I ask him my questions again. I won't be distracted like I was the other night under the tree.

"Griffin, you have to tell me. Who is the assassin? And how do you know I met Vienne today?"

Griffin looks to his left over his shoulder, away from me.

"Come on," I say. "I'll take care of it. You won't have to do anything. Just give me the name."

"That's what I worry about." Griffin chooses to answer my second question first. "Okay, I know Vienne. I've known who she was since she first moved into the White House fourteen years ago."

I'm shocked at this. "You have? She's been there for that long?"

"I've spent a lot of time wandering the halls of your house, waiting for my father. I couldn't help notice Vienne's studies were different from other kids'. She took something called psychology lessons. Normal kids don't get that training. Believe me."

"You've made a pastime of watching me and my future wife," I grumble.

"Just as you made a pastime of watching me."

Again, I'm embarrassed. I can feel the color rise in my cheeks to a hot crimson. I sense his arm braced up against mine. The skin tingles, making my arm feel more alive than the rest of my body. I'm conscious, not for the first time, that the man I've thought about from afar for the past four years is now close enough to touch. It's a dangerously delicious feeling that continues to threaten my future. I tamp down the thought of his skin's proximity to mine and continue a now gentler line of questioning.

"So, if you won't hand over the assassin, it means you must have already taken care of him?"

Griffin winces like I've hit him in the gut. He doesn't say anything.

"So I'm right," I say.

Griffin looks back at me ruefully. "Sort of. I... neutralized the situation."

I'm quiet for a moment, letting the idea I might be safe ease its way through my nerve endings. My hands, which I didn't even realize were pinched into fists, automatically release. Maybe I can trust Griffin. He admits he knows who the traitor is, but he says he's found a way to protect me from the threat. I don't relish the thought of watching another prisoner die today. Maybe however Griffin's rectified the situation is good enough for now.

My next words come out so fast I don't even pause to think them through. "I think you should be part of my personal guard."

Griffin grins, his happiness causing me to smile too. "That's the best idea I've heard all day."

12

I STAND UP, BRUSHING fragments of concrete off my pants.

"Guards, please come in!" I call in a loud voice. Immediately, Tomlin and the two guards who were with him earlier enter the room. "Release Griffin."

"Elected?" Tomlin asks, clearly bewildered.

"Griffin doesn't know what I thought he knew." It's a lie, and I look away from Tomlin as I say it. "But I have other plans for him. He's going to be one of my bodyguards."

Tomlin looks down at the ground, trying hard to suppress a smile. "Whatever you wish, Elected."

The two guards on either side of Tomlin unshackle Griffin's arms. Griffin pulls at his wrists, stretching them for the first time.

I start to walk out of the prisoner's room with Griffin close behind me. But I turn my head back and say to Tomlin, "And the Multiplier..."

He stops to look at me again. "Yes?"

"*No* one should wear the Mind Multiplier again."

Tomlin coughs, aware this is a subtle reprimand of the callous way he disregarded my personal safety in order to try the device. I look into his eyes, trying to guess if he tried the Multiplier himself before putting it on my head.

The way he avoids my gaze gives away the answer. I wonder what he's seen.

"It's too dangerous," I say.

Tomlin nods, feeling my recrimination. "Do you want me to destroy it?"

"No, please give it to Vienne. I trust she'll keep it safe and out of anyone's hands."

Tomlin nods again. "Of course, Elected." He bows slightly, a gesture I'm not familiar with yet, especially from my long-time teacher.

The group of us returns through the long corridor of the prison, back into the lobby and then outside. As we walk, our boots churn up a billowing cloud of dust and dirt. We're about halfway across the wide lawn when I see a maid running toward us.

"Elected," she chokes out, breathless.

I stop in my tracks and put both of my hands on her shoulders. "What's wrong?"

"It's Vienne..." Worry is etched across her forehead. Her outstretched arm points toward the White House.

Before she can even finish her statement, I'm running. I feel the thud of earth behind me as Griffin, the two guards, and Tomlin run after me, their footsteps falling heavy on the ground. From my smaller frame and long hours of play fighting, I'm faster than any of them.

I reach the front doors of the house first. In the foyer, I look frantically left and right, realizing I don't know exactly where Vienne stays now that she's almost the Madame Elected.

The maid is close behind us and points me to the left. "She's in her quarters."

I follow the maid to a set of double doors. Our whole party trails close behind. I throw open the doors, not even bothering with a polite knock.

Vienne looks up sharply as we all rumble into the room.

"Are you okay?" My question comes out as a gasp.

"Of course," she says. Her hands are folded against her stomach in what seems to be a relaxed state, but as I stare at her, I see she's clasping them so hard, her nails make white imprints into the skin.

I look around the room, searching for the danger, confused. "The maid said something... was wrong."

Vienne stands up from her seated position in a chair and wipes a hand across her brow.

"Don't worry. I'm fine."

But, it's not just me who's worried. Griffin walks past me to where Vienne leans her hand against a table. "You don't look so good," he says, his concern for her also apparent.

In that instant, I remember that Griffin and Vienne know each other. It's obvious in the way Griffin lays a hand delicately on her arm.

100

All of a sudden, I feel like a third party in the room. It makes me feel like spiders are crawling up my arms. The tingle of jealousy and my own shame threaten to topple me.

Vienne looks up at Griffin with a tentative smile. "I'm truly fine. Just a fainting spell."

"She collapsed?" I ask the maid, coming out of my stupor.

"Yes, while dressing the dead prisoner," the maid says.

I take the silver key from the string around my neck, ready to open our family's vault and retrieve a purple pill for Vienne even though I realize it's overkill.

"That won't be necessary," Vienne says, looking directly into my eyes. She knows exactly what I was about to do. "I was just startled when I saw this."

My eyes move down to where Vienne is looking. On the table before her is something wrapped in a cloth.

Griffin lifts the fabric and picks up the small object, confused what to do with it.

Tomlin walks closer, his earnestness for learning taking precedent. "It's a gun. Vienne, did it hurt you?" He looks over her arms and legs for any sign of injury.

"No, I barely touched it. It fell out of Imogene's jacket pocket."

"From Imogene?" I ask, incredulous. "How did she have a gun on her?"

The guards shake their heads in response, as flummoxed as I am. "I need answers to that," I say to them.

The head guard nods, bows to me, and says, "Elected, we'll give you a report by tonight." Both guards exit the room to start their investigation.

"A gun," Tomlin says again in awe. He lifts a hand to his forehead. "I haven't seen a gun for years. Your father led the melting party years ago."

"Just like our stores of long arrows were destroyed?" I ask, disheartened.

Griffin grimaces, but I don't have time for his discomfort over the assassin right now. I settle my eyes back on Vienne.

"But, were you hurt by it in any way?" I ask her again. I don't completely understand how guns work. Just that they can fire and cause holes in people. Holes that kill people instantly.

Vienne shakes her head again. "It just clattered to the floor as I was preparing Imogene for burial."

Tomlin opens the gun's casing to inspect it.

"How do we now have guns in our country?" I ask him. "This is spinning out of control."

He nods in agreement. "We are certainly seeing an uptick in technology use." We all look down, acknowledging this fact with grimly set lips. Finally, Tomlin says, "I'm going to follow the guards to investigate. If you'll excuse me?" He bows toward me and exits the room.

"Do you think we should do a metal scan?" Vienne asks.

A metal scan is when guards walk around the entire country, using a chemical compound to detect the presence of metal. It's a process that doesn't rely on technology to work. Only science. While technology is outlawed, science and chemistry are subjects we study and revere. To us, technology is anything run with oil or electricity. But, the art of natural science, the study of plants, and the understanding of the environment is dear to our society.

I nod toward Vienne in acceptance of her idea. "I hate to do it, but we need to know if there are other guns out there."

"I'll round up a squad of guards to start the country-wide search," Griffin says.

"And you'll need to talk about this at our next town hall," Vienne says, walking up next to me. "If we're starting a wide-spread scan, it'll frighten our countrymen. They'll need some kind of explanation."

Griffin puts a hand on my shoulder. "Do you think Imogene was planning to use the gun on you?" Griffin's worry for me now shows itself in a deep crease between his eyebrows.

I like his attention centered on me, instead of Vienne. But I instantly feel selfish and look away. "I don't think so. Imogene wasn't in a state to do harm to anyone else besides herself."

Griffin slings an arm across my shoulder. The warmth from his body touching me again feels good, but I can't let my future wife notice how I like it. I turn slightly so Griffin's arm is forced to fall away.

"Protecting you and Vienne is going to be a full time job, isn't it?" Griffin says.

"What does he mean?" Vienne asks.

I smile awkwardly, not wanting to reveal to her I want Griffin near me and have figured out a way to make it happen. "Griffin is one of our new bodyguards."

"Oh!" she says without a hint of reservation. "I thought he already was. He's always in the house, you know."

I smile back at her more fully. "Yes, he's certainly a fixture here." Then I pause, knowing for once what Vienne would appreciate me saying to her. "As are you."

Vienne beams at me, the color now back in her cheeks. "I promise to be a good wife to you." She kisses me on the temple, her lips leaving a tingle where they brush the skin.

I blush, not sure what to do with this new sign of affection. I haven't felt someone kiss me in years, if ever. I try to think back to a time when lips touched my skin, but I can't remember any instance. Her kiss makes me remember my duty, though.

I look at the ground as I say the next words, trying to keep my voice steady. I can't look at either Vienne or Griffin as I say them. It's like the second the sentence escapes my mouth, imaginary chains will come down to bind my neck, wrists, and ankles. I swallow, already feeling constricted. "We need to have our wedding sooner rather than later."

"I'll start the preparations immediately," Vienne says, pleasure clear across her face.

"So soon?" Griffin asks. He grimaces once in Vienne's direction but then looks quickly away from both of us.

"Yes, of course," Vienne says, giving him a pointed look.

I take advantage of the chill passing through the room to interject another piece of uncomfortable information. "Oh, and... I should tell you," I say, glancing around to ensure only Griffin and Vienne are left in the room. "Griffin knows I'm a... girl." I swallow thickly again, wishing there was a glass of water or some other, stronger liquid in the room.

Vienne stands back from the table, her right hand resting on her hip. She speaks slowly, focusing on me. "You told him? Why?"

"No! I didn't... I..."

"She didn't tell me. I figured it out," Griffin says. Thankfully, he doesn't tell her about seeing the decisive evidence of my femininity up close. "I don't think anyone else knows besides me. I've been listening for rumors of it, but no one suspects."

"Okay," says Vienne. "Then it stays between us and Tomlin. That's it."

I remember my gender endangers not just myself, but if my secret were publicized, Vienne would be executed too.

"Agreed," says Griffin.

Vienne looks back and forth from me to Griffin. She puts a hand on my forehead. "Why don't you get some sleep, Aloy. You haven't had much rest over the past few nights."

It's true. My eyes feel droopy. I think of my mother, tucking me into bed the day of the first assassination attempt, and I miss her again. I swallow hard, trying to resolve my feelings of missing my parents, knowing it was only today they left. All I want to do is curl up under soft blankets and block out reality.

I exit the room, glancing back at Vienne and Griffin for the briefest of seconds. The two of them stare after me. I give them a small smile, then turn around the doorframe, about to head to my room.

But, I can't help overhearing their hushed voices coming through the cracked doorway. I pause a moment, feeling conflicted about listening to their obviously private conversation. But Vienne's next words keep me at the door, my ear pressed up against the wall.

"You always knew, didn't you?" she asks.

Griffin says something in return, but I can't make out his words. I lean a little closer to the door.

"Even though it's confirmed, it doesn't make a difference," Vienne says.

Griffin's voice is quiet, but this time I can hear some of his response. "...ultimately her decision..."

"You can't. You just can't," says Vienne.

Suddenly, I'm tapped on the shoulder. "Elected!" says a young maid, surprised to see me with my ear up against the wall. "Can I get you anything?"

I cough slightly, looking away from the door. "Oh, ummm... no thanks, no tea for me. Thanks for checking, though. I'm just heading to my room." My words rush out fast.

I whirl on my heels before the maid can say anything more. I know she must be looking at me like I'm crazy, since she didn't ask me anything about tea. The maid bows, keeping wary eyes on me. I proceed in my original direction, left wondering what exactly Griffin can't do. And, if I'd rather he tried whatever it is.

13

IT'S BEEN DAYS SINCE my parents left. Days since I hit Griffin. Days since Vienne found the gun among Imogene's things. It feels like an eternity.

We've been making wedding preparations non-stop for a week, and the town is about ready to celebrate. The bakers and cooks were hard at work, molding marzipan and sugar into elaborate three-dimensional confections. The divers cast nets into the Chesapeake Bay continuously for the past few days, bringing up scores of seafood delicacies like fresh crab and trout—indulgences we don't usually afford ourselves as a nation. There haven't been any assassination attempts this week. And, no weapons found. People are busy getting ready for the celebration, migrating to the city center on their nirogene-shined bikes, camping out on the Ellipse in wait.

With all of the country's children close together, people are even going out of their way to teach extra lessons. Our education system consists of sharing knowledge. Everyone is a teacher. People sign up to show a group of children their trade, whether it be chemistry, mining, or planting. Around age twelve, children are expected to choose one line of work and study as an apprentice, so it's the younger kids who receive the benefit of the varied classes. These sessions are happening more often than usual this week.

For my part of the wedding preparations, I immerse myself in our few orchards, picking lemons like they're going out of season. I'm making vats upon vats of lemonade, my mother's recipe. From up in one of the gnarled lemon trees, I stop my picking for a moment to look over the horizon. The sun is setting a hot pink against the blue sky, turning everything a confectionery shade of purple. It's gorgeous, or at least I'd let myself think it was if I didn't know the stunning colors were indications of pollution. I still stare at the sky, letting the last rays of sun hit my upturned face. I don't look down until I hear voices below me. In the pasture, I see Griffin surrounded by a small group of children. I peer down from my enclosed spot in the tree, watching without being seen.

"What kind of bird is that?" asks one of the kids.

"A hawk," says Griffin. "You want to see its wings extended?"

"Yes!" come the responses of several younger children who cluster around Griffin's out-of-the-ordinary bird.

"Do you always get to play with animals?" asks one girl.

"Yep, I do. I'm really lucky to know about all kinds of animals. Long ago, people used to call it being a veterinarian."

A five-year-old pulls on Griffin's pants leg and looks up at him with big eyes. "I have a pet animal at home too. A cockroach!"

I grimace. Many kids keep roaches because they're hearty and plentiful. They're some of the only animals that survived after the eco-crisis. They could live through anything.

"Would you like to hold the bird?" Griffin asks the boy. The child's head bobs up and down as Griffin places the tame hawk's feet upon the boy's shoulder.

"Wow!" say the other children in unison. "Can we? Can we have a turn? Please!"

My arms are weary from all of the grating, squeezing, and picking I've done this week, but I hold tight to the tree branch anyway, continuing to watch Griffin's impromptu class with earnestness.

"Have you decided what you want to do when you grow up?" he asks one of the girls sitting cross-legged around his ankles.

"Have babies," she says matter-of-factly.

"Ah, I see," Griffin says, smiling down at her. "Well, I'm sure you'll make a great mother."

"I want to be an ama too!" shouts one of the youngest boys.

"You can't be a mommy, stupid!" the girl sneers back.

I crinkle my nose, wondering how Griffin will deal with this awkward tangent.

"You want to know something?" Griffin asks, his voice low and controlled. "I lost my mother when I was really young. My father served as both my ama and apa."

"But I want to do the most important job," the boy cries. "I want to make more babies so our species won't die out."

I shudder, knowing this young boy is parroting the words of some other grown-up. I hate that our country's children are burdened with problems I can't fix.

"You can still help make them," Griffin says.

"How can the boys make babies?" asks the girl again, her hip stuck out impertinently.

"I don't know, but you girls will learn when you're older, all right? Can we get back to the animals, please? This hawk wants to eat." The kids spring up again, each vying to see the hawk devour its meal. "Who wants to let it eat beetles out of their hand?"

The issue of reproduction is lost amongst the squeals of the children, as both girls and boys alike clamor to feel the hawk's beak pecking carefully against their palms.

I watch for a little while, suspended in the tree, not wanting to give away the fact I've been here this whole time. Finally, as the sun descends under the horizon, parents come to collect their children.

"Want me to walk you home?" Griffin asks the last boy left.

"Yes," he answers without hesitating. The five-year-old who has a cockroach for a pet slides his small hand into Griffin's. The hawk is on Griffin's right shoulder, and the boy is fastened to Griffin's left.

"The big wedding is tomorrow," says the boy.

Griffin looks up at the sky. His face is pointed away from me, but I can't help squinting to try and catch his expression anyway. I'm desperate to know what he really thinks about Vienne's and my wedding. And who he's more upset is getting married, me or Vienne. "I know," he says.

"Everyone's going. You are, too, right?"

I hold my breath up in the tree, listening for the response.

"Of course."

"I can't wait to see the Madame Elected! She's the most perfect girl in the whole world. I'll marry a girl like that someday."

The boy's infatuation with Vienne is to be expected. I've never seen my people throw themselves into something or someone as fully as they've done with her.

"She is wonderful," Griffin says. "But, there are other perfect girls too."

I stay up in the tree for a full ten minutes after Griffin and the boy are far enough away they won't have a chance of seeing me descend. Does he mean me? Or was he just talking in generalities about the boy's future marriage prospects. Or does Griffin have another woman he thinks is perfect?

I try not to think about it for the rest of the evening. I lie in my bed staring at the ceiling, the blankets pulled up tight under my chin. This is my last night without a wife. I think it'll take me hours to fall asleep, but instead, after a few minutes torturing myself yet again with Griffin's words, I do sleep.

Much later when I crack one eye to guess the time, golden sunlight is streaming through my windows. It is an auspicious day for a wedding. Tomlin knocks once at my door as if he could somehow tell I'd just woken.

"Ready for all the festivities?" A wide smile is spread across his face.

"It'll be a glorious day for our people." I don't say anything about it being a glorious day for me.

"Certainly. Now let's get you ready and into the customary garb."

I'm carted off behind Tomlin and a squad of four handlers who will whip my appearance into shape for the wedding.

After stepping out of a steamy bath, which I'm at least allowed to administer myself, they set a goose egg on a piece of toast in my lap and start on my hair. I devour the food, feeling famished from the long hours picking lemons this past week and hardly notice their work on my head... until they present a mirror in front of me.

"My hair is dark brown!" I say, surprised.

"Indeed," says Tomlin, bemused along with me.

"We're making you dark, and Vienne will be light," says one stylist. "Like yin and yang. Don't worry, it's not permanent. It's just for the ceremony."

They continue to make me darker throughout the day. A dark paint is brushed onto my nails, with red swirls painted on top of it. The same red swirls are painted on my hands and temples with henna. I eye myself in the mirror, sizing up my face. Yes, they're making me the customary opposite of my mate, but are they making me handsome? If one looked beyond my coarsely chopped hair, I do have some depth to my face—high cheekbones and bright eyes, but I don't think I look beautiful by any means.

I wonder for a moment what preparations are being enacted on Vienne—if they will change her perfect hair or her already perfect skin. Thinking of her draws nervous shivers down my spine.

The handlers dress me in the outer robes for the wedding. They wrap me in an elaborate brown linen shift, embroidered with the same red swirls covering my fingernails. They lace up long boots over woolen socks that ride up to my calves. Even with the sun shining, it's still cold outside, and they are taking all precautions to ensure I'll be warm. I wonder how much they'll cover up Vienne or if they'll keep her cold just to be able to dress her in a traditional wedding gown.

I don't have long to find out. When I'm finished, my team marches out behind me to the pastures near the north side of town, where the first part of the wedding ritual will take place. I'm hidden behind a white linen fabric, hung high so you can see the sun shining through it and only make out my silhouette from the one side. Townspeople gather on either side of the pasture with ample room to see the festivities. Vienne is already there, behind another white screen, but on the opposite side of the field.

They'll whisk away the screens, and then we'll walk toward each other alone. Tomlin told me that in weddings of the past, women were walked down aisles and 'given away' by their parents. For many of us, our parents are no longer alive when we turn eighteen. That ritual doesn't make sense for us anymore. Yes, our parents are important to us. They even have a say in our marriages, but the matches concocted at the annual dances are only finalized if the young man and woman agree. There is no one giving away our brides and grooms anymore. We stand on our own.

I think of free will as I stare ahead of me, trying to see through my white screen and past Vienne's for even one precursory glimpse. The idea of free will has always been a mystery to me. I look forward to partaking of it someday, but for me, there's only destiny, family, honor, and duty. It's duty calling me to get married today, not love. My parents may not be here, but they'll be figuratively walking next to me all the way across the pasture, ensuring that I fulfill my obligations.

I shake off the feeling. When I meet Vienne, I don't want to view our marriage as a chain around my ankle.

But at the same time, my eyes scan the crowd, searching for the one face I long to see. Griffin's kept a respectful distance from me all week—staying near but not close enough to talk. We were never alone, and he didn't make a specific attempt to seek me out. I don't spot him now.

I force my lips into a big smile even though I feel queasy inside. The people, at least, need to see my resolve in the matter of my wedding.

After thunderous applause from the townspeople on both sides, the curtains in front of me and Vienne are finally lifted. Mine swirls up in the wind as soon as they untether it. I glance around, trying to see

Vienne, but the fabric ripples in the gusts of air and flies in front of my face. I push the linen off with one hand, stepping around it.

At once there is an *aaahhh* from the townspeople as they see the pair of us. Me with my newly darkened image and Vienne with her... her... I squint into the sunlight in front of me to see.

She is the embodiment of pure white. As they've turned me darker, they've somehow managed to make Vienne lighter. Her hair is the color of the inside of an almond, sleek and long over her back. It whisks down like a froth of egg white on top of lemon meringue pie. It's tied back at the top with a line of pink roses across her forehead, just like the first day I met her.

And her robes. Can they really even be called robes? They billow around her in sheaths of many layers. The bottom layer is a pale yellow. The next a pastel pink. And the topmost layer is translucent white, so thin and gossamer it reminds me of a butterfly's wing. Each layer is delicately thin, as I can almost make out her precise figure under the swaths of fabric. I see her long legs walking steadily toward me.

The top of her robes are gathered above her breasts in a tight knot, one I know is a ritual for us to untie later when we're alone in bed. I swallow hard at the thought, not sure yet how I will handle that particular call to action.

Vienne holds a small woven basket in her hands, as do I. We make our way toward each other slowly, and the pasture feels long. I sense thousands of eyes on me, and I instinctively stand up straighter. When Vienne and I are the customary few inches away from each other, I reach for Vienne's basket, and she hands it to me with a smile. This is the first step. The mutual exchange of seeds. She takes my basket from me, and we bend down onto the white sheet that is laid on the pasture floor. Vienne eyes the red embroidery on my brown robes and fingers it with her thumb appreciatively.

"They made you look quite handsome," she says.

At once, I wish I'd complimented her first—not the other way around. "And you...," I say, breathless. "It's beyond words. You are... an angel."

Vienne smiles and takes my hand in hers. With her other hand she pulls a small, pink rose from behind her left ear, brushes it across her lips, and places it in the lapel of my robes. I nod thanks to her, and then we get back to the task at hand.

I'm to plant the seeds from her basket, and she mine. Together they signify the joining of our lives and the hope for a fruitful marriage. Tomorrow East Country planters will fill out the rest of the open pasture with more of the same seeds. They'll water the crop laboriously, watching for shifts in the moon and tide to make sure the land is sufficiently irrigated.

Vienne stands first, as I lay the last handful of dirt on top of the seeds I've just planted. Then I brush my hands along the sheet, ensuring not a single seed is wasted and rise as well. We clasp hands again and give our townspeople the first greeting as man and wife.

We bow to each other and then, back to back, we face our countrymen and say at the same time, "A new day to you all!" There's a mighty cheer that erupts from our people, and then, as custom dictates, they rush toward us, carefully avoiding the newly planted seeds. We let them come. I've already told the guards to stand aside, even though they argued against it. Considering the attempts against my life, it would be prudent to abandon the ritual mass embrace, but that would grant the assassin a hold over us. I can't allow my people to think we're manipulated or scared of the attacker. Instead, my guards hover nearby, eyeing everyone with hawk-like focus.

The townspeople come with exuberance, wrapping us both in their arms and well wishes. I'm hugged so many times and kissed on the cheeks both left and right I feel like I might fall over. After at least a half hour, Tomlin shouts over the crowd that the banquet is about to start in the Ellipse. People finally let go of us, and I'm quick to grab Vienne's hand again to steady myself.

She's busy securing locks of her hair back into place after the onslaught, and I laugh easily, finally enjoying myself. I look forward to trying the vats of lemonade that have been cooled all week long in the deepest of our buried pits. I'm thirsty beyond belief. My mouth salivates, imagining the array of fruits, vegetables, and fish piled high for our wedding feast.

We are the only country in the world, I think, still with fish of any kind. Back when oceanic pipelines first ruptured, our ancestors had the presence of mind to dam the Bay. Because the Chesapeake's sea opening was relatively small, and thanks to the effort of thousands of volunteers, they were able to prevent oil seepage. We are careful not to wipe out any variety of fish through overharvesting, so crab and other delicacies are only available on grand occasions. This is why my stomach piques now at the smell of the roasting trout.

Together, Vienne and I walk to the Ellipse, on our way to the buffets. A cup is thrust into my open hand as soon as I round the corner. I look to see who's answered my unspoken wish for something to drink, and my heart can't help beating out of rhythm for a moment.

It's the one person I so wanted to see.

"I may not be the first to congratulate you," Griffin says, "but I hope mine is the most..." He pauses, looking away from us. "Heartfelt." His voice is low and resonant like always, but his normally golden-brown eyes are darker underneath his eyelashes. He looks conflicted, and I wonder again whom he thinks he's losing because of today's wedding. Vienne or me.

"Of course it is," says Vienne, stepping forward to give him an embrace. She reaches up, grasping the back of Griffin's neck and burying her face in the slope of his shoulder. I stand still, my arms rooted to my sides as Griffin returns her hug. He leans down to whisper in her ear. Behind Vienne's waterfall of hair, I can see his lips move but can't make out the words. Vienne smiles demurely, her cheeks glowing pink.

I can't look at them any longer.

"I'm going to get us some food," I say. I start to turn away, but Vienne catches my arm.

"No, let me." She doesn't give me a moment to object, gliding off in the direction of the buffet tables before I even take a step. Griffin and I walk over to a bench away from the crowds but still within sight of several guards. I've wanted to talk to Griffin all week, but now that we're finally together, I can't quite think of what to say.

"Where've you been?" I ask him, absently thumbing a piece of hardened, dyed hair above my ear. "You're supposed to be guarding us, today of all days."

He erupts with a slight laugh and looks away from me toward the horizon. "Today of all days..." He doesn't finish the sentence. "I didn't think you'd actually go through with the wedding."

I look down. Maybe it'll come out now—this thing in the air between the three of us. "Vienne and I needed to marry. You know that."

"I knew you had to go through with a marriage. I just didn't picture it would be like this. I thought you would..." He stops, his breath catching. I still can't tell if he's more upset Vienne is now accounted for or if I'm the one he wishes was still single. "You break rules. I thought that meant you'd..." He doesn't complete the thought, leaving me leaning forward to catch the fragments of his unspoken words suspended in the air.

I don't know how to respond. And I don't know what I was hoping to see on his face when I looked for him in the crowd earlier. Acceptance? Reassurance that I was doing the right thing? But I hadn't seen him, and I'd gone forward on my own volition.

"Now you need to get married too," I say finally.

Griffin turns to me abruptly. "I will not." His tone is hard, like rocks colliding.

"You must!" I answer with surprise. "It's your duty. You need to have babies. Repopulate the earth." I can see the disappointment spread across his face, and I can't bear to maintain eye contact. I'm obviously not the rule-breaker he thought I was.

"Not quite yet." His words are quiet, contrasting with the heavier ones spoken just seconds earlier. Each breath he takes now is measured and soft, and it reminds me of my mother laying out a yellowed lace doily over one of our living room end tables. I don't know why I've just pictured her at this very second, but the memory is unsettling. I wrap my arms around myself and continue to stare over the top of Griffin's shoulder.

We sit in silence like this for only a few seconds, but it feels like time stops while I watch the rise and fall of Griffin's chest on each breath. The festivities roar around us, but it all seems far away, as if there's cotton clogging my ears. When I think I can't stand the awkward stillness for a moment longer, I feel a light touch on my hand. My head jolts down to see Griffin's thumb tracing the line of my own finger. It's a small gesture, but this one pass of his thumb across mine is electrifying. Then just as abruptly, Griffin stands up, the sharp manner causing me to blink hard.

He bows to me, hardly meeting my eyes. Then he turns, walking away from the party. I'm left alone on the bench with my thoughts swirling.

I don't have much time to linger on them, though, because soon Vienne is back with two platefuls of food. "Here you are!" She hands me a plate piled high with apples and fish.

I nod my appreciation, trying to give her a smile for her wedding day. "Where did Griffin go?"

I tilt my head over my left shoulder, indicating he stalked off in the opposite direction from the party.

"I love him like a brother, but that one... he's trouble."

"Yes, trouble," I say, eyes on the ground.

14

TROUBLE, IN ANY FORM, is nowhere to be found during the wedding celebrations. We dance the evening away, and the moon is now high in the sky. It's almost time for our goodbyes to the townspeople—time for us to sequester ourselves for the first night as a married couple. I give a little shudder, which Vienne perceives, with her hand resting on my right shoulder as part of the last dance.

"Are you all right?" she asks.

"Yes, just thinking about tonight," I say without thinking at all.

Her whole body slows as she's deep in thought. When I don't say anything more, she leans in close to my ear and whispers, "We can just sleep, Aloy. Just sleep is all."

I lean back so I can look at her, and we make the next turn together in our dance. I can't help but breathe a sigh of relief at her words. But, what does she truly desire, I wonder? To merely sleep? What has she been trained to do? And what will she expect from me? Does she desire me? And there is the question niggling in my head since I met Vienne... do I desire her?

I ponder this last question, staring at her, as she twirls in front of me, the yellow, pink, and white of her robes hooking the twilight and throwing glimmering gold shadows across the ground. I sort of like the way she's reached out to me so far. It feels like the love my mother used to give me as a child—comforting and unconditional. And Vienne truly is exquisite. That's undeniable. Anyone in his right mind would want her.

I do want to touch her, I realize. But it's a desire more born from curiosity than lust. I covet her beauty. I want to protect her. Hold her. See what it feels like to be hugged. But do I want to kiss her passionately?

That I don't know.

Vienne gives me a demure bow. "Are you ready, Aloy?" I nod at her, swallowing thickly. "Then let us say our goodbyes to the people." Vienne pulls me with her across the wooden dance floor set up beneath fragrant pine boughs. It is only the second time in my life that I've stood on a dance floor, and the memory of the first instance burns in the back of my mind. I walk with Vienne under the canopy to where Tomlin sits with a group of guards. "Tomlin, we're going home now."

He rises and kisses both of Vienne's hands. Then he turns to me. "Elected, are you ready for the last ritual of the night?"

At first, I think he means me and Vienne getting into bed together, and I blush. I've been obsessing over that aspect of our marriage too much, and it's like Tomlin's read my mind. But when he starts leading us to a nearby podium and gathering up a set of talkers, I realize he's not referring to Vienne's and my coupling. I'm expected to give the last speech of the night, blessing our people and the seeds we harvested today. Then, Vienne and I will be bound in one last ceremony before they allow us the privacy of our bedroom. I shudder at the thought of this one last public ritual. It's barbaric really.

I walk up to one of the talkers and look out to the crowd. I gather my thoughts, so I'm no longer worrying about Vienne's and my night together. Now it's about thanking my people. "Countrymen and women of East, thank you for joining us in celebration today."

There is a rumble of applause as people nearby answer back, and the people farther away hear my words a moment later from a talker. Their applause comes with a few seconds delay. I wait for it and then continue.

"Vienne and I are so blessed to share this moment with you—the commencement of our marriage and start of our family. We will try our best to fulfill our duty to have many sons and daughters. Ones who will carry our country and species into the future for years to come. It's unions such as these that propel our society forward and grant assurance that we prosper as a people!" There is more applause from the crowd. "If you would be so kind as to share one last ceremony with us, Vienne and I will now receive the ritual binding."

Instead of the metal bands people used to wear around their ring fingers, East Country prefers to "bind" a married couple with something more permanent. I've been dreading this particular ritual, but all married people endure it, so I tell myself to be strong.

116

A wheelbarrow full of molten hot ash is being guided through the crowd toward us. I look over at Vienne to see how she's faring with the ritual about to be administered. She seems serene, staring up at the few stars in the sky, concentrating on them instead of the hot metal making its way to her arm.

A long, hot poker juts out of the top of the wheelbarrow. A metal worker picks up the poker and comes toward Vienne. It's quite cruel they make the woman go first. But Vienne looks perfectly calm. A doctor walks up next to her and grasps hold of her right shoulder with one hand. He swabs her biceps with alcohol-soaked gauze.

Then the metalworker holds up his poker, which was sitting in the pile of ash. He comes close to Vienne's arm. The tip is almost white it's so hot. I look away, not wanting to see the actual act, but the smell hits me. I swallow, trying to close off my nose from the sickening stench of burning flesh.

I'm curious how it will look. Our brands will be identical. Each married couple is given an identical mark as their spouse, and no two in the country are alike. Often the metal is molded into hearts with arrows through them, a certain animal from past legends, or other symbols of love. I've told them I want our symbol to be a flower, and I'm anxious to see what my request will ultimately look like.

There's a silly superstition among my people: if you marry your true love and harm befalls him or her, you'll feel their pain in the brand along your own arm. I instinctively put my hand up to my biceps as Vienne's skin bubbles and turns black under the poker.

When the "binding" is set, the metal worker puts the poker back inside the wheelbarrow and moves close to me.

Please don't let me faint, I beg to the heavens. Not now. Please don't let a little hot poker do me in. I try to stay strong, taking Vienne's lead to look upwards into the night sky.

The doctor comes close to me, and before I know it, he's prepared my arm as well. I suck in air, trying to catch my breath before the grotesque act. Then I feel the heat searing as the poker rests its burning head against my skin. It takes all my energy not to scream out, but I bite my bottom lip to stop myself. Once the act is complete, the whole party backs away from us.

I stand inches from Vienne, and we grab our good hands, holding the inflamed arms out to our other side.

"You ok?" I ask her under my breath.

117

She just nods, as if opening her mouth in itself will elicit a scream. So I don't push it. I just nod too.

I try to smile toward the crowd, wondering how all the married couples in the audience put up with this same ritual, sometimes multiple times if they've been married more than once. My smile comes off as more of a grimace, and I know it's time to go.

We are helped onto two white horses, and we begin a slow canter back to the White House. When we're a good distance away from the crowds, I dare to look over at Vienne. She's already eyeing her wound, looking at the image they've burned onto us.

"What is it?" I ask her.

She doesn't answer at first, so I start to look down at my arm to try to make out the image in the darkness. It's hard to see, but I think I see something skinny and long etched horizontally across my biceps.

"It can't be," Vienne says. "I thought you said we were going to have a flower."

"I did. What can't be?"

"It's a..." She tries to get the words out.

"A what? I can't see it clearly. What is it? A heart?"

"No, it's a... long arrow."

"A WHAT!" I PRACTICALLY fall off the horse, wanting to get to the ground so I can see the blackened flesh in the light from the torches next to our front door. I twist the skin of my biceps so I can stare at the burn they've just embedded there. And, sure thing, the brand is in the perfect shape of a long arrow, its arm long and its tip sharp and triangular.

"Damn it!" I curse.

"Maybe it's not what we think it is. Maybe it's a special flower we don't recognize."

"No, it's surely a long arrow. How could they imprint that on us after the two assassination attempts on my life?"

"Maybe it's meant to be a sign of bravery. Just a misunderstanding? Let's not think of it now. It's been such a long day."

I look over at her face, weary behind her streaming blonde locks of hair. And suddenly I forget my anger, realizing I need to care for Vienne now, not focus on myself. She's right. We'll take care of the brands later.

I wrap an arm around her good shoulder and start to lead her into the house. A maid greets us in the front foyer, not quite sure where to lead us next. I'm not sure either. Am I taking Vienne to her quarters and leaving her there? Will she come to mine? Are we sleeping together or alone? How much of a farce do we need to uphold? I shudder thinking about the night ahead and what I'll have to do with Vienne. At the same time, I can't help feeling a little curious. Girls are taught about sex and reproduction, but throughout all my studies, no one told me a thing, shielding me from the topic in another exaggerated attempt to hide my gender.

Vienne takes my hand in hers and leads me to her quarters on the left. I follow blindly, happy to have someone else making the decision.

Entering her room, I'm struck by the strong smell of daisies. Vienne turns to me the second the door is shut and the maid is gone. "Let me help you," she says, taking my arm out from underneath my brown and red robe.

I jump back as if something hot has scalded me. "That's okay. I can do it." No one has ever helped me undress before. I'm not sure if this is what all married couples do or just what Vienne's been taught.

"Okay, anything you need." Her words are quiet, as though she's disappointed.

I don't want to offend Vienne, especially on our first night together, so I acquiesce and let her help me with my heavy robes.

"Maybe if you could just pull this off." I raise my right arm out to the side, leaning toward her. "Thank you."

"You're welcome. I just want to be a good wife to you."

Vienne bends down in front of me, helping unlace the boots next. "You will be. You are," I amend. I start to think maybe she's been given strict instructions on how to be "a good wife" in bed. My stomach flips again, thinking about what she's been taught to do to me and how I can stop Vienne without being rude.

She smiles up at me. "Would you like to sleep here tonight?"

"In here?" I look over at her bed, warm and inviting, its white comforter plump with massive amounts of feathers.

"Yes, in here. With me. Husbands and wives typically sleep together in the same bed." She sees I'm uncomfortable, so she tries to help me further. "It's all right. We don't have to do anything. We can just lie near each other. And talk maybe."

"Okay." I try to sound assured even though my stomach quivers. What are the things she's referring to exactly?

Vienne sits on the edge of the bed and removes the top two layers of her flowing robes with one swift gesture. The yellow layer is all she has left.

"Will you unknot the top of it? It's customary."

"I remember." I feel scandalous. Dirty. But innocent at the same time, as I truly have no idea what I'm doing in this area. I grab hold of the knot and tug. It unravels easily in my hand, causing the last layer to billow out and then disappear in a cloud on the mattress behind her.

Vienne's white skin is illuminated in front of me, pearly and smooth as the inside of a clamshell. She's completely nude. Vienne lifts a section of her hair in both hands, raising her arms so her entire body is exposed in front of me. I see everything. The curve of her shoulders. The roundness of her chest. The flatness of her lean stomach. Vienne lies down on the bed and pulls me with her so we're facing each another, nose to nose.

"What are you thinking?" she asks.

I don't answer for a second and then say the first thing that crosses my mind. "You're beautiful."

She gives a small smile and leans forward to kiss me. The touch of her lips is so soft and light, I hardly feel it. But the sensation lingers, sending shivers across my cheeks and around the back of my neck. It's the first kiss I've ever received. It feels intimate. Like hot cocoa in the dead of winter. But, do I want more?

Vienne leans back, watching me. "Does this make you nervous? Sleeping near me?"

I wrinkle my brow, trying to figure out how best to answer her question. I decide to rely on honesty. "Yes, a little."

"That's all right. I've heard it's like this for all couples on their wedding night. It's always new and scary."

"I'm not scared," I say, lying.

"Me neither. Just curious."

"What are you curious about?" I suddenly really want to know.

"To see if I like you in that way."

She is so honest it hurts my heart. But, I want to hear more. "Like what way?"

"Like if you were a real man. I've been wondering how it will be."

"Me too," I admit.

"Do you like girls?"

"I don't know."

"Do you like boys, then?" These are the questions she could not possibly have gotten answered from Tomlin. So it's the only thing she doesn't already know about me.

"Yes, I suppose so. They're... interesting."

This causes her to pause, and then she says, "You like Griffin."

I splutter my answer, trying to erase the thought from her mind. "No! No... not Griffin."

"I've seen you look at him. It's ok."

I try to calm myself. This is not the serene bedtime I'd hoped for. It's leading down a dangerous path, and we've only just gotten married

121

and into bed.

Instead of answering her, I ask Vienne a question. "Do you like Griffin?"

"Me?" She laughs. "No, of course not. I'm married to you. It's my duty to like you."

I hate that she's used the word duty. I want her to be proud of her new role. I want her to embrace it. Every aspect.

I let the breath I didn't realize I was holding escape through my nostrils. "Do you want me to...?" I don't know what I'm even asking, but the words tumble out, skipping over each other like smooth stones I need to expel before they choke me. I force myself to look down at Vienne's outstretched body and then scrunch my eyes closed as I say the next words. "What would make you happy?"

I don't hear an answer right away so I peer at Vienne from behind a half-raised eyelid. I expect her to be looking up toward the ceiling or absently twirling a lock of hair, but instead her head is cocked to the side as she gazes at me with a soft expression. For a second, it seems as if she'll tell me exactly what I should do, but instead she just reaches a hand up to my face.

My body inches away automatically, hating itself for bracing against the trace of Vienne's fingertips, but flinching back nonetheless. Vienne's hand stops in mid-air, but she takes a deep breath and reaches further. The back of her hand grazes my cheek, her pinky just barely brushing across my chin and over my lips. "For you to be comfortable," she says.

As soon as she says the words, I realize I don't know how to feel like she does – perfectly relaxed in her own skin. Perhaps if I didn't have to live as someone I'm not, always playing a role, all of this would be easier. After a long moment, I open my eyes to tell her this, but realize she's eased onto her side, nestled close to me in the bed. Her back makes a crescent shape against my stomach. Vienne's one arm holds mine across her, and in my confusion I hadn't even felt her move it there.

I listen to her easy breathing and rest my head deeper into one of her pillows. I sweep my hand through her golden locks like a comb, mesmerized by how it feels like spun silk through my fingers. If I can't bring myself to let her touch me, at least I can reach to her. Vienne sighs, inching closer to me in the bed.

Right when I think Vienne is falling asleep, though, she says, "Why couldn't you rule as a woman, Aloy?"

This is a hard question right before we're nearly slumbering. It's steeped in political turmoil and history. Too much to encourage a good night's sleep, but I feel compelled to answer.

"It's not prejudice. When the Elected Accord was created there were many women in presidential roles. Actually, it was the women's idea to have females focus on reproduction since the human population was so low. They thought that role was more important than any leadership position."

"Hmmmm." Vienne's face burrows into her pillow.

I prop my head up with one arm, and my words bubble forward, trying to convey my own thoughts on the matter. "Even though the Elected is a man, the wife's thoughts are very much taken into account. She gets to make many of the decisions. You can make all the decisions you want. I'll listen to you."

"That's nice of you. Thank you." Vienne's words are soft and drowsy, muffled by the pillow.

As she drifts off to sleep finally, I whisper to myself, "You'd probably be a better leader than me anyway."

But, she doesn't hear. She's already breathing deeply, immersed in a dream.

16.

THE NEXT MORNING, WE have the joy of another day full of strong winter sun. It comes through the window in lush rays, electrifying the cream colored walls in a dazzle of rainbows. It's a perfect way to lazily wake up next to my new wife.

"You should always sleep next to me," Vienne says, propping herself up on one elbow.

"Why's that?"

"Because that's the best night's sleep I've had in a long time."

I realize the same goes for me. I slept soundly, not having woken in the middle of the night at all. I smile luxuriously in the healthy feeling of a good night's sleep.

"Agreed. Your room or mine tonight?"

"Mine again. My bed is bigger." Vienne laughs.

"Okay."

"So now we've settled that, next we figure out how to get me pregnant."

This is a question to which I have not a single answer. I sit up on the bed with my back to her, starting to grab up clothing strewn on the floor.

"Yes? And do you have any ideas?" I expect a resounding answer of no.

Vienne comes to sit behind me. "Well, yes, I do."

I turn to her, delighted. "You do? Really? Is there a way?"

She turns her whole body toward me so I have no other option but to look her in the eyes. "I need to have sex with a man." Her words are so blunt I feel like an idiot for not having seen them coming.

"Oh." I look down at the ground in front of me. Today was supposed to be a good day, and already my new wife is explaining how our union won't work.

"You know it's true." Recognizing my discomfort, she insists, "We can't put off this conversation."

"I know." I refuse to look up from my shoes. The thought of a man touching my beautiful Vienne—not only my wife but my first real friend and confidant—makes me suddenly sick. "Maybe we can talk about this later."

"Okay, but we *do* need to talk about it. Make some decisions." She sounds resolute. "Getting pregnant is my biggest role in this marriage. And we need to arrange it as fast as possible while I'm in my most fertile years."

"Maybe after breakfast," I say, putting on my other boot.

She laughs. "All right then, after breakfast."

When we arrive in the dining area, Griffin is already sitting at our breakfast table, eating a piece of toast and drinking out of a crystal glass filled with lemonade. He lifts his goblet to me as soon as we walk in, the awkwardness of our last exchange purposefully ignored.

"Good lemonade, Elected. And good morning, Madame Elected." Griffin tips his head toward Vienne.

She beams back at him. "Griffin. A new day to you."

"I have more security reports for you both." He slides a sheaf of papers across the table to me. While Vienne and Griffin order a variety of marzipan delicacies leftover from last night, I pore through the numerous reports.

"Tomlin has already read them too," Griffin says. Tomlin nods from across the breakfast table where he's just sat down to breakfast with an apple and a slice of pumpkin on his plate.

"I hope you enjoyed the festivities yesterday. I know the townspeople were buoyed by the celebration," he says.

I nod but am again reminded we need to make a baby as soon as possible if my countrymen's morale is to be bolstered for longer than a day. The hope of our country sits with two women who can't biologically have one baby, let alone scores of children together. I try to block out the thought as I read through Griffin's report on our collection of chemicals to conduct testing. Today is the town hall where I will explain to our people we're searching for metal. I still haven't decided whether I'll tell them about Imogene's gun.

I read the report about how Imogene found the weapon. Her children say they never saw a gun in the house. Her husband admits, though, Imogene brought home the helmet a day before she was taken to the prison. And she was acting strange, talking about objects falling from the sky. The same thing she told me at the prison compound. I shudder, remembering her prophesies.

I continue reading through inconclusive evidence. The second report talks about rumors brewing. Some people are saying the Technology Faction is manufacturing its own weaponry, although how they're making the metal is a complete mystery. Then there are other rumors Mid Country is arming itself against us. To take us over. To take over our precious water supply. That they're banding together with West Country to vanquish us. This last idea isn't one I've put a lot of thought into at all. I can almost deal with the internal threat of the Technology Faction. But what would we do with outside enemies too? I thought the days of intricate political conflicts were over. I thought we were in isolation now. That would be easier. New enemies, amorphous ones, are more worrisome than ones I can see and understand.

Somehow, I can almost come to terms with the ideals of the Technology Faction, no matter how much I won't let them win. I can understand how they think just a little technology use won't hurt anyone, how we could harness it to fix our population's decline, how we could make water purifiers and clean up the oceans. There are a million tempting ways we could use technology to better our situation.

What I can't understand is other countries banding together to eliminate my people. It doesn't make sense at all. And yet, where did the gun come from? The first report indicates Imogene's husband says she was in the hills the day she came home with the helmet. Perhaps this is where she found the gun too. The hills are on the border with Mid Country. If they're arming themselves against us, perhaps a gun made it over the border right there.

I put my head in my hands, trying to make sense of it all. And that's when two guards run into the room. We all glance up in haste.

"Elected, your parents' horses have returned," one says.

"And my parents? Have they come back too?" My voice conveys hope, and I don't even care who hears. My parents, above all others, will be able to help me think through these recent developments.

"No."

Vienne asks. "But why did it take so long?"

127

It's been weeks since my parents left. I'd almost forgotten the horses were trained to arrive back in East Country.

"I'll ask my father if they look all right," Griffin says, rising from his seat at the table. "He'll be checking them over right now, I'm sure." He looks over at me, remnants of our disconcerting interlude at the wedding still cracking through his normal lightheartedness. "I'll meet you at the town hall." Then he nods at us and exits.

"I'm sure your parents are fine." Vienne stands by my side, putting a hand around my waist.

I try to nod in agreement, but it comes out stilted, a half bob of my head. I wish my parents were on the horses. I wish their mission to leave East Country failed and they returned. I could use their support now more than ever. I try to finish eating the dry toast I have in my hands, but it tastes like nothing so I just deposit it on my plate and a maid quickly takes it away. I have more things to think about today than eating, anyway.

As we leave the White House and near the Ellipse, I see most of our people are already at the town hall, sitting on the stone benches, their talkers spaced out every ten rows. Vienne and I dismount and walk up to the front at a fast pace. This time, Griffin is positioned directly to the right of us, already sitting on the stage. This comforts me somewhat. I have him next to Vienne with orders that, if there is another assassination attempt, he'll fly to her side first instead of mine.

"A new day to you all," my voice booms once we're onstage.

There's a murmur of happy agreement back to us. People are still in a good mood from the wedding yesterday. As I look out at their faces, I see many eyes droop from the late hours last night. Maybe their sleepiness will make my next announcements go over more smoothly.

"I'll get right to it. I have three pieces of business today. The first is that everyone will receive a packet of tree saplings. We really need some of these trees to take root. These saplings are from the heartiest of our current trees, so we're hoping at least twenty percent of these make it. Please plant them near your houses by the end of the week."

The talkers relay my message, and I wait for the words and precious saplings to get distributed—one sapling per family.

"The second topic is a reminder to conserve your nirogene. We're dangerously short on our supply. So there won't be any new cans of nirogene issued this month."

There's a rumble from the crowd as my warning makes it to their ears. I wait for an inevitable question. Rumblings always arouse questions. And if I know my people, they won't be mute on this subject. They'll want to preserve their bikes and other salvaged metal, and a reduced supply of nirogene will make this process harder.

The first question comes from a talker in the middle. "Elected, Dasan asks why the supply is low."

I answer after just a moment. "To tell the truth, I'm not positive. I'm going to visit the hills to look at our mines. If nirogene production is low, perhaps it's because of a reduced harvest. I'd like to turn the town hall over to Madame Elected now for our next topic."

Vienne stands, and the people smile back at her automatically. It's this response I'm relying on for the next announcement. I think it'll go over better coming from one who has become so beloved so quickly.

"Good day to you all," she says, smoothing one of her blonde locks behind an ear. "I have rather startling information. Unfortunately, I found a gun on a prisoner's body just last week."

There are loud eruptions of confusion from the crowd. Like me, they'd all assumed guns were a thing of the past.

"Yes, it's very troubling," Vienne says, her hands up to quiet the crowd. "Thus, we need to do a countrywide metal scan to ensure there are no more."

One of the talkers from the back stands, a question already upon his lips. "Madame Elected," he says, "why don't you and the Elected trust the people."

Vienne squints her eyes. "Can you clarify your question?"

The talker answers, "Only one gun was found. I don't understand why this constitutes a countrywide metal scan. Don't you trust that people will bring forth weapons if they're found?"

At this, I stand up beside Vienne. "Imogene carried the gun on her body. It went undetected for who knows how long, and she didn't bring it to anyone's attention. We don't have the full story on this. Since there may be other weapons in our country, we can't take any chances." There is widespread displeasure across the crowd at my last statement. And I realize I've just sent worry through the minds of my people.

"We don't think any of you are in danger," I say quickly. "To date, the only life-threatening violence this country has seen in the past thirty years was directed at me."

I hate to say this fact out loud, but it's true. The only assassination attempt—the only use of a weapon—was aimed at me. Twice now.

"I must take action," I say.

Someone shouts from within the crowd. I'm surprised because the voice isn't coming from one of the talkers. No one's ever spoken out of turn like this.

"You cannot hold us all responsible for the actions of one who went crazy!"

I look out into my people, searching for the voice. I don't find it, but instead I see Imogene's husband standing up, gesturing toward the crowd. "She wasn't crazy! I don't know how my wife got hold of the gun, but she wasn't crazy!"

Another man shouts out of turn, "A metal scan shows you don't trust us! Use of a weapon was the act of one person only!"

"We don't know that!" I answer. "Plus, the Technology Faction is growing." People give displeased rumbles. "It's true. Just yesterday there was a showing of the Faction at our wedding!" I grimace, covering the still puffy, raw flesh with my hand. "Vienne and I were imprinted with... unusual bindings."

I lift up my sleeve so the people in the front rows can see the shape burned on my arm. They give astonished gasps of understanding as they view the image.

"We were each given the symbol of a long arrow—the very weapon used against me in the attempt on my life!"

There are many shouts from the audience. One man stands and again doesn't wait for a talker to approach him. "Get the offender up on stage for questioning!" he yells.

"We'll speak to the metal worker this afternoon," Vienne starts to say. "I'm sure he was just confused..."

She's cut off midsentence by the very metal worker running forward. I think he's just trying to defend his name, but our guards catch him in their arms as he tries to leap onto the stage. Griffin and I both instinctively hover closer to Vienne.

"It's a warning from the Technology Faction to you, Elected!" he yells. "You cannot keep us down! A new day for technology!"

There's an uproar as a small group of people in the middle stand. "Technology now!" they yell in unison.

I realize the Technology Faction was waiting for the metal worker's signal. The guards rush at the Faction, providing a fence around the small group, roping them off with their bodies.

"We need technology!" the group yells again—in an obviously

orchestrated demonstration.

I try to shout over the mob. "You're out of line! Sit back down!"

And before I can stop him, the metal worker hits one of the guards holding him in the face, throwing the guard off balance. The man is free once more. He ascends the stage, lunging for me. I step back fast, wobbling over a few chairs, trying to keep my balance. I crash back against the podium, all the while yelling out to Vienne. "Get back!"

The metal worker is caught at once between the arms of Griffin and another guard. They hold him off the floor as he thrashes and kicks.

Most of the crowd rallies with me, shaking their fists at the mob in the center. A rock is sent flying in their direction. Then one of our precious saplings is lobbed at the head of one Technologist. And the Faction, held behind the circle, responds by throwing objects back out.

There's a sharp whack and everyone looks around, expecting another gun now the idea's been put in people's heads. Townspeople scream and cover their heads. I look around for a weapon in the circle of Technologists, but I don't see anything.

It seems every time we assemble now—every time we have a town hall—it erupts in violence. I cringe at the thought that our society is taking steps backward. Back to when we relied on technology to kill and maim each other.

"Calm down!" I shout. "This is folly! You're fighting against your own people! There are so few of us left!"

They don't hear me. There's chaos as the guards try to hold people back, but the group at large is pressing in on the Technology Faction. They'll crush them, I think. The protestors will be suffocated with the guards stuck right in the middle, about to be trampled. I can't believe it's come to this. A full-out riot.

"Stop!" I yell. "Stop right now!"

There's another dull thud, something thick hitting a hard object. I can't tell where it originated until I see a fist rising up amidst the crowd to hit another man in the back of his skull.

Now Vienne is yelling too. "Peace! Please, peace!" she shouts, but to no avail. So close to her, I'm the only one who has a chance of making out her words.

I see a circular orange object crashing toward the stage from the circle of technologists. The pumpkin hits a chair to my right. It splatters into four squishy sections, sending seeds flying. But it's not just a pumpkin. The squishy masses have shards of metal sticking out from them. I only have a few seconds to analyze what the pumpkin holds before more objects come flying from within the Technologists' circle. An apple hits me in the arm, hard, something sharp digging its way into my biceps. I'm cut, but worse, it's hit my upper biceps, colliding with the burnt flesh still healing from the marriage binding.

I yell backward again, warning Vienne to get down. I hold my arm, watching the Technologists closely to make sure nothing else is coming toward us. But there's no way to stop the onslaught now.

At once ten arms go up from the Faction's circle, and each holds a bunch of apples. All of the apples glint with bits of metal sticking out of their skin.

Before the surrounding guards can stop the Technologists, the apples are thrown with full force all at once on a single, coordinated command. They hit the stage with a multitude of thwacks. Some of the shards of metal stay attached to the fruit, but others fling outward once the apples hit the stage. None have hit me, and I stare back at once to show the group we're unhurt.

But we're not. Someone on stage has indeed been hurt. And it's the worst possible person.

Vienne.

17

SHE STUMBLED BACKWARD, AWAY from the onslaught of apples and tumbled off the raised stage. I hear a sickening yell, primal and wounded. It's my own voice as I run to Vienne. She lies still on the ground, her left arm sticking out grotesquely in an awkward position from her shoulder.

Griffin is already next to Vienne, having left the metal worker in the care of the other guard on stage. A few other people surround Vienne too, trying to revive her. I scream again, calling her name. She's been hit in the head and the shoulder. Already a large welt is bulging on her forehead. She's knocked out cold, but at least she's breathing, her chest rising and falling in even swells.

Tomlin rushes over with a glass of cold water. A doctor runs forward too, holding something fragrant, lemon rind, I think, under Vienne's nose. I don't even know what's going on offstage right now. All I can focus on is Vienne. The doctor turns her shoulder sharply in its socket. I hear bone and cartilage grind together, and the sound hurts my teeth. Vienne's shoulder clicks back into place, and the action revives her. She yells out in pain.

Griffin holds one hand on my shoulder to steady me and puts his other hand on Vienne's perspiring cheek.

"She's going to be okay, Aloy." He doesn't bother using my official name. I don't care. I just nod at him, unable to take my eyes off Vienne's face.

"She's going to be okay," he says again. Maybe he's trying to reassure himself. His eyes are stricken, round and wide in his face. It looks like he was the one who was hit, his cheeks are so red. Vienne going down, under his watch, is like a knife in his side, I realize.

I finally look into the crowd. Everyone is quiet, watching us with open mouths. They're all transfixed on Vienne, scared for her too. Even the Technology Faction is subdued. Nothing is being thrown anymore. All fist-fighting has ceased.

I'm not sure how to proceed. I don't know how to punish all of the Technologists who've thrown objects. East Country has never convicted more than one person at a time before. Mass execution is unthinkable. I turn to the guards. "Please take this man away," I say, gesturing to the metal worker. At least I know how to deal with the squirming man who's the one person still trying to get out of the guards' hold to attack me.

Vienne sits up in the dirt, groaning with the effort, and whispers close to me. "Did your arm hurt?" I think she's asking about the apple hitting my biceps, but then I wonder if she believes the superstition about feeling your true love's pain on the brand. My thoughts turn to my throbbing arm. In the middle of all this chaos is Vienne asking if we're true loves? Or does she just want to know if I've been hurt by a thrown object too?

I decide to go with the simplest answer possible to ease her tensions. "Yes, it hurts, but I'm fine."

She leans in again, whispering in my ear. I listen for a moment and shake my head at her in disagreement. Like me, she's thinking what to do with all of the people who threw the grotesque fruit.

"It's the only way," she pleads. "And you said you'd listen to me." I look at my new wife, lying on the ground beside me. She's the one who's been really hurt, and yet she's able to so quickly forgive.

I reluctantly heed her advice. I shout toward the Technology Faction, trying to make my voice sound calm. "I would like to throw the lot of you into prison, however Madame Elected has asked me to show mercy on this day after our wedding. This is not the correct way to demonstrate your dissent, but I'll host you in the White House to talk through your vision. Nothing good can come from violence. Instead, your words will be heard."

One man from the mob speaks for the group, his voice also tempered. "Thank you, Elected. We'll take you up on that offer. We have much to say to you. Much to suggest. Much technology to start producing." He pauses, seemingly embarrassed. "We're sorry Madame Elected was hit. She wasn't our intended target. We'll pay whatever penance you deem appropriate."

"I'll see you tomorrow," I say, not having decided yet what penance

134

I'll dispense to the people who obviously aimed their weapons at me. "Please disperse now."

I motion for the crowd to leave, keeping the Technology Faction within the circle of guards as people exit the Ellipse. Once the rest of the people are gone, the guards escort the Technologists out. For so long, these people kept hidden. Now the Technologists are so bold and so defiant of me, they feel they can unearth themselves. I can almost feel my power and influence waning, like they're tangible things that can be wrestled out of my hands.

Griffin, Tomlin, Vienne, a small group of guards, and I are left on stage. Besides us, the open air hall is empty. I wipe the back of a hand across my sweating brow.

"I'm sorry," says Vienne, sitting down heavily on one of the chairs. "Instead of announcing the metal scan in a noncontroversial manner, it seems I made it worse."

Griffin comes to her defense. "It wasn't you who made it worse. The Technology Faction obviously had something preplanned no matter what was said."

Comforting Vienne is my job. I come to stand near her, putting an arm on hers. "Their reaction had nothing to do with you. There are strange happenings across our country right now. People are worried."

"We need to investigate the nirogene supply as soon as possible," Tomlin says.

"Yes, today," I say. "And I want Vienne with me. The people need to see her as a partner by my side. Not as a delicate flower."

Vienne smiles up at me as I say this. I can tell it's what she wants even though she's hurt.

"I'd like to come too," says Griffin. "If there are indeed weapons stashed on the border, I'll bring the metal scanners and start the search there."

"Very well. First Vienne rests, then we'll set out on horses."

We wait two hours before Vienne finally convinces us she's fine. Griffin runs back to the White House to get a third horse for himself and two more for a set of guards. We ride off at a fast canter and, within the next hour, we're in front of the hills bordering East and Mid countries. I can smell the pungent odor of nirogene being harvested.

Griffin attaches his horse to a rock and starts the metal search, sprinkling chemical in lines across the dirt. Vienne and I walk directly to the mouth of a cavern, determined to talk to the miners. Two men meet

135

us at the cavern entrance, their shovels thrown over their shoulders.

"Quite a display at the town hall today, Electeds," says one.

"Yes," says Vienne. "That's why we're here." She shields her eyes from the glaring sun but at the same time covers herself more tightly with her jacket. The days are getting warmer but still there's a chill in the air.

"I should have come weeks ago," I say, apologizing for not investigating the nirogene supply as soon as my father and I heard about it. "I just didn't realize exactly how limited our supply was getting."

"We're reaping just as much of the mineral as normal, though," says the second man.

"Then where do you think it's going?"

"Beats us. Although, one of our newest harvesters, Camine, insists bottles are disappearing."

"From where do you think thieves are accessing the supply? The mines or in the chemist's shops?" Vienne asks.

"Not here," says the miner quickly. "Definitely not disappearing from the mines. We load buckets of the compound onto wheelbarrows and move them into town over a couple of days. Each wheelbarrow is guarded by two miners. I count them myself before they leave the hills."

"So you think the chemists are the thieves?" I ask.

"I didn't say that exactly. It's a mystery where the bottles are going."

"Can we speak to Camine?" asks Vienne.

The second man goes to fetch Camine, who returns in a few minutes, holding his lunch in one hand. He's all of fifteen years old.

"Am I in trouble?" he asks, looking up at me with a mixture of anxiety and sun in his eyes.

"No, but I have some questions for you. Were you working here the day Imogene visited the hills? Did you see her?"

"Yeah, it was odd she was here," he says. "We usually deliver the chemical straight to her in town, but she said she was here to see the supply firsthand."

"So she was investigating it too?" asks Vienne. "Or she was stealing it herself."

"Don't know. She was acting kinda weird."

I think back to my last day with her. Those phrases dripping out of her mouth like acid. The blurry look in her eyes. She must've used the helmet for a long time before she was discovered.

"She said things were falling from the sky," says the boy, lifting his hand to shadow his eyes from the sun.

"Have you seen things fall from the sky?" Vienne asks.

"Ummm... no. I'd have told someone about that, for sure. But, it would sort of explain where the pellets come from," Camine says, cautious with his response.

"Pellets? What do you mean?" asks the head miner, all of a sudden interested.

"I mean, these little pellet things." He cups his hands into a small circle. "I've never seen them fall from the sky. But sometimes when I get here in the morning for the early shift, I find a couple lying around."

As if on cue, I see Griffin running back toward us. "The ground," he calls out. "It's turned orange!"

I follow where he points and reach the orange dirt mound first and start kicking up the dirt stained with chemical. Griffin's metal scan has done its job, turning the dirt a reddish-orange color where metal's been found. The scan turned up four separate mounds. From a distance they look like large anthills, but upon closer inspection, they're lumpy, odd in their puffiness like each mound has pimples.

Griffin and I work to dislodge the dirt and, after a second, we see the "pellets" Camine was referring to.

"Is this what you saw before?" I ask him in disbelief.

"Yeah. What are they?" Camine bends down so he's kneeling in the dirt. He fingers one shiny pellet between his thumb and forefinger.

Having been schooled in history and past warfare techniques, I know right away, but it takes the others a moment to register what the odd metal cylinders are. I fall to my knees in the dirt, pulling out the cylinders handfuls at a time. I just can't believe how many of them there are.

Vienne breathes out one word as she too realizes. "Bullets."

18

THERE ARE HUNDREDS OF them. We scoop them out of the ground in handfuls, depositing them in wheelbarrows.

"What are we going to do with them?" asks Vienne, her hands covered in the chemically orange dirt.

Griffin answers for me. "Melt them down. Just like Aloy's father did years ago."

"I don't know how these got left out," I say, incredulous.

We send the miners all back to their work. Last thing we need are a few bullets straying into their hands as souvenirs. This thought worries me—I'm starting to distrust my people. I shake the notion from my head, intent on clearing out the ground of these vile cylinders as fast as possible.

"Can you imagine if Imogene had found these and loaded her gun?" asks Vienne.

No, I don't want to imagine. I roll one of the cylinders in between two of my fingers, pushing it back and forth across my palm, thinking fast.

"These are different than the ones my father melted," I say into the air.

"What do you mean 'different'?" Griffin asks.

"I've seen sketches of the old bullets. These are more circular, little ovals with a stamp in their side. I peer closer at the pellets to see the stamp. It's a ship cresting over a series of waves. This is strange too, as ships were also eradicated years ago.

Ships, of course, make me think of my brother.

"They're newly made?" asks Vienne, pulling me away from my

thoughts of Evan.

"Yes, I think so." The metal isn't corroded at all. See how shiny it is?"

"You think our people have the capability to construct these?" asks Griffin.

"No, we don't have the technology. I'm sure of it. Our people didn't make these. These came from somewhere else."

"Someone is hoarding them here. Getting ready for an ambush?" asks Vienne, a few bullets in her palm.

"Maybe," I say.

"If it's for an ambush," asks Vienne, "why now? We've maintained peace with the surrounding countries for so long. Why would they start a war with us now?"

"Maybe their resources are waning," I say. "Maybe they're desperate. That was how war started before. When the resources were so thin countries started stealing from one another via unmanned airrides."

Griffin picks up the metal scanner and begins sprinkling more chemical in outward circles. "I'll do a more extensive scan right now. And I'll come back later with a larger force. We'll scan up and down the hills."

"Yes," I agree. My head is lost in thoughts of Mid and West Countries arming themselves against us, intent on stealing our resources. We'll have to take some kind of defensive action, but I just don't know what yet.

We load three wheelbarrows full of bullets onto carts attached to our horses. We'll melt these down tonight. First I'll remove the gunpowder from the casings, as my textbooks instructed. Then the metal workers can heat the ovens to melt the gold shells.

The question is what I'll do with all the gunpowder. Where I'll put it. Later that afternoon when I've personally escorted the bullets to one of the metal worker's huts, I ask Tomlin to meet me and dispense his advice.

"I'd sprinkle the powder around. There will be so little in any area, it can't be swept up and collected," he says.

I nod, and Tomlin wordlessly helps me crack the casings and deposit the gunpowder in crude sandy piles. He scoops up a few heaps and starts sprinkling them outside. Tomlin does this methodically, distributing the gunpowder little by little as I continue to open the shells.

We're almost done as the burning ovens reach the required temperature. I think of all the firewood being wasted to fuel this huge bonfire. We could have used this wood in so many better ways.

The moon is high in the sky by the time we're loading all of the shells into the fire. My face is red from the effort and the heat. Tomlin stands beside me, scooping shovel after shovel into the fire. A metal worker churns the fire with a poker, turning over the wood, while I stir the shells inside the oven.

I watch as the flames lick and eat the golden metal. The fire is so hot, it's blue. It's mesmerizing to watch, and finally Tomlin taps me on the shoulder to indicate we're done. I turn, bright spots dancing in my vision from staring into the flames so long.

"It's finished. We can go home," he says.

I nod, wanting desperately to crawl into bed after today's riot and the ensuing treasure hunt at the hills.

As we walk back through town to the White House, I fill in Tomlin on our guesses regarding the bullets' origins.

"Very troubling," he says with a hand at his brow. "If Mid Country is planning an ambush, it's unprovoked to be sure."

"Unless..." I stop in my tracks. "Unless my parents incited it. Arrived there and made them mad?"

"Couldn't be," says Tomlin. "Your parents would die before causing trouble for East Country. And the timeline would be off. Imogene was investigating the nirogene supply at the hills long before your parents left."

"True. So now we have Mid Country dropping off bullets in the hills, my parents' whereabouts possibly adding to the tension with Mid, and a nirogene supply being stolen from somewhere inside our own country. I'm going to have to take some decisive action soon, don't you think? To ensure that we won't be defenseless?" We both grow silent, mixing these problems around in our heads to try to make sense of them.

As we near the house, I look up at the moon, round in the sky, and think of Vienne. She'll be in her quarters now, and that's where I'll be heading too. To sleep next to her, in her warm embrace. I remember what else I've been meaning to ask Tomlin.

"What happened to Vienne's parents?"

"Her parents?" He doesn't look directly at me.

"There aren't any graves for them."

Tomlin puts a hand to his chin, taking a moment before speaking. "I specifically picked a child who didn't have parents. Your father and I

141

thought it would be easier choosing someone... unencumbered. Someone whose parents wouldn't ask questions about you."

I nod. "Okay, but what happened to them? Why aren't there graves? Even if they just left and never came back, we'd have put in headstones for them. Like we've done with my parents."

Tomlin stops outside of the doors to the White House.

"You're very astute, Elected. You were always my brightest student. You pick up on things no one else does." He stops for a moment and looks up at the sky, worried. I prompt him.

"What is it? Where did she come from?"

"Vienne... well... we don't know what happened to her parents. They..." He stops again, swallowing hard. "I found her near the hills when she was about three years old. Wandering along the border. No one was with her. She doesn't even know."

"Know what... exactly?" I'm already worried about the answer I think is on the tip of Tomlin's tongue.

"She came from Mid Country."

19

"No!" I BREATHE OUT, willing it to be untrue.

"I am sorry I didn't tell you earlier. I swear to you she doesn't know, though."

I bob my head, confused at this new information, not sure how to respond. In light of finding the bullets, Vienne's heritage is that much worse.

"You can't tell her," Tomlin urges again. "She can't know. It would eat her up inside. She's loyal to our country. She thinks this is her home."

I look over at Tomlin, resolute. "She's right. East Country is her home. I won't spoil that for her. Especially now."

Tomlin shakes his head heartily in agreement.

"I'm sorry. Your parents didn't want you to know. But... they are no longer here."

I put a hand on Tomlin's shoulder, letting him know I understand. He nods and then proceeds into the open door I'm holding for him. He turns right, and I go left toward Vienne's room.

Outside her door, I rest a hand on the outer frame, leaning against it, thinking.

If she knew, would she want to go back? Look for her parents? I brush a hand across my forehead, contemplating this when Vienne's door opens wide.

"What are you doing out here?" she asks, placing an arm around my waist. "I thought I heard someone. Come inside. You must be exhausted!"

I push the thoughts of Mid Country from my mind and follow Vienne into the room. "I am exhausted."

"We all are. It's been a long day." She has a bandage over the side of her forehead, concealing the angry looking welt she received from the onslaught this morning. Vienne's previously dislocated shoulder is wrapped in a linen brace. I want to fuss over her, hold her head in my hands and make her feel better. But she's a step ahead of me, as usual.

"Here." She pushes a teacup into my hands with her good arm. "I made you some of your favorite mint tea. It's still warm."

"Thank you." I give Vienne an appreciative smile. She watches me as I put the teacup up to my lips.

"Your hands... they're red!"

"From the ovens. The fires to melt the cartridges were very hot."

"Well, we'll get a good night's sleep tonight, and hopefully they'll go back to their regular color tomorrow." She traces her fingertips over the palm of one of my outstretched hands.

I don't know why, but her warm touch makes me think of Griffin. Before I can stop myself, I blurt out my question.

"So where did Griffin go after the metal scanning? What's he doing tonight?"

"Went home to stay with his father, I think."

This is odd, since he now mostly stays in the White House. Where he sleeps, I'm not sure, as Vienne made the arrangements, but it's strange to think he's not here in the house with us tonight. Griffin's been our personal guard ever since he came back with me from the prison. Even though I know we have other protectors, Griffin's departure makes me feel a little less safe.

"He's turned your old room into a bachelor pad," says Vienne absently while pulling back the sheets on her bed.

"My room?" Well, there's my answer. "And bachelor pad? Didn't it look male enough when I lived in it?" My voice reveals irritation.

"I didn't mean it like that. Of course, the room looked like a bachelor pad when you were there too."

Now I know she's placating me, but I'm too tired to care. I wash off my face in a nearby basin and undress quickly. I still feel awkward taking off my clothes in front of Vienne. But the same isn't true for her. She's been schooled on her role as Madame Elected and is maybe even more loyal to her role than I am to mine. She follows the instructions to be my wife, no matter if I am a man or a woman.

She easily steps out of her flowing apricot dress, letting it pool by her feet. She wears a small slip underneath. Something silky. I realize that, instead of wanting to touch the luxurious fabric on Vienne, I'd rather be wearing it myself.

I chide myself on my selfishness and try to offset it with a compliment. "You truly are a vision."

She beams. "Thank you." She steps closer to the bed and pulls me down onto it.

I fall onto one of the soft pillows, burying my head in the crook of her arm and the clean cotton of the sheets. "You smell sweet. Like lavender. How do you always smell so good?" I mumble. I feel like we've grown close over the past weeks. At the same time, I am wary of our intimacy. I don't know how far she'll take the ruse of us as man and wife or what she's been taught to do. Maybe she's been told to flush the femininity out of me at any cost—to make me fall in love with her so I won't stray from our farce of a marriage.

She burrows closer to me, the heat from her body feeling good against my cold legs. "Because I want to be attractive to you. You like lavender, don't you?"

She knows me so well. I wonder if there's anything Tomlin didn't teach her about me. My favorite kind of tea. My favorite scents. It'll take me a lifetime to learn all of the specific things she likes and craves in return.

I don't answer her question but run my hands up her arms instead.

"One day, we'll have a bunch of children running around," she says, "and the girls will smell like lavender too."

I'm quiet, not sure how to respond to her comment about multiple children. It'll be hard enough to have one, let alone many. But I don't want to snap Vienne out of her seemingly harmless dream.

She does it for me, though. "Aloy, we need to talk about this." She abruptly sits up next to me, taking my aching hand in hers. She's gentle with her words, but they hurt all the same. "It's impossible for you and me. You just can't..."

"I don't have the right parts," I say.

"So we need to think of another way."

"I know."

Our words tumble together.

"I understand you don't want to talk about this, but you promised to help figure it out soon. And I might ovulate in the next few days. You know how hard it is to get pregnant. Each time I ovulate and don't get pregnant, it's one more chance gone forever."

I don't know much about reproduction. I don't know how many times Vienne will ovulate throughout her lifetime. The radiation effects have caused women's cycles to fluctuate randomly. Perhaps Vienne's ovulation is a thing that happens frequently or maybe just once a year. Maybe she doesn't even know herself.

"We have to figure this out in the next few days?"

"Yes, if at all possible," Vienne says, lying back down against my arm. "Do you have any ideas?"

"Not one. You?"

Vienne hesitates. She's usually forthright with me, so her pause is worrisome. I lean forward on an elbow and look into her eyes.

"You do!" My eyes are wide with expectation. "What is it?"

She blinks and breaks my gaze. "We have one option."

"That's great!" I prod. "So we'll make that happen. What is it? Is there something you can eat or drink to get pregnant on your own? Whatever it is, we'll get it."

Vienne gives a sharp, small laugh. It's more of a choke than laughter, I know, but I still want to hear her answer, so I don't say anything.

"No, I can't drink something. I need a man to get pregnant. They really didn't tell you a thing about reproduction, did they?"

"No." I look down at my hands, red and blistered in my lap.

"No, they didn't tell you anything? Or no, you won't let me include a man?"

"No, I wasn't told much of anything. I guess they didn't think I'd need the information. But..." I look over at her upturned face. She's staring at me now, waiting for my answer. "We can't involve anyone, Vienne. You know the risks in that. They'll find out I'm a girl. What if it gets out that the baby isn't mine? It won't stay a secret if there are more people involved than just you and me."

My words are pouring out, one after the other, thinking of multiple reasons why Vienne can't be shared with anyone. Why bringing a third person into the mix is hazardous. Vienne is mine, and the possessiveness I feel is a new, foreign emotion. I'm not quite sure what to do with it.

"I know someone who's good at keeping secrets," Vienne says, her head bent, eyes focused on her lap. I don't want to hear what she'll say next, but she goes on anyway, looking up at me again, trying to catch my gaze. "You know it too. You *know* he's our only choice."

I still don't say anything.

"He's not married yet. And he's the right age. Eighteen is when men are the most fertile. It's why we marry at this age. He's just a month away from eighteen now. He's the right one, Aloy."

Vienne takes my face in her hands and makes me look her in the eyes.

"You know who I'm talking about," she says.

She waits for my response a long time. It feels like nails on my tongue when I finally do open my mouth.

Vienne is still staring at me hard, willing me to voice our only option.

"Griffin," I say.

20

"IT WON'T WORK. HE won't do it," I say. Rather, I hope Griffin won't do it. But what man wouldn't want to be with Vienne?

"Won't he, though? He'll do anything for us. For you."

I'm confused about her meaning, but she goes on. "If you ask him, he'll do it for you."

Vienne is convinced, but I'm not as sure. I don't think Griffin is as devoted to me as Vienne seems to believe. She doesn't know, for instance, he refuses to give up the name of the assassin. If he cared about me so much, telling me the name of his friend, my attempted murderer, would be an easy task.

I shake my head back and forth, but Vienne catches my face again between her hands. "We need to ask him soon," she says. "Tomorrow. We can't waste any more time."

"This is the only way for you to get pregnant?"

"Without technology? Yes. If we used the old ways, I could be artificially inseminated, but that's off limits now. I must have sex with a man. And it has to be Griffin."

I don't know much about artificial insemination, but I know it requires refrigeration and some kind of centrifuge. Our society is far from having those capabilities. If that is Vienne's only other option, it's certainly off the table.

"Let me think about it overnight, ok?"

Vienne agrees and eventually falls into a deep sleep, her head still resting on my arm.

I don't sleep, though. All I can think about is Vienne in the arms of Griffin, their two perfect bodies close to each other. The picture makes

149

me want to throw up. Vienne is lovely and beautiful and untouchable. For years I've known the Madame Elected would be mine alone—raised just for me. Growing up, I had no friends of my own, so it's hard to willingly give my new best friend over into another's open arms now. What if she falls for Griffin and wants to spend all her time with him?

And Griffin. The thought of him with someone else is repugnant to me. I want to be the only one to run my fingertips down his back, feeling his strong spine and the curve of his shoulders. To feel his chest resting lightly against mine. I know I shouldn't be indulging in these thoughts, but in the dark like this, I let my mind wander. The images stir my mind so I can hardly keep still.

I picture his hair. The way it spikes across his forehead, unkempt and dark. His dusky eyes. The way they bore into mine when he looks at me. The way he's daring, throwing himself between me and a long arrow, but at the same time speaks to East's children with a patience I've only ever seen in Tomlin. He is a constant enigma of opposites. Mischievous but serious. Strong but gentle.

I sleep fitfully, rolling side to side, never getting comfortable. I don't know when I'm able to rest, but finally the room becomes bright, and I know it's morning. When I open my eyes, Vienne is already up and sitting in a chair close to the bed.

"Have you decided?" she asks. She's unwavering in her need for an answer. I've never seen her this insistent.

"I guess so." My eyes are still crusty from a hard slumber. I rub them and sit up on the bed, my feet falling over the side with a soft thud. "Tell me again. This is the only way?"

"Yes. If there was a better option, I would do it."

I think fast, as a last ditch effort to find an alternative. Who else knows I'm female and incapable of having a child with Vienne? "Tomlin!" I pronounce, before even thinking it through.

"Tomlin?" asks Vienne. "He's unable to have children. Have you never wondered why he's unmarried?"

I'm quiet, feeling insensitive. I'm surprised I never deduced this fact about Tomlin before. I'd always thought he was extremely dedicated to the country and my family, and that's why he didn't get married. But as stipulated by the Accords, marriage is exclusively about having children. People who can't produce offspring either wed someone else who's infertile or don't marry at all. Love has little to do with the concept of marriage, except that compassionate parents try to arrange an amiable

150

union. I look down, wondering if Tomlin ever loved someone and knew the person couldn't marry him. I grimace at the thought, realizing I'm the one who now has to uphold the Accord's harsh rules of population increase.

"It'll just be a business arrangement. It won't mean anything more," Vienne assures me.

I look at my hands, which are slowly returning to their regular flesh tone, as Vienne said they would. She thinks it's all business now. But in the arms of a muscular, virile man, she may change her mind. She may determine she loves Griffin.

And who couldn't resist Vienne? In saying yes, I'm risking the possibility of giving Griffin and Vienne over to each other. I will lose them both, I think.

This office of the Elected threatens to crush me under its weight. Over and over, I have to make decisions that go against my fiber. Watching people drink hemlock and die. Letting my parents leave. And now this. Allowing my wife, my friend, to be intimate with someone else. And not just with anyone. Griffin.

I nod my head without looking Vienne in the eyes. I don't want her to see how full they are, brimming with unease.

She yelps in happiness and gives me a hug. "You'll see. He'll say yes. And then you and I will have the most beautiful baby boy. A new ruler for East Country. He'll be wise, handsome, and strong!"

Vienne is bouncing in her exultation. She must be truly worried about making a baby. I realize her whole life is dedicated to figuring out a way for us to conceive. And I've just given her the key.

We make our way down to breakfast, Vienne hopping in her shoes and me shuffling over the floorboards like I'm a prisoner walking to my execution.

Griffin is already there, alone, with a bran muffin coated in honey. The nectar drips down the side of the muffin onto his hand. I stare at his fingers for a moment, lapping up the image of him as mine for the last time.

"Looks like you didn't get any sleep," Griffin says toward me.

I don't want to waste any time with small talk. Especially since the room is vacant except for the three of us. It's the perfect time.

"We have to talk to you about something," I mutter.

Griffin raises an eyebrow and lets the muffin fall down onto his plate. "Oh boy. What have I done now?" His smile is impish.

Vienne gives a small laugh and comes to stand by his side. I pull up a chair to his left. We're bordering him now like bookends.

Griffin stops smiling. "What is it?"

"Aloy has a question for you," Vienne says.

Griffin looks over at me. "Elected, you know I can't tell you... we've gone over this before." He's formal with me, thinking my request will again be for the name of the assassin.

"No, that's not what I need to ask you." I run my hands over my head, wiping the small spikes of my hair backward. I rest my fingers on my mouth.

"I need you to have sex with my wife." There. I've said it. My words hang in the air like a knife about to drop.

Griffin looks from me to Vienne and back again, his eyes wide. After a moment of quiet, he settles back over his muffin, pulling a finger through the honey. He doesn't say a word. Instead, after a solid pause, he laughs out loud, his shoulders shaking with the onslaught.

"We're not kidding," says Vienne, her voice serious and low.

"I need Vienne to get pregnant," I nod once to emphasize the reason and convince myself of its need at the same time.

"And we can't do it without you," says Vienne.

Griffin puts down the muffin again and looks at me square in the face. This time the hilarity is wiped off his face.

"Absolutely not."

I look away from the two of them, not wanting to show my relief or elation about the fact Griffin's said no. But when I look up, I see Vienne's face. It's twisted with intense sadness. I can tell she feels guilty for suggesting this option. But I know she won't easily give up. That I am not as resolved in making this child bothers me. I should be even more emphatic about the idea than Vienne.

"Why not?" asks Vienne.

"This is ludicrous. You want me to fake having the next Elected with Vienne?"

"Yes," I say, my head down. "Yes, that's exactly what we want you to do."

"You want this? Do you, Aloy? You want me to make *love* to Vienne?"

I swallow the lump in my throat and answer fast so I won't change my mind. "Yes."

"I can't. I won't do it."

"I told you he wouldn't do it," I say to Vienne.

Vienne turns to Griffin, forcing him to look at her instead of me. "I told Aloy you'd do this for her if she asked it of you. That it would be hard, but you'd agree."

"And I said you wouldn't do it," I respond.

"Well, it looks like Aloy knows me best," Griffin says, bitterness now dripping from his mouth, his muffin discarded on his plate, the napkin balled up in his fist.

"No, she doesn't," comes Vienne's voice from across the room. "I do."

I didn't even hear Vienne crossing the floor. But she's on the other side of the room now with something cupped inside her hands.

"What do you have?" I ask.

She comes forward, holding out a small box.

Griffin groans.

"What?" I look back and forth between the two of them. They obviously both recognize this object, whereas it's importance is a complete mystery to me.

"Something Griffin keeps in his room," Vienne says. "Something of yours, Aloy."

"Mine?" I ask, my eyebrows scrunched together in a tight crease.

"Vienne, did you really have to go looking through my things?" Griffin asks, his brow tensing.

She comes forward, holding the box out to me. But she's speaking to Griffin. "I'm the only one who's supposed to care for the Elected, Griffin. The only one who is, by duty, supposed to be by her side. But it seems I've had competition long before I was ever Aloy's wife. You've coveted her for years."

I open the box, the old hinge squealing as the lid lifts. In it are five small wooden toys—a crudely fashioned bird, whistle, bicycle, horse, and a figure of a little girl.

"These are mine," I say. "They disappeared a long time ago. I thought... Ama threw them out."

"I'm sure she did," says Vienne. "However, each time your mother threw out the figurines you whittled, Griffin found a way to save them."

"My toys," I marvel. I'd given up whittling anything that looked like a play thing. Ama didn't approve.

Griffin is looking down at the table, but without shame he says, "I rescued them for you... so you could have them back one day."

"You see, he does want you." Vienne looks over at Griffin, her eyes narrowed. "Don't you? You'd do anything for Aloy. Anything to protect her and help her keep her secret going. Even help her have a baby."

"I... I...," Griffin stammers.

I stare at him. Maybe he does care for me as much as Vienne thinks.

"So will you do it, Griffin?" asks Vienne again, her voice like a piston, steadfast and rapid. "Will you do the one thing Aloy asks of you? Will you help us have a baby?"

He sits quietly in his chair, his hands square on the table. He's looking at me again. The world seems to stand still. It's only him and me in the room. No table. No breakfast. No Vienne. There is just Griffin's full, dark eyes locking with mine.

"Aloy," he says, his voice low. "This is really what you desire of me?"

His use of the words "desire" and "me" in the same sentence threaten to squeeze my stomach in on itself.

I stare back at him, setting my jaw resolutely even though I don't feel sure of my words at all. "Yes, it is."

Maybe he'll still love me even after having sex with Vienne. Maybe I'll get Vienne and Griffin and a new baby. Maybe everything will be perfect.

"Then I'll do it. I'll make love to Vienne, over and over again, as many times as it takes for her to get pregnant."

His words, "as many times as it takes," slice me in two. Like a sword has just lashed through my guts, flaying me open like a fish. *As many times as it takes.* Vienne and Griffin making love over and over again as I wait in the wings for the act to be finished. I feel the bile rising in my throat, and I don't dare wait for it. I excuse myself from the table, backing up the chair so it makes a sharp scratching sound on the wood floor. I look straight ahead as I exit the room.

21

I THINK I'M ALONE, leaning against the wall with one hand when Tomlin turns a corner and almost bumps into me.

"Oh, Elected! Good. The Technology Faction rioters from the town hall are here for your meeting."

I'd almost forgotten about that.

"Right. Let's get to it."

I follow Tomlin to another part of the White House into what used to be a conference room, or war room, off the oval office. Already there are fifteen people, a mix of men and woman of various ages, seated around the table. One man sits near the head, but the prime seat is left open for me. I walk to it right away, sitting down as the other meeting participants start to stand in deference.

So, they do still regard me with some degree of respect, I muse. Or they must feel bad about causing Vienne harm.

On cue, the group's representative, Grobe, inquires, "How is Madame Elected? We hope she wasn't hurt badly."

"She's fine," I say, my words clipped. "She has a small welt."

"We apologize again, Elected. And we brought something for Madame Elected." One of the women, Margareath, whom I recognize as one of our planters, brings out a plump, spikey green shrub in a terra-cotta pot. She sets it down in the middle of the table, and it's passed over to me.

"An aloe plant," Margareath explains. "Its leaves, if broken in half, give healing lotion to the skin. It will help Madame Elected's scrape on her head."

"Thank you," I say. "She'll appreciate it." I don't say I'll appreciate it, as I don't think I can like anything from these people. For all I know, one of them might be my assassin. In fact, I decide to ask outright.

"If we knew who it was," says Grobe, "we would hand him or her over to you. It would be the patriotic thing to do. Again, we didn't mean to hit Madame Elected. And we didn't think the metal-laced fruit would really hurt you. We just meant to capture your attention enough so you'd understand our dissent."

I don't believe him, as I remember the trajectory of the fruit laced with metal. It was all aimed for my head. "It could have been voiced through more productive means," I say, bitterness in my tone.

"Well," says Grobe, "thank you for meeting us today. Your father never would."

That sounds like Apa. He was opposed to even discussing the use of technology, as any violation of the Technology Accord went against his morality. He, like me, was schooled in history better than anyone in our country. He'd seen pictures of our world before climate change was brought on by the pollutant, carbon dioxide. I'd seen the same worn and tattered snapshots. Lush, green fields. Flowers aplenty. Great snow-capped mountains. Now our world is barren. Dirt fields. Mountains under so much snow that they're now entirely unscalable. And flowers. So precious to us now, they're hardly ever picked to go in a vase and die.

"I won't bend easily either," I say, looking once again into Grobe's eyes. "I don't think you'll change my mind about using technology. I'm not going to be responsible for the destruction of our people."

"We don't see it that way. We see it as an improvement. Our people could prosper with just a bit of technology use."

"We're not advocating a return to the old ways," says another man. "We don't want to start using cars again. Nothing like that." He winces at even the mention of vehicles.

"Just a few items," says another man.

"Such as?" I ask.

"Defense systems, for one thing," says Grobe. "If Mid and West Countries are arming themselves against us, we need to be prepared."

"Who says they're arming themselves?" I ask, reproachful as it sounds like Grobe has helped spread the news.

"It's a rumor," says Margareath.

"We're not saying we should manufacture weapons ourselves," says one of the men. "But some force field exploration maybe—"

I cut him off. "You know what you're asking for? Force fields require electricity. That's a slippery slope. If we start manufacturing any of it, we'll need electricity. Some of the old machines. Oil to run those machines. Where are we going to get oil anyway?"

"It could be harvested from the Atlantic," says Grobe. "If we used ships."

"I don't think so," I say quickly. They've thought all this through too completely. Even Tomlin, sitting in the corner of the room, looks uncomfortable. "This is all too much."

"And health technology," says Margareath. "Manufacturing the purple pills. Don't you want to help your people, Elected?" She almost gets me with this one, as I've thought about the same thing in the past. If there's anything that would get me to advocate for technology, it's the health of my people. But I have my answer ready.

"We don't have the ingredients for those pills anymore. Those plants died out years ago."

"We could try emulating the ingredients," she says. "With what we have."

"Creation of those pills would, again, require electricity," I say.

"And so what?" says Grobe, angry this time. "What's so wrong with electricity?"

"What's so wrong with it?" I say, aghast. "Electricity is generated at a power station by electromechanical generators. Primarily driven by heat engines, fueled by chemical combustion or nuclear fission. We can't turn that on."

I can tell they're impressed with my understanding of science. A few of the men look up at me with greater respect.

"Yes," says Margareath. "But it can also be created by the kinetic energy of flowing water."

She too is learned. I am taken aback by Margareath's intellect. In just a few moments she's not only appealed to the one thing I care most about—my people's health, but she's also shown the range of her scientific understanding.

"We would need a waterfall to create enough force for the kind of flowing water you're describing," I say. "We've looked for waterfalls. There aren't any left in East Country. They've dried up."

"We could create one," says Margareath.

"Enough!" I say. "We just keep going around in circles. Anything we want to create would require the use of other technology to build it. I appreciate you telling me your thoughts, but I can't give the answer you want to hear. I'm not about to reverse a century's worth of decisions just because a small group of our people wish it."

Grobe stands. "We see. Well. We agree to disagree." The line of his mouth is taut. "Just because a small group of people are forward thinking and the majority wants to stay stuck in the past is not a reason to resist advancement. I'd heard you were reasonable—that you might not be as rule-fearing as your father, but apparently that was inaccurate." He is agitated, rocking back on his heels.

I nod. "Well, we can at least keep this dialogue open. We can meet periodically. But before you leave, there's the penance you must pay for hurting Madame Elected." I don't mention anything about the hurt they caused my arm.

"Yes," says Grobe who sits back down, rightfully admonished.

I've been thinking of a suitable punishment for their use of violence. It doesn't warrant death, but I do have to take some action. Punish them. Deter others. But also show these people that I do believe in them and their intrinsic goodness. I hope trusting this group now isn't a mistake.

"I need you to take shifts at night, watching the hills."

"Whatever the country needs," Grobe says, "we'll gladly help." His eyes are wide, clearly surprised at the tame retribution I seek.

"Good. We need teams of extra people to help the guards watch the hills. We need to ensure Mid Country isn't dropping off bullets or stockpiling weapons near the area."

"So I was right!" exclaims Margareath.

"We don't know for sure," I say. "But we need people to watch at night and report back to me. There just aren't enough guards to cover the entire border."

"We'll accomplish that," says Grobe. He slaps his palms on the table, like the meeting is over and he's preparing to leave.

"There's more," I say, grimacing as I dispense the last part of their punishment. "Each of you must pay another penance for throwing the metal-laced fruit. It was dangerous and shows vast disrespect for the Elected family. You must each be branded with the symbol of an apple on your stomach."

I see a few of the technologists cringe. I've picked the fleshiest part of the body for the branding. One that will surely hurt when touched with the hot poker.

"As you wish," says Grobe. His eyes squint at me.

I nod at the guards who open the conference room doors. The group stands and Tomlin ushers them out of the room in an orderly fashion.

I turn around, my hands resting on the table in front of me. I stare at the wood grain on the surface, following the horizontal lines with my eyes. I've assumed the room is empty, so when a voice flutters close to my ear, I jump.

"It's not so hard to build a waterfall," says Margareath. She's too close for comfort.

"Back up slowly," I say to her, wondering for a split second if she could be the assassin.

"I've brought one with me," she says, so excited about the contraption she's about to show me she ignores my command for space. From beneath her cloak, Margareath pulls out a small bird whose wings are tied down at its sides. She attaches the bird, via a wire and some sort of battery, to a small bucket of drinking water set out for the meeting. She unwraps the bird's wings, which begin to flap furiously with great whooshes of air. I start to protest, but at once a few drops of water from the bucket burst straight up, like it's raining upside down. The droplets hang in midair for a split second before plopping back down into the larger pool again.

"See?" she says.

I stand next to her, speechless. What I can't decide is if Margareath is a genius or if she's gone ahead and demonstrated explicit use of technology right in front of her Elected, an act so foolish, I can't even comprehend her motivations. I stare at the device, full of silver wires.

"Where did you get these?" I finger one of the thin cables in my fingers.

"Oh..." Margareath blanches at this. She doesn't continue with an answer.

"You took these from a bike."

Margareath licks her lips. "I didn't think... it's my own family's bike... I can put them back on..."

And then I focus on the battery. "And this?"

Margareath stumbles backward, eyes down. "Oh that... I found it."

I can't decide what to do. If I turn a blind eye, word will get out I let her dismantle our precious resources to create inventions. And I find it highly unlikely Margareath found a working battery. Batteries left from previous centuries would have lost their energy by now, even if they

159

could power an entire rocket ship back in the old days. I can't let her walk out of this room and tell people I approved this contraption. And by doing nothing, it would be as good as giving implicit approval. It'll start an avalanche of Elected-approved technology creation.

I frown at her, thinking fast about my options. About the Accords and the harsh implications of breaking them. About breaking the Fertility and Elected Accords myself. About showing my countrymen what happens when they tinker with technology. About the threat from Mid Country and our lack of defense. And about Margareath herself. Her warm, expectant smile as she passed the aloe plant across the table to me. Her learned response about kinetic energy. Her anxiety now that I figured out she broke the Technology Accord.

A plan forms in my head, something of which I'm sure my father would disapprove. I must deter my people from creating technology, but for the first time, I decide to defy the Accords on my own.

"Guards!" I yell.

22

MARGAREATH STARTS TO PROTEST, looking at me with wide eyes. She didn't expected this reaction from me. As two guards burst into the room and look at her invention on the table, they immediately understand their task. They take both of Margareath's arms by the elbows, leading her out of the room.

She tries to reason with me, even as she is being pulled out the door toward the prison. I stand in the frame, watching her as they go. She twists her head around to see me, still pleading, calling out the Elected's name for mercy.

I stare at her, my face blank so as not to give away my new idea to either Margareath or the guards. I try to imagine my father's voice in my head. What would he think of my new ideas, the way I'm starting to think my own thoughts instead of just being his parrot. I can almost hear the deep mesmerizing way he spoke, but his voice is like a butterfly flitting away. I have it and yet it's gone again.

I carefully untangle the wires from the bird's wings and set it free through an open window on my walk out of the war room.

I proceed toward the one person with whom I can discuss my idea. Who, no matter what she might think personally, will have to go along with my plans. I just hope Vienne agrees with my decision of her own free will. My stomach knots, imagining how it will feel to force her to defy laws on my behalf once again. I find her in her quarters, a book open on her lap.

"Aloy!" she says, surprised and pleased at the same time. "I'm so glad you're here. I thought you might be upset after our conversation at breakfast."

Her face is earnest and open. I try to smile back at her, but again the thought of Griffin with her threatens to turn my stomach. I concentrate instead on the task at hand.

"I just met with the Technology Faction, and one of them was daring enough to show me an invention she created."

"Oh no," says Vienne, rising out of her chair by the window. "Is she at the prison now?"

"Yes, but there's something I want to discuss with you. Something I want you to do with all of our criminals going forward."

I move closer to Vienne and pull her gently down to sit on the bed next to me. She faces me, listening to every nuance of my plan. Her eyes never move from my face, and I'm at once overwhelmed again at her level of loyalty to me and this country. She doesn't just hear my words. She listens to them, takes them in, and processes them. She refrains from commenting until the end, but when I'm finished, I look to her for an answer.

She'll have a key role in this plan, and I need to know if she's on board. Vienne doesn't take more than a second to give me her reply.

"I'll do it. Of course."

I smile, a heavy weight lifting from my shoulders. I grab her toward me, almost crushing her shoulders as I envelop her in a hug.

"Thank you." Then I pull back and look at her face again. "I know this goes against everything you were taught. But I think it's where our society needs to go next."

Vienne bites her bottom lip, pausing for a moment before speaking. When she does, her answer, as so much of her, surprises me. "It may have been what I was taught, but I never agreed with it."

In that one second I realize Vienne and I may be more alike than I thought.

✦⟨✦⟩✦

Over the next few weeks, rumors that Mid Country is stockpiling bullets against East rise up like an infection in the minds of my people. The miners who saw us dig out the bullets, the Technology Faction, and the metal workers can't be quieted. Before long, the entire country knows about the threat of Mid Country. We have multiple town halls. People don't even bother going home in between the meetings. Many of them camp out with their bikes on the Ellipse, crafting makeshift tents out of fabric borrowed from other countrymen.

And their questions about our defense systems mount. Now the rumors that West Country is in on the coup also take shape in their minds. The questions bubble up at the town halls so fast the talkers hardly have time to repeat a question before the next one is asked. People don't even wait for the talkers anymore. They just yell out their questions, and others in the audience propel the words forward like children's balls bouncing on raised, outstretched arms. Many times I have to call order to the proceedings before my countrymen become so flustered they start fighting amongst themselves again.

The Technology Faction comes forward, more and more people outing themselves, and the small group I believed existed, grows larger. They speak at the town halls about creating defense systems. Grobe talks about manufacturing force fields and more purple pills. But, to the credit of my people, discussion and conversation is all the fighting that breaks out. There are no physical assaults. No one throws anything. The words are heated, but people maintain decorum.

Members of the Technology Faction watch the border day and night, working in shifts to ensure no other stockpiles of weapons are deposited. I have no fears the Technologists are finding weapons, keeping them a secret, or hiding them for future use, because I also employ as many guards as possible to help during each border shift. The guards watch both the hills and the Technologists. The teams report the arrival of no other bullets, and metal scans show nothing more.

Additional people, besides the Technology Faction rioters, offer to watch the hills and play guard. The outpouring of volunteers is high, and I'm buoyed by the care our people have for the country.

Everyone seems more diligent in their work. More focused. The planters grow twice the amount of greenery, throwing themselves into digging holes and watering the land. The chemists take the additional vegetation and mix it to stockpile homeopathic medicines, in case we'll need them later. And the guards maintain a quiet presence everywhere. Wherever I turn, there are a couple who trail me dutifully.

The one person who doesn't trail me is Griffin. We've avoided each other for days. I'm almost thankful for that, as I imagine Vienne's fertile period is coming soon and it'll start their intimacy. I can't bear to look at him, so I'm grateful for the reprieve. He is there, still watching us, on the sidelines, but he doesn't guard me specifically. He doesn't guard Vienne either, almost like he's trying not to show a preference for her. And I'm distracted enough by the proceedings in the country that I'm almost okay with this.

My plan with Margareath in the prisoner's quarters goes off without a hitch. I'm there as she drinks the mouthful of clear liquid, the tears welling up in her eyes as she thinks it is her last moment. I just nod at her encouragingly, not giving in to emotion. Only I know what will happen next, and this affords me the luxury of looking past her fear, knowing in the end she'll be okay. Vienne dresses the body, as we discussed, and this too goes as well as we could imagine.

I visit Margareath's family afterwards, apologizing to them, listening to them tell me stories of her bravery and devotion to her children. I hold their hands as the youngest child cries, his tears falling like raindrops on the top of my thighs. I grasp tightly to his shoulders, telling them everything will be all right. As I watch them deep in despair, I try to remember I know things that will make them feel better later— that Margareath will eventually return. I try not to dwell on their despair further as I step out of their small house, into their side garden that is now overrun. It used to be one of the best personal gardens in the country, but without Margareath there, no one has thought to care for her plants. The space is closed off by a thick fence on all sides, allowing me a moment of semi-privacy to collect myself as a pair of guards wait on the other side of the high walls.

I bend down and brush dirt off the tender petals of a few plants. The sun beats down on my uncovered head. The air has grown hot now, in stark contrast to the unwavering cold of one month ago. I'm not sufficiently prepared to work outdoors in the garden, but I lose myself in caring for Margareath's plants. I stay there longer than I should, the harsh rays of the sun starting to burn my neck.

"You should take more caution," says a voice over my shoulder.

I don't look up, already knowing who it is.

"What do you care?"

"I care a lot," says Griffin.

He gives the two guards who are watching me through the garden gate a curt nod, relieving them of duty. The guards bow in my direction and make themselves scarce. Griffin and I are alone for the first time in a long while, but I don't look at him. I keep my hands deep in the dirt of Margareath's garden, pulling at a rock that just won't come loose.

"Here, let me help," he says, squatting down next to me. He holds his hands out, meaning to dig the rock from the earth. Our fingers touch, just the slightest inch of his skin brushing against mine, and I'm paralyzed with the sensation.

"No, don't!" My voice comes out like a bark. "I don't need your help."

He eases up, rocking back on his heels and then standing. "Well, it looked like you did."

"Don't let this little stone fool you. I don't need you." I yank on it hard until it puckers from the ground and tumbles into my hand.

"You certainly need me for something," he grumbles, angst in his tone.

I stand up fast, the blood rushing to my head. I'm wobbly on my legs but I overlook the feeling, too angry at Griffin to notice my own body's needs.

"Yes, over and over again, like you said," I hiss.

"Yes, that." Griffin looks down at the dirt on the ground between us.

"Why did you have to rub it in? *Over and over again?*"

Griffin sighs. "I wanted you to be mad enough to change your mind."

"You could have refused either way. Everyone is free here."

"It's like Vienne says, though. If you need something desperately, you know I won't refuse you." He pauses for a moment, looking up at the high sun instead of at me. "And yet you ask this of me, knowing I will ultimately do what you want."

My barrier of anger falters slightly. "I *need* this, yes, but that doesn't mean I *want* it. The thought of you and Vienne..."

My voice falls off. I can't finish my sentence.

"The thought of us making a baby together makes you want to choke, to throw up, to keel over, your stomach lurch?"

Yes. How does he know me so well?

"And does it elicit the same reaction in you?" I ask, knowing already any answer other than yes will cause me to wilt in this hot sun, the same as the plants on the ground in front of us.

Griffin doesn't answer for a moment and instead looks down at Margareath's garden. "To tell you the truth, the physical act of being intimate with Vienne doesn't bother me in that same way. She's a beautiful woman. Any man would want her."

He's just voiced my exact worry. I kick up the dirt in billows, knowing this is the ultimate truth. He will enjoy this. He will fall in love with her.

"But," he says, "the thought of what this does to you... that I'd rather be intimate with you... how even though you've requested this, you'll hate me for it. That turns my stomach."

He catches my face in his hands, and before I know it, Griffin's kissing me. It's like a million fires spontaneously crackling as his embrace grows deeper. Like a wave of water crashing down on my body. Like I am on the ground but floating at the same time.

I kiss back, my lips working perfectly with his in an amazing symphony of rhythm. All of my questions about what gender I like, or if I even want to feel someone's touch, are answered in a split second. I know I'm trying to leave a passionate impression on him, so I have a slightest chance of Griffin remembering me after being with Vienne. I take in the taste of his lips on mine, the feel of his warm hands as they grasp my upper arms in the embrace.

After what feels like mere seconds and eons all at once, I hear a bird in the distance caw. It breaks my concentration enough that I reluctantly take a step back. We may have relative privacy, but what we're doing still isn't safe. I cough, stepping back from Griffin and look up at the sky instead of meeting his eyes.

"We shouldn't," I say.

Griffin slowly lets go of my arm and rubs one hand over his forehead. "I came here to tell you Vienne and I will be together tonight. I thought you deserved to know. I will be... as fast as possible."

I turn red at the thought. My next words are stilted, caught in my throat. "Thank you... for the heads up."

He nods, mouth set in a grim line. "I guess I'll see you around." Griffin brushes a strand of hair from his forehead. It refuses to budge, clinging to his skin in a moon shaped curl. I want to brush it away for him, but I hold back.

I blink, trying to block out my feelings as Griffin starts to walk away, out of the enclosed garden. Then he turns and his whispered words burn a hole into my heart.

"You know, we could make love too."

23

I DON'T EVEN KNOW how to physically do what he's talking about, but I have to admit the thought has crossed my mind. I want so much to run into his arms and tell him it's a fantastic idea.

I can't speak for fear I'll say yes, so I just shake my head back and forth. It's all I can manage.

Griffin nods back at me, like he knew I'd say no. Then he turns again and exits through the gate.

Does he know my "no" isn't my real answer? I want to tell him in other circumstances I'd, of course, want to be with him. But I've already told him we cannot act on our feelings together. I'm the Elected now, and I'm married. Any indiscretion I do with Griffin is not only a slight against my country; it's a betrayal of my wife. Vienne's having sex with Griffin is different than my being together with him. For her it's a duty. For me it would be a desire.

I wipe my hand in frustration across my lips and refrain from running after Griffin. I keep myself busy for the rest of the day, trying not to think of the impending evening when Vienne and Griffin will be together. Vienne tells me since I've moved into her quarters, she and Griffin will use my old room. I don't want to be in the house when it's happening, and I rack my brain trying to think of what I can do with my time. Something that will erase their images from my mind.

I refrain from having dinner with them, instead sequestering myself in Vienne's quarters, flipping blindly through her books, trying to find one that will sufficiently pique my interest. And as I root through Vienne's things, what I will do tonight is suddenly clear. I grab the circular metal object I'd placed into Vienne's care weeks ago, carefully hiding it

167

in a dark, canvas bag. I pull a tunic with a hood over my head, covering myself so I won't be recognized. I want to be outside, under the stars and beneath the tree where Griffin's hand first brushed my face. I know sitting under the tree will be my own unique form of torture, but it's the place I want to be tonight.

The moon is high but heavy clouds block its light, as well as any glow from the stars. The evening is dark, so my guards don't even see me sneak out of the front door and across the Ellipse. My escape reminds me of five years ago, when I last snuck out of my own house.

The townspeople are tucked away in their makeshift tents on the lawn or in their houses a mile away. Even the few people who are out roaming the grounds this evening don't pay me any attention. I gather the bag closer to my chest, afraid to leave it bumping against my side like a normal bundle. I hold it in the crook of my elbow as I find the deep, thick roots of the oak tree. The ground is still warm from today's heat, and this is fine with me, as the dirt feels pliable and soft against the back of my bare legs.

I know what I'm about to do is dangerous, but right now I don't care. I realize I vowed not to use the Mind Multiplier again, but I feel like defying something, even if it is just my own decree. I need to know a few things, and this is as good a time as any to find them out. I want to know what's happened to my parents. And I need to understand if Mid Country is our enemy or not.

I strap on the helmet, connecting the plastic tubes into their various ports. I look around once more just to double check no one can see me within the shadows of the tree. Satisfied I'm truly alone, I switch on the contraption.

Instantly the helmet vibrates against my head, humming with power. I'm struck with an intense feeling of physicality. An image of Vienne and Griffin holding each other close crosses past my eyes with such allure I almost reach out to touch them—pull them apart. The two of them touch each other's hands, arms, and necks. I see Griffin look at Vienne with tenderness and see her look up at him beneath long, batting eyelashes.

This is not what I wanted to see! I close my eyes and push hard at the thought, thrusting it far back into the recesses of my brain. The strain of the concentration causes my eyes to water, but I'm rewarded with a different picture instead. In fact, there are three images dancing across my brain at the same time. One is Vienne dressing Margareath's supposedly dead body, Margareath suddenly gasping awake, clutching at Vienne's blouse. I know that one is true already.

The next picture is one I really want to see. It's of my parents, alive and well. They're walking hand-in-hand past a set of fir trees. The lusciousness of their surroundings gives me pause. The ground is shiny, green and fresh. I can almost smell the pine cones. It's moist where they are. In a forest. A cornucopia of greenery. With waterfalls and ponds. They're happy. How they've found such a paradise is beyond me, but at least they're safe.

I try to hone in on this particular thought stream, stay with it for a while, figure out where they are, but the third picture burns into my retinas, pushing at the other images, setting fire to the image of my parents like a piece of paper engulfed in flames. The edges of that thought twist and curl up in orange licks. Try as I might to hold on to it, my parents fly off like a piece of ash. So I concentrate on the other image instead—this third one that so badly wants to get in.

I'm glad it's been persistent; I need to see this one. This image shows me the hills along the border of East and Mid Countries. A dark figure walks cautiously over the top of one of the highest peaks. The figure carries a bucket. At the bottom of the hills on our side of the border he sinks down to his knees, the bucket beside him on the ground. The man begins digging with his hands and then pulls out a small metal object, which gleams in the moonlight.

I look hard to see what the man is holding. It has a small handle with a pointed metal triangle at its base. I prickle as I easily become aware of its name. A shovel. We have these in East Country too. However, this shovel is different. At once it comes to life, vibrating in the man's hands. The shovel starts moving great masses of dirt, more than a person could dig by oneself. In just a few seconds a large hole is made in the earth. The figure sets down the automated shovel and dumps the contents of the bucket into the hole.

On instinct, I put my hands to my temples, just below the helmet, pushing on my brain, trying to see more. I think I know what is being poured into the hole, but I need to be sure. I make the Multiplier show me the hole's interior. And, of course, the objects inside are bullets. The man backs up, starting to kick dirt over the hole. He finishes and then looks left and right, suspicious of being seen. Finally, he starts running back up the hill, eager to reach the other side.

That's when it happens. I hear two sharp cracks in my head. The sounds hurt my brain as they reverberate between my ears. I try to discern if the cracks come from the real world or from the world the Multiplier is showing me. It's hard to tell, but when I see the man lying on his stomach, I'm instantly watching by his side, looking down at his body. There's blood leaking from his heart. It pools next to him, and I'm confused why we didn't find this man weeks ago. His body should be lying out in the open, on our side of the border. He is certainly dead. Our patrols should have found him the second the sun came up, at least.

But then the answer becomes shockingly clear.

An airride whirls into view, silently descending out of nowhere. It lands next to the still body. As I watch dumbfounded, the jet's doors open and another metal object slides out. It looks like a steel box, but it moves. The box starts its work, sliding over the pooling blood, leaving nothing but dirt in its wake. Then it attaches itself to the figure's limp body and hefts the man along the ground to the side of the airride. The box is having a hard time, as the body is obviously too heavy for it. The man is crammed inside until the door has room to close. After a moment the aircraft ascends again, disappearing behind the clouds in a matter of seconds. I look down at the ground in front of me, but there are no traces of the man. He and his blood are both gone.

I try to focus, figure out what's happened, but my head is beginning to hurt. In fact, it pounds; I can hear my heartbeat in my ears. But I keep trying to focus through the constant throbbing. Why would Mid Country send in a man to deposit the bullets but then gun him down and take his body? Is he a rebel, hoarding ammunition to take over his own country? Is he Mid Country's form of a Technologist?

If Mid Country picked up his body via an airride, they have to be using technology too. So is the man not following orders correctly? Was he punished for depositing the bullets? Or maybe he stole the bullets from Mid Country. And maybe the airride didn't come from Mid Country at all? Who knows who else is out there?

This is all so confusing. My mind pulses, trying to take it all in, decipher what I've just seen through the haze falling over my brain.

And all of a sudden there's a sharp pink light crashing through my head, like a tidal wave breaking over a beach. Then a yellow light. Like a pulsing jackhammer, the light flashes behind my eyes. I know it's coming from inside my own head, but I claw at it with vigor. I can't stop myself from pulling at the skin on my own face. I scratch my nails across my cheeks. I need the light to stop! I'll go blind! I pull at the sides of the helmet, but suddenly I can't seem to pry it from my head.

Other images bombard me, coming at rapid speeds. Vienne's future baby crying. Griffin's father hosing down one of our horses and then ramming a long arrow into its side, blood gushing from the horse's guts. Margareath screaming behind the armor glass in the prisoner's quarters. Imogene breaking the armor glass and running at me with hands at my throat.

I can't seem to get the images to stop coming. They're horrible, garish pictures. They don't even make sense, but the most alarming part is in between the bright flashes of light and these repugnant thoughts, I can't seem to remember how I'm supposed to get this helmet off my head. I can't seem to think about anything except for the barrage of pictures floating behind my eyes.

I feel my own hands pulling at the helmet, grasping at the plastic tubes, trying to pry them loose too. But a flash of dark red light crosses over my forehead, moving from right to left. I feel myself slump against the tree, my head falling first. I want to help myself, but it's like I'm seeing my body from the outside looking in. I can't do a thing. I just watch myself fall onto my side, the helmet still securely attached to my head.

And then everything goes black.

24

HANDS ARE ON MY face. At my sides. They're pulling at me, jostling me. I want to ask them to stop. To tell them they're hurting me, but I can't speak. And I can't see. All I feel is heat beating down on me. I'm so hot. So hot! I reach up, trying to cool myself. But my hands are caught. I hear a voice at my side, deep and vibrating in the recesses of my mind.

"Lie still, Aloy. For God's sake, stop trying to pull out your own hair!"

It's Griffin. At his voice, I try even harder to open my eyes. I manage to inch the eyelids apart a bit, but the searing sun threatens to burn them, so I shut my eyes hard again.

"Can you talk, Aloy?" asks Vienne. "Thank goodness you're all right!"

All right? I'm far from all right.

Vienne is on the opposite side of me, her knees in the dirt to my left. She bends over me, running a hand through my hair and putting a cool, wet cloth on my brow. I try to sit up, positioning a hand in back of myself. It's hard, but I force myself to balance on my arm and once again try to open my eyes. I see Griffin, Vienne, Tomlin, and four guards all encircling me. I'm sitting on the ground underneath the big oak tree.

"Be careful," Vienne insists. "I think you bumped your head."

Bumped my head? I glance around, trying to get my bearings. And then I remember using the Multiplier and thrash my arms around, feeling for it next to me. When I can't feel metal under my fingertips, I make myself move my head down even though it causes waves of pain to crash through my brain.

I need to find that helmet! If they know I've used it, then I'm just as bad as Imogene. I've used technology! I flinch in big awkward spasms.

"What are you looking for, Elected?" Griffin asks, using my formal name now, to jar me back into acting composed.

I look up at him with wide eyes, trying to convey my needs without saying them. But he doesn't understand. He doesn't know the Multiplier even exists, so he can't decipher my strange actions. Instead, he looks at me with concern.

I scan the ground in front of me and to my sides, but nothing's there except for the empty canvas bag. It lies dirty and open a few inches away from me. The helmet is nowhere to be found.

I look over at Tomlin, thinking he's taken it. He'll wink at me or give me some sign he's taken care of it. But he just looks at me with worry on his face—his eyes innocent of any knowledge I've used the helmet.

Everything feels fuzzy. The images of last night still flash across my brain, but thankfully the bright, earth-shattering colors have dissipated. Griffin and Vienne help me to my feet. They walk me at an exceedingly slow pace back to the house with Tomlin and the guards making a semicircle in back of us.

I spend the rest of the day indoors with either Griffin pacing at my side or Vienne gingerly stepping around, offering me mint tea. I need to be alone to digest the images of last night—the implications of Mid Country arming itself or killing off a defector who was hoarding weapons—the picture of my parents holding hands in a green forest. When the sun is finally setting, Griffin and Vienne make their excuses, mumbling something about eating in the dining room. They leave the room, and I'm alone for the first time all day. I sigh, sitting back on my elbows.

I try to concentrate on the images I can remember, but they're still just pictures roaming in and out of my consciousness. I can't seem to grasp them fully. What I need is real information. And so, without thinking further, I stand up and exit the room. I tell the wary guards this time I'm staying within the borders of the estate, so they let me leave without them.

I'm not lying to them. I make my way past the foyer, through the conference room on the first floor, and out toward the kitchen. On my walk, I glance past the open door of the dining room, but I see no one inside. No matter, I think. Griffin and Vienne probably already finished. The good thing is I have at least a few minutes more to myself. They aren't around to fuss after me or follow me where I'm going next.

174

I nod at the kitchen staff as I pad through on soft soled shoes. I grab a couple of apples from a satchel and a few sugar cubes from a bowl on the counter. And then I proceed out the side door into the stables. My mind is still foggy, but as I guessed, Griffin's father, Maran, is the only one in the stables, washing off the horses and grooming them until their coats shine. I'm reminded of the gruesome picture of him piercing one of our horses with a long arrow, but I blink to rid the ridiculous thought from my head.

"Hi," I say as I walk up behind him.

He turns slowly, a water bucket still in his hands. When he sees me, he doesn't smile as I expect. I watch as he flinches slightly, like he's not sure whether to lower the bucket or let its water splash all over me. I furrow my brow for a split second and this seems to snap Maran out of staring. He lowers the bucket to the ground, water sloshing out of the side in a wave.

"Shouldn't you be inside, Elected?" he asks. "I heard you suffered a nasty fall. Bumped your head." His words are careful. They are devoid of warmth or comfort, like I'm talking to a different person from the caretaker I've known for years.

I absently drag a sugar cube across the bottom of my lip, feeling the course texture, tasting just a hint of the sweetness.

"No, I'm fine," I say. Then I lift my hand with the food in it. "I brought you an apple. And some sugar cubes for the horses." I hand him the red fruit and wordlessly walk to the closest horse, offering a treat. I turn back around and see Maran rolling the apple over and over in his hands. I suddenly wonder if he's upset Vienne and I somehow stole Griffin from him. Since Griffin started living in the White House, he sees his father less. He's no longer Maran's veterinary partner. Maybe this accounts for his cool demeanor. I start to say something about it but then decide to leave it up to father and son. Griffin is his own man. He can make his own decisions.

So I delve into the main subject of my visit instead. "My parents' horses," I start, "can you tell me more about their condition?"

Maran leans against the side wall, still rolling the apple in his left hand. "They're both in good shape. I already told the guards all that for their report."

"Yes, I know. I read it. But I was hoping you could tell me more. Like their hooves, for instance. Did they have anything unusual caught in their feet? Blades of grass maybe? Or pine needles stuck in their coats?"

I'm thinking of the lush forest where I saw my parents.

"Needles? Where would they have run into pine trees?"

"Who knows what's out there in the wilderness, where my parents went?"

"I didn't see anything out of the ordinary. Why do you want to know? It's not like you're looking for your parents so you can make them return and tell you how to run the country."

His voice is like an accusation. I look up, surprised at his tone. And at the fact he's guessed my intention.

"That's not your concern," I say, my words flowing slowly over my tongue.

Maran continues, unruffled. "Because the Electeds before you relied on their own minds and the thoughts of their own people to make decisions. They didn't go running back for their parents."

"Maran?" I'm taken aback by his rudeness.

He is undeterred. "Because the Electeds before you knew where they stood on the issues. And if they didn't, they got their advice from the people themselves, not from their parents. They were not dictators."

I'm not sure what he's talking about, but I wasn't expecting this line of conversation from him.

It's my duty to listen to individuals. So I force myself to listen to Maran now, even though my head is still throbbing, and now I desperately want to leave the stables.

Maran's voice strengthens, growing higher with his obvious frustration. "You don't listen. More of the people want to start bolstering our defenses. You don't hear them out. We should be manufacturing weapons. We are left like sitting ducks." He tosses the apple into a stack of hay at his side.

I stare at Maran for a minute. When I do speak again, my voice is measured. "We haven't been attacked by anyone. There's no need to manufacture weapons."

His voice is almost a growl. "That's incorrect."

I look over at him skeptically, wondering what information he has that I don't. "No one's been attacked," I say again.

His response is stark. "You have." Maran meets my eyes directly.

"That wasn't an attack on our people. Only me."

Maran looks back at one of the horses, idly running his hand over its flank. "You'd think that would be enough to incite you, but still no."

"I won't be incited to create technology easily. Not even by that."

"A real leader would take action."

"I am taking action. Setting up shifts to patrol the hills. Destroying the bullets." I choose my next words carefully, trying to distill truth from him even though it is hard for me to hear. "You don't think I'm a good leader?"

He looks at me again. His lips edge into the slightest indentation of a smile, happy to have the opportunity to finally tell me to my face. His one word is crystal clear as it comes out of his mouth.

"No."

I turn on my heels, not wanting to hear more right now. I know I should ask Maran more questions. Or stay and just listen. My father told me he often didn't agree with the views of his people, but he always listened to everyone... except the Technologists. It goes with the office, he'd said. But the thought that Maran, my parents' trusted veterinarian and Griffin's father, should think this low of me is too much right now. I will follow-up with him later when my head is in a better condition.

I walk around the back of the house, shuffling my feet as I go. I can't reconcile the two personalities my people expect of me. I can't be decisive but also waffle back and forth on the whim of the crowd. I can't bend to the tyranny of the minority, the Technology Faction. I remind myself the majority of my people still want to follow the Accords. I can't be the puppet of the Technologists, forfeiting the Accords of long ago.

But maybe there is some way I can provide a concession. Some way to show them I'm taking defensive action to protect us. Some way to make them happy. Bring them hope. I think of my plan with Margareath. That would suffice, but people won't know the outcome of that endeavor for a long time, and it still needs to be a secret. They need something now.

I'm racking my brain, walking back and forth in front of one of our park benches. That's when I hear giggling coming from a shed on the grounds. I walk toward it fast, thinking it's some kids messing around on the property.

"Hey, you guys, come out of there," I call as I get closer. The giggling stops immediately.

I venture closer and pull hard on one of the shed doors. It doesn't give; something's pushed up against it. I stand on my tiptoes, rubbing through years of dirt filmed on the shed's one window. When I see skin, I jump back. It's white and creamy, and I'd know it anywhere.

"Aloy!" comes Vienne's startled voice as she throws open the shed doors to peek out at me.

177

I stand open-mouthed as she buttons her shirt, and I watch as Griffin fumbles, tying the drawstring of his pants.

"We thought you were in bed," she says, guilt written all over her face.

"Enjoying yourself, are you? Sounds like you're both having a pretty good time. And you certainly weren't kidding about over and over again."

"It's not like that," Griffin says, his voice gruff.

"Not like that? I heard you two laughing back here. Having the time of your lives." My words are like tiny pins, each one pricking my lips as I say them.

Vienne moves to my side, reaching for my arm. She holds out a stick of paper. "It's this. This is why we were laughing. Out of joy. I'm pregnant!"

She thrusts the paper under my eyes. It's a thin sheet of litmus with neon green in the center.

"I don't understand," I say, quieted. "I don't know what this is."

"It's a birth predictor. You lick it right after... after... you know." She doesn't want to state out loud that she and Griffin just finished having sex. "It lets you know instantly if the woman's egg was fertilized."

I swallow hard. The paper in front of me flaps in the soft breeze, but I hold onto it like a lifeline so it has no chance of flying off. "It's really true? You're pregnant?"

"Yes!" Vienne jumps up, wrapping her arms around my neck, her elation bold and bright now that I seem to grasp the import.

I swing her around, forgetting everything about Maran, my anger at Griffin and Vienne's stolen moments, or even my aching head. Madame Elected is pregnant!

"And after only two times," says Griffin, a devilish smile spread over his face. "Not over and over again."

I look over at him and set Vienne down on her feet. I walk to Griffin, so we're standing straight in front of each other. "Thank you, Griffin. Thank you so much." I say it slowly so he'll feel the depth of my gratitude down to his core.

He smiles wider, embarrassed. "Sure thing. No problem." He brushes a hand through the hair in front of his eyes, trying to take the attention off himself, break my intense gaze.

I am so happy it's finished, I can think of nothing else. This will be what unites our people. Gives them something to hope for. How can they not band around Vienne and me after this? This is what will stave off the Technology Faction, letting them know there won't be chaos after my term is over.

I reach up and hug Griffin hard. He's surprised at my sudden, whole-hearted embrace and even more surprised when I let him extend the hug into something more. He pulls me closer, burying his face in my neck. After a moment Vienne clears her throat, and I let go of Griffin, almost embarrassed Vienne has witnessed this moment between us.

The largest smile bursts through my cheeks as I take Vienne's outstretched hand. "Come. Let's go tell Tomlin," I say.

The three of us walk as a happy trio back to the house. We ask where Tomlin is, almost bursting to tell the first people we see. Instead, we hold back, wanting Tomlin to hear it first.

A maid points us in the direction of the old oval office. I almost run over to it, with Vienne and Griffin quick on my trail. I fling open the door, ready to pronounce our good fortune before Tomlin can read it on our faces and guess for himself. But, as I heave open the heavy wooden doors and the three of us look into the stately room, we realize there is no good fortune waiting for us inside.

25

I SEE TOMLIN FIRST, his back to us, one hand on his hip, the other on his forehead. Then I see five guards. They're crowded around Tomlin. For a second I have a sickening feeling they're arresting my tutor. My friend. This is the second time now I've been worried for him. I want to reach out and pull him away from the guards. I'm about to do so, with one arm already outstretched to him, when I see the guards surrounding someone else. Someone else has his hands tied behind his back in thick ropes. Someone else is the prisoner.

And before I can actually see who it is, Griffin pushes past me into the room.

"Apa!" he exclaims.

Vienne puts a hand to her mouth, suppressing a gasp. I don't speak, but I watch as Griffin pulls the guards apart so he can get to Maran. Whatever Maran has done, I'm suddenly worried Griffin will do something now to defend his father and throw himself in harm's way. That he'll attack the guards to get his father free.

But he doesn't. Once in front of his father, Griffin closes in, standing with his face mere centimeters away from his father. He growls much like his father's voice sounded when speaking to me in the stable less than an hour ago.

"How could you?" Griffin asks. "You promised me you'd stop after the town hall attempt!"

Maran gives a harsh, guttural laugh. "You would protect this weakling? This one who will pull our country down into the mud? I step up for righteousness. I take action to give us a future."

I walk up close to Griffin and Maran. The guards stand by to protect me, even though Maran's hands are sufficiently bound.

"Maran, you were the assassin?" My voice is tight.

"I'm surprised you didn't figure it out in the stable today," he says, expelling his words so spittle lands on my cheek.

I wipe it off roughly. "No, I would never have guessed that about you, no matter what your opinions. You've worked loyally for my parents for years. And this whole time you've been plotting against us?"

He guffaws. "Plotting *for* this country. I thought the assassination attempts would confuse you into blaming Mid Country. Then you'd have at least begun building defenses and using technology again. But no, still you did nothing. You protect your precious Accords, but you do nothing to propel your people to greatness. You would rather uphold an outdated policy than begin building again—begin creation of technology that will let your people survive. That will let your people procreate safely. Griffin's mother could have been saved! We could be years ahead of the other countries if your family just let us build unfettered. East Country could take back the entire continent, if you'd only let it!"

My voice is thick as I respond to him, wanting everyone in the room to hear my side. My reasons. "This is exactly why the Accords must be upheld. You talk like you've walked straight out of the twenty-first century. When countries competed to see who could build the bigger weapons. Machines that caused our eventual destruction. You would send us straight back to a time when pollution, oil consumption, war, and greed caused the collapse of our environment. My goal is not to rise up against Mid and West Countries so East Country can rule the continent. My goal is for East Country to live in peace. In isolation. You are in the minority, Maran. You alone want these things for us. Even the Technology Faction doesn't wish for what you do."

He laughs, a high pitched, crazy hoot. "They are weaklings too! I go to them, angry at you, ready to make a real attempt right this instant with their help, and what do they do? Instead of banding behind me, giving me the recognition and help I deserve, they turn me in. They lead me straight into the hands of the guards."

"Enough!" yells Griffin. "You do not speak to the Elected like this! Apa, I stood by you. I didn't turn you in when I found out you were the assassin. Because you got down on your knees to me. Promised no other attempts would be made. Said you'd made a mistake. But you were lying! I came here to be the Electeds' bodyguard, to specifically guard them against you. To make doubly sure you would cause them no harm. And you try again? Damn you to hell!"

He stares down at his father with such hate in his eyes I fear it will eat him from the inside out. That this hate will come back to haunt him later when he remembers his dead father. I must diffuse this, if only for Griffin's sake.

"Maran," I say. "You know what you've done. You'll be sentenced to the prison. This is your last chance to speak to your son. Do you have any last words for him?"

I hope what he will say will be kind. That it will be enough for Griffin to remember his father with at least some good thoughts in the years to come.

Maran is checked by this, at least somewhat. "Griffin, I always kept you in mind. I was always thinking of your future. Your family. Your future sons and daughters. You may not realize it now, but one day you'll know I was right. You'll look back upon this moment and know East Country needed to build technology again. To guard itself against intruders. I only hope it isn't too late—that you realize all this while there's still time to take action."

He leans forward to kiss Griffin's cheek. Griffin deftly moves out of the way, avoiding his father's touch.

Maran looks at Griffin with a crooked smile. "I understand, Son. I know why you guard the Elected. It wasn't just a way to protect them from me. There is more. But you are wrong to be so infatuated with them. They'll cross you. Leave you desolate. I, alone, love you. I did all this for you."

Griffin refuses to meet his father's eyes, but I see his eyes welling. He struggles to hold back. Vienne walks forward and puts an arm around Griffin. He doesn't shake off this embrace.

"Take him away now." Griffin gestures at the other guards.

Tomlin nods to them in agreement, and they take Maran by the arms, leading him out of the room.

I look at Vienne. She knows now is not a good time to tell our news. We both turn to look at Griffin. He's fallen onto the big couch by the unused fireplace and stares blankly ahead.

Tomlin puts one hand on Griffin's shoulder. Then he glances toward me and Vienne, and without speaking, takes his leave.

I sit across from Griffin, but Vienne is the first to talk, "I'm sorry, Griffin. So sorry."

He just nods, eyes still glazed and unblinking.

Then he turns to look at me. "I knew, and I didn't tell you."

"Now I understand why you couldn't tell me. Why you didn't turn in your own father." I speak softly, trying to convey the depth of my feeling. I can understand a relationship with one's parents is complicated. That we have such a short time with them as it is.

But he shakes his head at me. "I'm an accomplice because I didn't give you his name. You have every right to put me in prison too."

At one time this is what I would've wanted. But now it's different. I care for this man. He's fathering my child. I couldn't sentence him now.

Vienne breaks in, picking up on all of this too. "Never, Griffin. We would never."

"And your father is wrong," I say. "We won't forsake you. Vienne and I will stand with you to our dying breaths. We're a team now."

"I wanted to keep you safe," he says. "I thought my father was telling me the truth. That he gave up the idea of assassinating you. That his views weren't quite so strong after all. But I was wrong. He was still a threat."

"He will no longer be a threat," says Vienne. "But we still want you to guard us. To stay here with us." She looks over at me for confirmation. "Isn't that right, Aloy?"

"Right," I say.

We leave the room, Griffin and Vienne going together to tell Griffin's stepmother, Brinn, what happened. I stay behind in the house, thinking about what it will be like to preside over Maran's suicide. Griffin might be upset with his father, but Maran will always be his Apa. And no matter what, I'm afraid Griffin will hold the fact I presided over Maran's death against me. I will always be his father's killer. It all feels like a seam slowly ripping, the threads starting to tug in opposite directions.

As custom dictates with a violent offense, I will preside over Maran's assisted suicide this same day. So I only have a few excruciating hours to think about it before walking over to the prison.

I leave the White House, worry over the "bump" on my head now far in the past. No one frets as I leave through the front door. A set of guards come with me, but now that the assassin is found, they are more relaxed.

I wander through the town, not knowing where I'm heading, nodding at the townspeople who smile at me. I think about the fact I'll soon be a parent. That Vienne will be the best mother ever to bear a child. That I will make sure Vienne has the utmost in medical care we have to offer. That I'll have the purple pills ready if she shows the slightest sign of needing one.

I make my way to the edge of the town and realize where I've been going the whole time. It's the graveyard. The plot is located behind a short iron gate that's always left open. I step through it and find the specific stones I've yet to visit. They are side by side and bear the names Claraleese and Soyor. The given names of my parents.

I sit down in front of them and notice my guards have made themselves scarce, standing at the entrance to the graveyard with their backs to me.

Even though my parents technically left, didn't die, our custom is to forge gravestones for them anyway. As far as East Country is concerned, they are dead.

I touch the hard stones and start talking to them. "Ama and Apa, I know you're still alive. I know it in my soul. But your being gone hurts just like you're dead. I miss you so much. The things I've done, you wouldn't believe. In just a few hours I have to put Maran to death. How can I do it? How can I watch him suffer? How can I watch any of our people suffer?"

I look to my left and see a small boy talking to a grave a few hundred yards away from me. Every now and then he waits, listening for a response. Then he laughs out loud like his dead companion just said something funny.

I turn back to the stones signifying my parents.

"Vienne is having a baby, Ama. We've done it. We figured it out. Thing is, it's not really my baby. But I'll treat him or her like she is. And I'm not even hoping for a boy. I'll be happy with either. I don't think it's right only boys can rule. Vienne would do a fine job, even if she's focusing on getting pregnant."

I'm rambling. Telling my parents everything in my head. Spilling my thoughts out like sand coursing through fingers. I gush about my feelings for Vienne. And my feelings for Griffin. How I love and want to protect one. And how I long to kiss the other. I wonder what Maran would think if he knew Griffin were to be the father of the next Elected. I stay bent over my parents' graves, continuing to talk, even as my calves begin to scream. As the sun begins to set, I know it's time to say goodbye to my parents and head over to the prison. I stare at their fake gravestones and then turn, not looking back.

Once outside the Old Executive Office Building, I walk up the old steps like it's my own execution. I keep my head down as I pass by the guards in the lobby. They don't say anything as I make my way through the narrow corridor and am led to Maran's door. I stand outside of it for a few seconds, longer than normal, trying to take a last, deep breath before going inside. I glance at the guard to my side, say thank you, and turn the door handle.

My side of the room is set up as usual, with one wooden bench facing the glass. I peer in to see Maran standing on his side of the clear wall, palms planted against the glass, waiting for me. He bangs on the armor glass as he sees me. I'm sure he's hitting it hard, but I don't hear anything. I see his lips moving, but I can't hear his words. My room is bizarrely quiet in contrast, almost church-like in its reverence to the scene unfolding.

From the door off of Maran's side, a guard brings in a small crystal glass filled with the clear liquid. He sets it down on the floor and then quickly exits again as Maran starts to rush at him. Maran looks at the glass and then laughs, banging on our separation again, clearly trying to get my attention. He opens his mouth wide and gives a primal yell, although I still can't hear a sound.

I see him move sideways and swiftly kick the crystal cup. It launches across the room, shattering on the armor glass in tiny pieces. I'm startled, jumping backward off my small, wood bench. I watch as the hemlock streams over the floor in stripes and Maran steps on the liquid, scattering the droplets with the sole of his boot.

In the assisted suicides I witnessed, I've yet to see someone refuse the drink. I know the mechanics of the following custom, though. As if I could predict the script in a play, I watch the next scene commence. This time, two guards walk into Maran's room. They bring him a second glass full of hemlock. They set it down on the floor and exit again.

Maran looks at the second cup and gives another yell. This time he must also let out a high-pitched laugh because the octave of his voice does resonate slightly through the glass. He beats against the material, and I think of my father's reassurances weeks ago—armor glass won't break.

Maran picks up the cup, and I think this time will be it. He'll drink it down, and this gruesome episode will be finished. I take a deep breath.

But instead of lifting the cup to his lips, Maran smashes it down against the ground. It breaks, not into a hundred small shards, as it did on the armor glass, but into three sharp pieces. Maran picks up the largest shard and presses it to his arm. I think maybe he's choosing his own method of dying. Perhaps he means to take his life by cutting into a vein instead of drinking the poison. This too will be gruesome, but I hope it'll happen quickly. That it will not, in fact, cause him too much pain.

Maran doesn't cut into his wrist, though. I watch with wide eyes as he draws blood from his arm, slicing the glass through the skin from the inside of his elbow down his arm. He lets the blood bubble up for a minute and then sticks a finger into the long wound. He draws his pointer finger out again and wipes his own blood on the armor glass.

I don't understand what he means to do, but soon his intentions are clear. He's writing a word on the glass, so he'll be able to communicate one final message to me.

I watch in horror as Maran goes back, again and again, to his bleeding arm to gather more writing material. Each time he comes up with a finger full of blood and smears it on the barrier between us. When he finishes, there are seven letters on the wall. I can't see them clearly, so I stand up from the bench, moving closer to the glass.

He's written a word, but it faces him, so I'm forced to interpret the slanted letters backward. Maran stands there, watching me, with a slight smile on his face.

When I finally decipher it, I'm appalled—furious he would write out this word as his life's last communication. But I'm more furious he's guessed my true gender and written it out for others to see.

The glass reads, "LESBIAN."

26

SOCIETY OUTGREW THE WORD years ago. No one felt the need to label people for who or how they love. At the same time, our world is so dependent on population growth there's a constant conflict between necessity and our desire to accept people as they are. I don't worry about Maran's use of the word, itself. But this final betrayal of my gender causes my heart to quicken so much that I can hear the rush of blood in my ears. Maran knows I'm breaking two of our most sacred laws; the Elected Accord and the Fertility Accord, and his final act is to announce I'm an imposter. I guess if he couldn't kill me, he's now trying to unseat me legally.

His eyes are alight with amusement as I stare at his art. His mouth opens and he gives big guffaws, laughing at me. I glare at him, unsure what to do next, bracing myself for the guards' response. Three guards enter the room, beginning the next phase of the custom. They glance at the word written in blood on the glass, but their eyes are uncomprehending. Maran stares at them forcefully, pointing to the word and becoming more frustrated when they seemingly don't understand its meaning. He starts to frantically explain it, but the guards are resolute about their role. They proceed with robotic precision, ignoring Maran's pleas. Because of the nature of the coming ritual, I assume they're trained to block out a prisoner's verbal defiance. Or perhaps they choose to discount what they don't want to hear. It's a relief they don't acknowledge the word, but I wonder if I'll have to provide answers later.

One of the guards holds a third cup of hemlock. The forthcoming ritual is what I've feared with each of the suicides I've witnessed. But this is the first time I see it first-hand. This time, it's not an assisted suicide. I am watching my first government-sanctioned kill. The two other guards hold Maran down on the floor, his arms and legs pinned with the guards' own bodies. Then the third guard forces Maran's mouth open, twisting his arm to keep Maran's teeth from biting down on him. He quickly pours the drink between Maran's lips. All the while, Maran is spitting, trying to clamp his mouth shut, resisting.

However, he's not strong enough to stave off the three guards. They continue to hold him down as the hemlock's juice begins exercising its power. Maran's body convulses under the guards. I see his legs twist in pain and his arms spasm. I don't watch his face, only imagine the look of it. His eyes turning white, rolling to the back of his head, his facial muscles contorting into something monstrous.

I don't fully look. Don't afford the prisoner the respect of my full attention. I don't stare into his eyes, acknowledging his life lost.

Instead, I sit down on the bench, bent over with my head between my knees. And I think of the only thing that could truly distract me right now. Griffin.

How Griffin is the opposite of his father. How he is warm and tender and caring. How two men could be of the same blood but share so few personal qualities. I see Griffin's arms in my head. His legs. His face. I concentrate on this last picture the longest. Griffin's face with a smile on his lips, the sun shining down on his brow. I figure this image is the best offering from Maran's life. The best and only way I can pay homage to his life. To think of the thing he created that will live past him. That will offer something good to the world.

Finally, I raise my head and see the guards picking up Maran's body. They'll bring him to Vienne's quarters so she can dress him for burial. I know it won't be the same ritual as when Vienne cared for Margareath's body. We did not fulfill my new plan for prisoners with Griffin's father.

I sigh deeply, letting the weight of what I just saw course out of my limbs in waves. Finally, I stand up, and I know there's only one place I need to be right now—one family I need to console tonight. I make the steady, sure walk toward Maran's cottage where I know Griffin will be waiting for me. In front of their hut, I raise my hand to rap on the thatched door. It opens before I have a chance to knock. Griffin stands before me, looking so much like his father it hurts my head.

"Come in," he says. His voice is even. It doesn't carry the distress I thought it would. Vienne must have talked with him earlier to help Griffin get through his father's execution.

"Is your stepmother here?" I ask.

"She's in the living room. We've been waiting for you." Griffin pauses, and a long sigh escapes his mouth. "So... it's... finished?"

"Yes, your father's gone."

Griffin nods wordlessly and leads me deeper into the house to where his stepmother sits before a fire. The warmth isn't needed, but she stares into the flickering flames anyway.

"I'm sorry, Brinn," I say from behind her.

She doesn't respond—just keeps staring into the flames. It's incredibly warm in the house. I can already feel beads of perspiration trailing down my forehead. I wipe them off with the back of my palm and walk around Brinn's rocking chair to face her.

"Brinn, I apologize..."

She breaks me off with a hand. "Don't, Elected. Don't say you're sorry. It was his own fault. He brought this on himself." She pauses. I'm about to say more but she continues, "Technology use would be one thing. But violence against the Elected? That is unforgivable."

"And yet, we must forgive him." I quote my mother's words when she spoke of prisoners in the past.

"Eventually, I am sure I will. But not now. This is not an excuse, you know, but he had cancer. He knew he didn't have long. It started a year ago."

I look to Griffin and he nods. "I'm sorry to hear that." I'm surprised Griffin never told me.

"A tumor in his head. Perhaps that changed him somewhat. Affected him in ways our doctors can't even comprehend. Changed his personality a bit. When he hit Griffin—"

This time I interrupt her. "Hit Griffin?" I look over at him for confirmation.

But Brinn is the one to answer, still absently staring into the fire, "Yes, hit him in the face."

"So you didn't get a black eye from fencing?" I ask him.

"No. He came at me when I refused to help with the assassination attempts."

I look down. I should have known. Griffin, with his fighting skills and quick agility, would never fare badly enough at fencing to get a black eye.

Brinn stirs. "Elected, thank you for coming here tonight, but would you leave me now? I wish to be alone."

I shake my head yes. "Brinn, again I'm sorry. If you need anything, please tell me or Madame Elected."

She nods but continues to stare at the flames. I look at Griffin and he gestures with a slight nod toward the door.

Once we're out of the living room and away from his stepmother I ask, "Are you going to stay with her for a while?"

"She wants me to remain at the White House. She keeps looking at my face, saying it reminds her of my father."

"Would you walk back with me now then?" I ask. "Or will you stay with her for a few more minutes?"

"I'll come with you. Just let me say goodbye."

He leaves to give parting thoughts to his stepmother. From around the corner I see him pulling a blanket over her legs, even though it's not cold. He wraps it around her and gives Brinn a small hug. When Brinn doesn't move or embrace him back, Griffin visibly winces. I wonder if Griffin, like me, was also refused affection by his parents. Maran hit him and now Brinn won't offer him love even after his father's just died.

At their front door, I say, "She seems frail."

"Brinn has cancer too," Griffin says. "It won't be long now."

Griffin's step-mother is nearing forty so I'm not altogether surprised at this explanation, but it's sad anyway. Our people die much too young.

"I'm sorry." I feel like I've said the same words a million times today.

Griffin takes my hand and leads me out of the house. Now that we're alone, my guards finally leaving me be, I fear Griffin will ask about his father's final moments. I steel myself for his inquiry, wondering what I'll say in return. How I'll characterize it. If I'll tell Griffin about the word written on the armor glass. If I'll tell him Maran had to be killed in the end.

"Aloy," Griffin begins, his voice unsteady. In this second I make up my mind not to further chill Griffin's view of his father. I won't give him the gory details of his father's execution.

"Do we have a little while? There's something I want to show you." He doesn't ask about his father. In fact, as I walk with him farther out of the town and into the bordering swampland, I realize Griffin may never ask about his father's last moments. He doesn't seem to want to know.

We walk hand-in-hand through the brown, spindly plants lining the dirt floor. The feel of his palm against mine is soothing. I never want to let go.

The ground, hard where we first started walking, begins to soften and grow soggy as we keep venturing farther away from the town. My boots slog into the earth, leaving small footprints, which are slurped back into the mud a second after they've been made. After a good thirty minutes we arrive at a broken down shack nestled on the side of a marsh. The air here is musky and humid.

"What is this place?" I ask. No one in East Country lives alone, so this bedraggled shack is out of place by itself in the middle of a swamp. It should have been knocked down years ago, the wood used for some other industrious purpose.

"It's mine. I come here to think."

"Here? But it's abandoned?"

"I found it years ago." His next words are deliberate. "I didn't report it because there was a group that needed somewhere private to meet. After a certain night—in fact, the night you and I met at the dance—this group needed a more discrete meeting place."

I look at Griffin, only starting to comprehend his meaning. I swallow and nod slowly, subconsciously pulling my body away from Griffin's. I look back and forth from Griffin's face to the house in front of us. I drop his hand, cinching my own arm hard against my stomach.

"Please don't tell me you're part of them." I can't look him in the eye. I'm already subtly searching for the best escape route. Which way can I run where he won't be able to catch me?

"No, not just part." His voice quickens. "I know your secrets, so it's only fair you know mine too. I'm not part of the Technology Faction. I lead it."

27

I STARE AT GRIFFIN hard and then in an instant, I turn. I start to pick up my feet to run, but they slog in the mud. I feel like I'm being pulled under. I yell out, trying to get help, but we're in the middle of nowhere. I know my shouting is a futile effort, but I do it anyway.

"Help!" I scream.

Griffin is behind me. He catches my arm. Not hard, but his hand wraps around my wrist.

I don't try to pull away from him. I know it will be useless to run at this point, but my voice catches in my throat as I say, "So this is it then? You were lying to me? You were in on the attempts with your father? You're going to kill me now?"

He pulls me close to him, and I have such mixed feelings I think my heart might split in two. Here is my would-be murderer, the man I think I have loved for years, pulling me close, hugging me. And in the next second he could be thrusting a knife into my side.

Griffin buries his face in my neck and talks straight into my ear so I'll be sure to hear. His words come fast. "Please, let me explain. I would never in a million years hurt you. How can you not realize that by now? But I can't help who I am and who my father was, just like you couldn't help who your parents were. I believe in the use of some technology. I believe we should invest in procreation technology to keep our women safe in childbirth. My mother could have been saved." Griffin's voice breaks, but he continues, "I believe environmental greed destroyed our race, but not all technology is bad. We can find ways to use it wisely. To make electricity through the use of solar energy, for instance. We can find responsible ways to advance our people."

I'm shaking, trying to take in everything he's saying. He leans back to look at my face.

"I didn't choose to be the Faction's leader. Just like you didn't choose to be the Elected. My father was the leader for many years."

I remember back to the voice I heard after I snuck out to the dance. The hoarse, determined voice coming from one of the village huts, showing the Faction a battery-powered tool. That was Maran. I wish I'd recognized it then.

Griffin continues, "But when my father started showing signs of radiation poisoning, he handed the leadership role to me. I didn't want it at first. I'd grown up on my father's heels, watching him run these meetings, knowing I wasn't like him. I didn't want the things he wanted. So I said no. I told him to choose someone else as his successor. When he insisted I take the role, though, I thought I could maybe change the Faction from within."

I grimace again, not yet willing to believe him.

"And you have to understand," Griffin says. "I'm the only person in this whole country, besides Vienne, who's seen exactly what it's taken for you to do what you believe in, no matter the costs. We're the same that way. To help your country, you were forced to step into a leadership role you never wanted, and I had to put aside my own reservations about the Faction to do the same.

I finally find my voice, interrupting his monologue. "But you lead the people who started a riot. Who threw metal laced fruit at the Elected family. Who break the laws governing our society! You endorse this group!"

"I don't endorse everything they do. There are two different sects growing within the Technologists. I would have stopped the town hall riot if I'd heard about it ahead of time. But that was a small subset of the Faction. There are many more of us who believe in trying to change your mind, change the minds of all our people through talk, not violence."

"Is this why you wanted to get close to me and Vienne?" My voice is stiff, my eyes squinting into thin lines. "So you could get into our heads? To convince us the Accords should be abandoned?"

"No, that's not why I wanted to get close to you and Vienne. Remember, it was your idea to have me stay in the White House as your guard."

"Maybe so, but you... under the tree. Your seduction was a set-up."

I think of the position Vienne and I locked ourselves into. That Griffin stepped into, seemingly unwillingly, but that will serve him to a huge advantage if the country rebels against me. He will now have claim over the next Elected baby, should he choose to contest its parentage at a later date.

I say as much to him.

Griffin backs up and looks at me so our eyes are focused on each other. "You have to know I didn't engineer this. Yes, I am part of this baby, but you were the one who begged me to be so."

"We didn't have all of the information. If I knew..."

"You would have chosen someone else?" he finishes for me.

I cannot think of who else we could have involved. Griffin was the only choice.

I look away. "You know things about me that render my position invalid. I'm a woman. If you just tell people, you can have me taken out of office. There'd have to be an election. The Technology Faction could win. You could take over. Why haven't you said anything yet? What are you waiting for?" I ball up my fists at my sides.

"I'm not waiting for anything. You still don't understand. I may be head of the Technology Faction, but I support you as the country's leader. I won't interfere with that."

I try to wrap my head around this conundrum. I've always thought the Technology Faction wanted to take office. To pull my family down. I put my hand to my head, trying to figure it out. "But the faction has always wished for the downfall of the Elected leader. And even if that's not your intention now, you want me to be a different leader!" My voice grows higher as I try to wade through my confusion. "To start creating technology!"

"Not all technology. I want you to pick and choose. I think you, specifically, because of the chances you've taken, will be able to lead us through the gray areas. You gave the sick girl one of the pills. You are breaking the Fertility Accord. You, better than anyone, will know how to wade through the intricacies of the Accords. What parts need to be enforced. What parts are outdated."

I take the opportunity to move a step back from him. I see Griffin wince, anticipating I'll run—that this time I'll break away for real and not turn back.

Yes, I kissed him once, but that was before I knew he was leader of this faction. Everything he says to me, everything he does, could be designed to snare me. And yet, Vienne found my whittled toys Griffin kept since I was young. His ruse couldn't have been going on for that long.

Griffin gives one last plea. A final statement to gain my trust. It's heartfelt, but it doesn't sound like he's begging. It sounds like the most honest words I've ever heard in my life. "Aloy, please don't leave me. I love you."

I'm flooded with emotions. I try to parry out my feelings, to differentiate lust and love, but my mind won't work that way. The two are interlaced.

I step forward before I can put rationality above my desire. I reach out and pull Griffin's face toward mine, making a final, undeterred decision.

Rigid with concern a moment earlier, I feel the muscles in Griffin's arms relax as I now step into them. We move our lips together and begin something from which I know I can't return. I feel his fingertips lightly trace my stomach. He inches my shirt upwards, and I let him, even helping him lift it over my head. It lands on the soft earth by our sides. In the moonlight, I see him remove his own shirt, the stars reflecting off the curve of the smooth muscles on his abdomen.

I remember the images I saw in the helmet, this time relishing that they're real. Griffin deftly unties the cloth binding my chest. He begins unraveling the fabric, and I turn in small circles, still enclosed within his arms. The long white strip flutters to the ground as he loosens his grip on it.

I'm left naked from my waist up, and for once I'm not nervous my chest will be exposed. I like the feeling of the warm night wind on my skin. More than that even, I like the feeling of Griffin's kisses on my cheek, on my shoulder, and on my collarbone.

In one swift movement, he picks me up so I'm cradled in his arms. He walks me wordlessly into the deserted house. I stare up at him, not wanting to break eye contact. I think it will be pitch black in the small house, but as we cross the threshold, I'm surprised to see tiny globes of light bouncing off the walls. I can't help myself; I move my eyes from Griffin's face and look around with curiosity.

Griffin sets me down on the floor, which is covered by a thin bamboo mat. He sits down next to me and watches as I glance around. Everywhere I turn there are little orbs of light floating in the air. The room is illuminated with hundreds of these hanging glass jars, giving the rundown shack an ethereal feel.

"What are they?" I whisper.

Griffin gives a soft laugh and wraps a warm arm around my back.

"They're fireflies. We breed them for light."

I hear the quiet interwoven hum of their wings. "They're beautiful."

"As are you. I meant what I said that time on your stairs." He looks at me with soft lidded eyes, his lashes illuminated to seem longer in this half-light.

I take him in like I'm starving. What starts out as a gentle embrace becomes more. I squeeze his upper arm, holding him to me so our bodies are closer still. I run my hands down his back, like in my dream. I wrap my legs around him.

He gently lies me down so I feel the hard wood under my back.

"Do you want this?" he asks, cautious.

I contemplate what he's asking. I'm cheating on Vienne. I know this. And yet, I cannot stop what I've set in motion. I don't wish to stop it. I may be the Elected, but I'm Aloy too. Just like Griffin cannot separate who he is from his beliefs, I cannot separate my passion from my responsibility.

"I want you."

He gently takes my head in his hand, moving downward, kissing me lightly. Everything is foreign. The touches. How it feels to have skin connect with the flesh all over my body. The tingling it produces from my scalp all the way down to my toes. I shiver with the ache of Griffin's skin on mine.

We are one. I feel like there is no separation from where my body ends and his begins. The world stands still as Griffin and I are together. The room falls away from my view. All I can see when I open my eyes is Griffin's face and the orbs of light hanging in the distance. The world is light and love and perfection.

All fear I had about the physicality of this act—how to do it, the mechanics—are nonexistent. We flow together like our bodies were made to fit together. The crook of his arm rests in the curve of my side. His head fits perfectly in the space over my shoulder. His legs and mine curl together so I'm unsure which body part is mine and which is his.

I'm overcome by a rainbow of light and a steady drumbeat flowing through my head. It's like I'm traveling down the sky as a droplet of rain. It's the kind of light and burst of energy I saw through the Multiplier. But this time it doesn't hurt my head. It's the opposite of pain. I think of the steel roller coasters I saw in a book, ascending higher and higher into the sky until one final peak, which sends a rider diving back down to earth. I feel like that now. A welling deep within my stomach, building until I can hardly breathe.

Fireworks go off all over my body. I'm still, not wanting this sensation to end. And then it does, slowly coasting downward, giving me power over my muscles once again.

Finally we ease away from each other. We lie side by side on the mat, our hands clasped. We stare straight ahead at the fireflies and the light they're emitting.

"I wish the rest of our lives could be just like this," I say. "That we could turn into fireflies and stay right here."

Griffin sighs. "That doesn't sound so bad." He gives a small laugh and squeezes my hand tighter. He turns onto his side, facing me. "Whatever happens after this, do you promise you'll know I love you?"

I look at him, wondering what he means. How anything foreboding could happen after the beauty we just shared together. "Nothing will happen."

He leans over me so our faces are close. Griffin runs a finger down my cheek. "Everything is perfect now, but nothing stays the same." His words carry an intensity. A worry. "Will you promise me something? One day when we're much older, when the burdens of your position are no longer valid. When our country is stable. When you're free to acknowledge your gender. Will you marry me?"

I'm quiet for a moment, for so long I can sense Griffin growing uncomfortable. I look into his eyes, sorry to bring up my thoughts. "By that time, you'll already be married to someone else."

"No, I won't. I'll wait for you."

"Eighteen years from now? When our baby takes office?"

"Yes, if that's what it takes to have you. I can't marry another. It must be you."

"A lot can happen within eighteen years. I'll be much older. Maybe our love will have waned by then."

"No, it won't matter our age or the timespan. Do I have your agreement? Your promise?" He raises his arm to me in the marriage proposal of our time. The back of his biceps is facing me.

I look at him and then lean down, kissing the spot where a marriage binding would be placed.

Officially accepting his proposal.

28

GRIFFIN GIVES ME HIS hand to pull me to my feet. I can't erase the smile from my face and find he can't either. We start buttoning up each other's clothes. I tie the string on his pants, wanting to prolong our intimacy.

"There is one more thing I must show you," he says. This time, though, his words don't carry worry. He's excited to show me this new object.

"Okay, what is it?"

He leads me across the room to one of the glass vases that seems to hold another firefly. "This firefly is brighter than the others!" I say. My eyes focus on the most intense of the lights.

"That's because this one isn't an insect."

I look at him with raised eyebrows.

"It's electricity... I made it."

"But Griffin, this... isn't... you shouldn't have..."

"I found a way to harness the sun." He's so proud of his work, he doesn't even acknowledge the knot forming on my brow.

"How is that possible? Wouldn't that require panels and metal and... and... technology?" My words pour out over each other.

"Sort of." He opens the glass jar and shows me a dark square on its bottom. "I did have to make this part."

He takes out the copper square and places it in my palm. I feel the illicit metal resting in my hand. Threatening me with its illegality.

My voice shakes. "This is against the law."

He looks at me, still calm. Still having faith in my love for him. Hoping this will be one of those instances where I ease the meaning of the Technology Accord and make accommodations.

"This tiny piece of metal isn't hurting anyone. It's not spewing pollution into the air. It's just a piece of metal, broken down, and shaped back into the right sized square."

"But it is not just a piece of regular metal, is it?" I already know the properties needed to harness solar power. "There is silicon in this."

"Just an ounce. It won't hurt anyone."

I'm conflicted. Manufacturing these materials is off limits. But Griffin's right. With so little a chunk of metal, there were no harmful by-products created in the dividing of these pieces. It's indeed a technology but not one that will hurt our environment. The only harm done is a violation of the meaning of the Technology Accord.

"You can't make any more of this."

"I can't anyway. We don't have any more nirogene component. That's what was needed to piece this together."

"Nirogene? Nirogene can do this? Were you stealing it? Was the Technology Faction taking it to make solar panels?"

"No. This is the only panel. One of its kind. The supplies of nirogene are diminished, but it's not because of the Technology Faction. All I can think is the people are right. Mid Country is taking it."

"By using airrides?"

"We haven't seen any airrides, though, right?"

I picture the airride I saw in the Multiplier. The little robot opening the airride door and scooping up the blood of the unlucky man with the bullets. My spine involuntarily gives a shiver.

"No, I haven't seen one," I say, thinking it's true I haven't seen one in person. I don't know why I lie about the Multiplier, but for some reason, I keep it my secret.

He nods. "We need to get back." Then he stops and holds both of my hands out in front of me. "It was all right to show you the light, wasn't it?"

I know what he's asking. If I'll turn him in. If our marriage proposal still stands.

I think of the other prisoners who I've seen die because of their creations. Then I remember my and Vienne's plan for all prisoners going forward, and I know Griffin is right about me. I am starting to see gray areas in the Accords. Starting to buck the system to create my own rules.

"I won't tell anyone. Just promise me again you won't make any more electricity."

"I promise."

My decision to be faithful to him comes at all costs. I realize there's nothing he can do now that will change the way I feel about him.

He walks me back to the house and leaves me in the front hallway with a light kiss on my forehead. It's tender but noncontroversial if anyone were to see us. He turns right and I go left toward Vienne's room.

She's already in bed. I slip under the cool sheet, hoping not to wake her, but she whispers my name.

I turn over to look at her, wondering if she's just saying my name in her sleep. Vienne's eyes stay closed, but she wraps an arm around me, burrowing against me even though it's so warm outside. She's in a semi-sleep, close to nodding off but not entirely there yet.

"I'm here," I say.

"Mmmm," she mumbles. She's falling deeper into dreamland.

I take the opportunity to look at her in the moonlight streaming through our uncurtained window. As I stare at her serene face I think of the actions I've taken against our marriage tonight. Do I feel badly for acting on my feelings with Griffin now that my wife is back in my arms?

I want to keep her happy, but I realize Vienne was never the porcelain figure whom I needed to protect on a pedestal. She knows what she's doing. She's stronger and more determined than any of us. She grew up lonely in this place, not being able to tell a soul, aside from Tomlin, who she was to become. It was an even lonelier life than mine. Yet, she doesn't complain of it. Whereas I often feel the burdens of the Elected position hanging over my head, Vienne seems to embrace it willingly. Happily.

And she knows how to turn situations to her advantage. She was so easily able to convince me and Griffin to go along with her plan for making a baby. She was not a fragile, delicate angel there. I don't resent her for manipulating us into the strategy. In contrast, I respect her will— her ability to get things done when they need to happen. Vienne may be beautiful and delicate, but she's no wilting flower. She has more iron in her stomach than in my whole being.

I touch her cheek, barely grazing it with my fingernail. One day I hope to be as strong in my loyalty and conviction as she is. But for now, I am just happy to have made a few more decisions of my own.

At the next town hall I will tell my people they can start creating armor glass. Griffin is right. I do find the gray areas within the Accords. And my mother hinted at the Accords' antiquity too. At some point they will become outdated. Maybe the time is now.

We will band together as a country to ensure our survival against whatever powers out there might be aiming to violate our sanctuary. We can't remain defenseless.

The web of lies I've sanctioned can't be for nothing. I risk my own life to violate the Fertility Accord and pose as a boy. I risk Griffin and Vienne's lives to create a child who will take over my office eighteen years from now. All of this could be for naught if our country is overtaken.

This country. It is the one thing I will not risk.

29

A FEW WEEKS PASS without much incident. We still monitor the hills nightly and there still remains a fierce sense of patriotism across the country. Somehow, though, everyone's private stores of nirogene are entirely depleted. All we have left is protected under lock and key at the chemists' workspace. It's not much, so we don't use it for the bikes anymore.

Today is the next town hall, and we plan to tell everyone about my acceptance of armor glass manufacturing. Vienne will also announce her pregnancy. She's slept more than usual lately, which she says is normal for the first trimester of the gestation. But I still watch her closely for any signs she's growing sick or unable to carry the baby. In fact, I watch her so much, Vienne sweetly scolds me when she sees me staring at her. Just yesterday at the breakfast table, Vienne turned to me over her tea.

"I'm fine!" she moaned with mock exasperation. "You don't have to stare at me quite so intensely. You look at me like I'm a ticking time bomb about to explode. I'm doing very well. Don't worry!"

I try to take her advice, but the statistics are just so daunting. Only about half of our pregnancies come to fruition. And of the fifty percent of women whose pregnancies end early, five percent of those women die because of the strain on their bodies.

I've taken to waking early and immediately turning to look at Vienne. I watch her stomach rise and fall until I'm convinced she's breathing normally and is okay. This morning, Vienne is still sleeping when I wake. After watching her for a full minute, I slip out of bed and head straight to the kitchen.

"Dorine," I say from the kitchen entryway, "can I ask for something?"

The tiny, elderly woman in her forties, who's been our cook for many years, walks toward me, balancing on her one good leg.

"Whatever you wish, Elected. Are you going out? Would you like me to pack you a breakfast?"

For some reason, I hadn't thought about my own need to eat at all. But when she asks me, I picture poached eggs on toast. The idea of the slimy eggs running off the edges of the toast makes me feel queasy, so I decline.

"No, thank you. I'd actually like a couple of baskets. The kind my mother used to give sick or grieving people."

"Ah, you are doing some ministering then, I assume?"

"Yes, I'd like to stop at two houses this morning. Bring them something."

Dorine starts puttering around the kitchen, pulling out drawers and opening cabinets until she's arranged items into two overflowing wicker baskets. Within minutes, both baskets are full with a few squash, apples, homemade bread slices, and a packet of assorted nuts.

"You might be ministering to my house at some point soon." Dorine's voice cracks in the back of her throat as she hands me the baskets.

My eyebrows furrow. "Someone in your family is sick?"

"Yes, my son." Dorine looks up to the heavens, like she's asking the very skies above for mercy. "He has cancer. Got it just this year at age twenty-five."

She makes a guttural tutting sound. I want to say something about how miracles can happen, but I know it's useless. No one gets better from cancer here except for the Elected family.

I go to pat Dorine's arm as a method of soothing her, but she takes a step back.

"And you, Elected? How are you feeling lately?"

"All right, I suppose."

"Your plates are coming back full. Do you not enjoy what I've been cooking recently?"

Again I think of slimy food resting like gel on a piece of bread and have to force back the urge to be sick.

"No, no. I just haven't been as hungry lately."

I thank Dorine for the baskets and then start my walk into town. I didn't want to get into a specific conversation with her about the kitchen's latest culinary concoctions. I'm sure she has bigger issues, such as her son's health, on her mind, and that's the reason why everything she makes me nowadays tastes like wet slugs.

In about ten minutes, I've walked down into the town. People are starting to come outside now, gathering full milk bottles left on their front stoops. A few of the townspeople stop to wave at me as I go by, surprised to see me walking around the neighborhood this early. I'm repulsed by the frothy milk in these jugs laid out each morning. Since the country no longer has many animals, like goats or cows, which can offer us milk, we use what we have. We don't let any resource go to waste. Our women are so often pregnant and nursing that leftover breast milk is distributed around the village. People swear by it, saying the sweet milk is a creamy version of water. I know it's supposed to be nutritious, but I've never been able to make myself drink a glass.

Perhaps it's because I know I will never be able to produce my own milk. Maybe I'm jealous and my feelings manifest themselves in my utter distaste for the stuff. Either way, I'm more turned off today than usual. I walk faster by the homes with the milk on the doorstep, not wanting to see the way it bubbles at the top of the glass jugs.

My first stop is Margareath's house. I almost want to tell her family she'll be back one day. They just need to be strong right now. But I can't give them that yet. For all I know, my plan will fail. It would be wrong to give them false hope now.

I find my second destination at Brinn's house. I can see she isn't well, but I don't know if it's more from the loss of Maran or the result of her illness. I suggest ways her pain could be alleviated, but she says she doesn't want anything prolonged. I leave just as her sickness forces her to vomit.

I make my way back to the White House, faster now without the heavy bundles bobbing at my sides. I run through the village, past the houses that still haven't taken the milk inside. In just a few minutes time, I'm panting as I reach the doors to Vienne's rooms.

"Ah, there you are!" Vienne remarks with vigor when I step inside.

"You're looking well." With glowing face and skin, she's radiant in pregnancy. She's a complete contrast to Brinn's sickly demeanor. I'm silly to worry about her having a baby. Vienne is made for this. Her hair is even silkier than ever, flowing down her back like it's grown a few more inches in just a month.

"Today's the day we get to tell people about our baby! Breakfast first and then into town. I'm famished!"

Thinking about breakfast again gives me a slight chill. After seeing Brinn throw up, I know I can't eat a bite. But I douse my face in water, pull on a new shirt, and follow Vienne to the dining room. Breakfast is an intense affair now we all know Griffin's status as the Technology Faction's leader. I brace myself for the philosophical discussion we're most likely going to have again today.

Griffin and Tomlin aren't in the room yet, so there's nothing to distract Vienne from beginning to eat. I watch as she rips into a fragrant croissant even before settling down into her seat.

As soon as she swallows a few mouthfuls, she says, "Are we also still announcing Griffin's role at today's town hall?"

"Well, it'll allow us to bridge the gap between the Technology Faction and the rest of our people. Have more open discussion. If more people know who he is and that we still accept him, they'll be more inclined to tell us their true opinions too. And Griffin is moderate on his views of technology creation. He is not unreasonable."

"I'm not?" comes his voice from behind us. "You were listing off my good attributes?" He pretends to tick them off on his fingers, grinning wide. "Reasonable. Go on."

"No, that's not exactly what we were doing." I roll my eyes, but I can't help showing a big grin of my own. Like Vienne, Griffin is the picture of good health. He's clean shaven and freshly washed. I catch the faint whiff of fresh grass coming off his skin. Since the night in the abandoned shack, Griffin and I haven't met alone again. I want him. Desperately. The skin on my entire body seems to vibrate when he walks into the room. But another indiscretion is too dangerous to take lightly.

"You're still okay with standing up, telling everyone you lead the Faction, right?" I ask for the fifth time this week.

"Yes, but hopefully people won't react as badly as when I told Vienne a couple of weeks ago."

I remember her response well. Griffin said he wanted to be the one to tell Vienne and Tomlin. So over breakfast he'd dropped the bombshell in between taking bites of egg, trying to nonchalantly throw it into conversation. Tomlin dropped his muffin on the floor, too shocked to respond. And Vienne paced around the table, detailing all the minutia of how Griffin single-handedly ruined our baby's future.

"Look," she says now, defending herself. "I'm pregnant... a bit more ferocious than normal because of the hormones. You took me by surprise, is all."

"I'll say," mutters Griffin.

"Hey, I didn't react too well when you first told me, either," I interject. Then I change the subject before we can delve into where exactly Griffin broke the news to me. I've yet to tell Vienne about Griffin's and my intimacy that night at the shack. "Come on, we've got to get going. Tomlin's already there, getting the stage ready."

We move out together, a tight-knit threesome ready to let the rest of the population in on our news. Griffin's role, my new policy, and Vienne's baby. If ever the three of us were a trio of power, this is it.

When we reach the top of the town hall pavilion, I'm amazed at the sight. Tomlin has arranged crisscrossing beams over the stage like a large trellis. And from these beams hundreds of bright flowers delicately hang. It's a deluge of color.

From behind Vienne, Griffin looks over to me and shrugs with a big smile on his face. "Surprise!" he says. "We've all been gathering the flowers for a while. Even Brinn helped out. Tomlin wouldn't tell anyone why we needed them, but I think people might be catching on now."

Tomlin stands with one hand on a wooden, hand-crafted baby basket that I realize he must have whittled himself. I continue to hold Vienne's hand as we descend the pavilion stairs, passing by our people who can't help staring at Vienne to see if she looks different.

Vienne immediately walks up to Tomlin who's beaming off to the side of the stage. He keeps looking up at the flowers, like he could keep them aloft just with determination.

"Thank you," she says and kisses him on the cheek. "It's gorgeous."

"This is a momentous occasion," he says, looking happier than I've seen him in a long time. He looks back and forth between me and Vienne. "We displayed flowers at your birth announcement, Elected. Lilacs and peonies, if I remember correctly." He pauses and puts a hand on both our shoulders. "Your parents would be so proud. So overjoyed."

"Yes, they would have loved this." I try to think of something else besides my parents so I won't become wistful.

"Well, it looks like paradise," says Vienne. "I could lie on the ground and stare up at these all day."

I'm reminded of saying almost the same thing to Griffin a month ago. My heart flutters in my chest, out of rhythm for a moment, as I remember our exchange. All of this—the flowers, thoughts of my parents, Griffin's closeness—threatens to unhinge my guarded emotions. It's even harder than usual to keep my feelings tamped down.

So instead of delaying, I start the town hall meeting. "People of East Country! We can no longer keep our joy from all of you. We have much to celebrate with you today!"

I wait for the talkers to excitedly pass my words back. There's a rumble of anticipation from the crowd. A wave of elation, rising slowly toward the front.

I laugh out loud, cheered even more by their expectancy. Vienne stands farther up on the stage, ready to share the full extent of our news, as we previously agreed.

"We will be welcoming a new child into the world in eight months' time!"

Even before the talkers have finished relaying her news, there's a gush of cheering rising from our countrymen. People yell out their congratulations.

One man stands up and shouts, "To the Electeds!" More people rise and echo his toast, lifting both of their arms in the air in the traditional greeting. "To the Electeds!" they yell back.

It's a thrill to see all of our people standing for us, exulting in their good wishes for our new baby. As I hoped, this will be a unifying event.

I put up my hands to quiet the audience, but it takes a few moments before it is quiet enough for me to speak again. "We must all watch over Madame Elected. Make sure she's safe at all times. As we must always do for all of our pregnant women. We will monitor her health closely. She will be healthy, as will this new baby!"

People cheer again in agreement. I put up my hands for quiet, and the pavilion settles. "I have more news to share with you today. It's all not as joyous as Madame Elected's, but it's essential to the good of our nation. I know there are many rumors of Mid Country trying to infiltrate us. To launch an attack, perhaps. We know none of this for certain, but after much thought I've decided on a defense strategy."

I pause, running a hand over my forehead, determining how best to explain I'm now advocating breakage of our most sacred Accord.

"The Technology Accord was created to ensure we didn't emulate the mistakes of the past." I pause, looking into the audience to gauge their reactions. People sit on the edge of the stone benches, waiting for me to go on. "It didn't fulfill its designed mission. Without isolation the countries couldn't remain peaceful. Thus, the Ship Accord was established. Finally countries were able to let down their defenses and stop relying on technology to guard against other entities. But now our isolation is infringed upon again. We don't know how they're doing it, but Mid Country is infiltrating us. Stealing nirogene. Depositing bullets on our land. We cannot continue to allow this."

I stop for effect.

"You don't know how much it pains me to say this, but we must break the Technology Accord."

There's a rise of agitation from the crowd. People look to their neighbors in confusion, then back to me with raised eyebrows. They're surprised about my decision. I don't give them much time to reflect upon it. I lift up my hands to regain quiet.

"I don't wish to disregard it entirely. I just want us to build one thing. I know it's asking a lot to forego our rituals, but we need to build a wall between us and Mid Country. Something that cannot be knocked down, pushed through, or excavated. We must manufacture armor glass."

There are more ripples through the crowd as people take in my words.

"Armor glass will keep them out. Stop any invasions if they are forthcoming. I'm advocating one full-scale push to build a long wall of armor glass for our border, and then we'll stop production again. I'm not allowing creation of any other technology. Everything else is still off limits."

I let the ripples of talk from the audience come forward to me in waves. I let everyone ruminate on what I've just said, knowing I can't hold back their conversation anymore. Questions fly at the talkers from all around the pavilion. To the credit of our people, the inquiries reach me in an orderly fashion, one at a time. I answer them as fast as possible.

Yes, Zet, we'll harness all forms of technology needed to create armor glass.

No, Grobe, we won't use these other forms of technology for anything else except this project. Not even to produce more medicine. No.

Yes, Delia, the chemists and metal workers will focus on this project for the next few months.

No, Albine, everyone else will help as needed, but there is still a requirement for our planters to work the fields. We cannot let our stores of food deplete.

Finally the questions dwindle to one. I see a boy in the back of the room gesture toward a talker who shimmies over to him to hear his words. After listening for a moment, the talker walks back to the side and sends the question up to me. I look into the crowd to see the boy whose question I will soon be answering.

A slight movement identifies him. A cockroach walks lightly around the crown of the child's head. It's the boy who held hands with Griffin under the lemon trees.

The closest talker to me brings forth the question. "Will this keep us safe?"

I look down at the stage floor while I think about my answer. I want to give my people hope, but I also want to speak the truth. Will it keep us safe? How can I guarantee something I don't know for sure? What can I say now that's honest, but heartfelt?

When I have the words I need, I look out toward the boy.

"With all my heart and soul, I certainly hope so."

The audience is quieted by my response. But there's still something I need to share with my people. I glance over at Griffin who walks forward. I start the introduction.

"We have one last piece of news before we break for the day and get down to business with the new projects. Recently, it came to my attention that someone close to me and Madame Elected was also close to the Technology Faction. We'd like to completely open lines of communication with this group."

I nod to Griffin. He steps closer to me and looks out into the crowd. I see his throat constrict as he swallows. I lock eyes with him, thinking about Griffin's bravery throughout the last few months. The loss of his father, which he accepts even though he doesn't agree with the Technology Accord that sent his father to death. How he walks two lines. The one where he protects me and Vienne with his entire being. And the one where he meets secretly with the group that wants to defy our rule. He talks of a bridge I must find. But he is the bridge. He is the one who has the power to gather acceptance of the rules I set forth.

With his next words, Griffin's two personas will come crashing down.

"It is high time I tell you who I am. I've been keeping it a secret for too long. Many of you were brave enough to step forward and reveal yourselves. Now I must be equally strong. I'm not just a guard to the Electeds. I'm also the Technology Faction's Leader."

Shouts erupt from the audience as a few people pump their hands in the air in deference to Griffin. The rest of the audience either looks side-to-side to see which of their yet undisclosed Technology Faction

212

neighbors just revealed themselves. Or they yell out their surprise and reluctance to receive this new information about Griffin. To have the Technology Faction Leader, and one whose father tried to assassinate the Elected, so close to the ruling family is unsettling to them.

There is confusion as people try to determine what this new information will mean. If the Technology Faction is infiltrating the Elected Office. If I've already bowed to their requests and am a puppet. If that's why I now advocate manufacturing armor glass. Or if the Technology Faction has just officially given up and vows to follow all of my dictates. If they are now the puppet.

I realize the people who raised their hands to cheer for Griffin are not the entirety of the Technology Faction. As I stare into the agitated crowd, I hear a mixture of shouts denouncing Griffin as the Faction leader, saying he's given in, shown weakness. I didn't picture what Griffin's announcement would do to him, only what I would gain. Now I wonder if we've been wrong to bring his affiliation forward. I am spellbound, listening to the rumblings of my people as best I can.

So I don't see Vienne looking toward me imploringly. It's only when her hand touches my upper arm, the tender spot of the brand, that I spin toward her.

"Aloy, we should go. It's not safe here for us right now."

I purse my lips at her in consternation, upset that just a few minutes ago the crowd was fully behind us and our new baby. Now I see my people entering into chaos once again. I don't want to let it go unchecked. "Maybe just a few minutes more," I implore, hoping I can bring order quickly.

"No, I must go. The baby. It isn't safe. I can't stand in the middle of another riot."

I know she's right to be prudent. I picture her knocked down by thrown objects, and this pushes me forward. At once, I gesture to the guards and they surround her in a tight circle, ushering her off the stage. I follow quickly, looking back at Griffin. I mouth the words, "I'm sorry," to him.

He shrugs, not exactly giving me his usual mischievous grin, but not defeated. "I'm not," he mouths back.

Vienne and I are led out of the pavilion. It's not until we're at the top, me looking down at the four thousand people below us, that my stomach turns in on itself. Already a few of the flowers in the trellis above the stage have started to fall. Instead of the pretty picture the

flowers made before, now they look decayed, like something has rotted and begun to disintegrate.

Tomlin meets me and Vienne at the top of the pavilion. "Come," he says, sounding an awful lot like my mother. "Let them talk it out. They need to make sense of this. Come to some kind of new political order where the Technology Faction means something different than it did fifty years ago."

"Talk?" I scoff. "They're not exactly talking. I thought..." I can't finish my words.

"Let Griffin work out the next part."

Griffin. I stare onto the stage where he's standing alone. His hands are up, trying to bring a semblance of quiet so he can start answering questions. The talkers are no longer used. People yell out questions, but Griffin can't fully hear a question to answer it. And even if he could, few would be able to hear his response.

Then a voice from the audience rises above the others and it stops me in my tracks.

"Guards, arrest Griffin!" the voice screeches.

I swivel around, looking for the person who's just asked for something only I can order. How dare he. My eyes squint, looking for the person I will mow down with my words in a second.

I'm not entirely surprised to see Grobe standing on top of one of the rock benches. He gestures toward the stage, and the audience quiets to hear his accusation.

"Do you deny it, Griffin? Have you not played with electricity?" Grobe's voice is loud and authoritative.

Griffin focuses on Grobe for a second, but then his eyes find their way back to me. The audience follows Griffin's gaze, glancing back and forth from one of us to another. At first I think Griffin is asking for my help, but then when I see the slight movement of his head back and forth I realize he's doing the exact opposite.

This can't be happening.

"Elected," Grobe says, looking toward the back of the Ellipse at me. "Moments ago, you said no other technology should be made except for armor glass. Yet, Griffin created technology and must pay for his crimes!"

I am speechless, wondering how Griffin was so lax as to show someone else his invention. And that's when I think of it. It'll be Griffin's word against Grobe's. I'll just side with Griffin. No big deal.

I look at Griffin, trying to send my thoughts across the expanse to his brain. Please be complicit with this, I silently beg.

"It's only you accusing Griffin," I say toward Grobe. "I cannot enact the justice you seek without seeing evidence."

Then I look at Griffin again, my eyes bright with the easy solution I've just concocted. But Griffin is looking down at the floor. He won't meet my eyes, and it's just seconds before I understand why.

"I've seen it too," says a man standing near Grobe. The man looks toward Griffin in apology. "I also advocate technology creation, but Grobe is right. Until the Elected tells us we can create the machines, we are only allowed to talk about it. Griffin did more than that."

Another woman near Grobe steps forward. "It's true," she says.

I look back at Vienne and Tomlin, and see they've both turned white. If I denounce the evidence of three people, which I know they can showcase if asked, and instead advocate for Griffin, I'll be tearing apart the very framework of laws our society needs to stay intact. And if I do come to Griffin's aid now, it will seem like favoritism. Possibly even more. Like love.

Maybe they'll even be able to guess I'm a woman. Then nothing will matter anymore. Not only will Griffin go to prison and be executed, but Vienne and I will too. Vienne's baby will be stripped of its future title. And all because of my love for one man.

I look at Griffin once more. This time he's staring straight at me. He mouths one sentence in my direction.

You know what you have to do.

No one else seems to notice his mouth move since the entire country is staring at me, waiting for my decision.

Griffin's right. Unfortunately, I know all too well what this job makes me do. Over and over again, I have to pick my position over my own heart.

I look at Griffin one last time, ignoring the eyes of my four thousand townspeople. I try to tell him I'm sorry, and I think he does understand. He nods again and gives me a slight smile. It's almost like a goodbye.

"Guards, arrest Griffin," I say.

30

"Don't worry," Vienne says, reading my mind as she props me up on our way to the Old Executive Building. I feel sick all of a sudden, as if I might throw up right in the dirt at our feet. We're following the path of the guards who, just an hour ago, took Griffin to the prison.

"Vienne, we can't live without him," I say into her ear.

I look away from her so she won't see a tear as it's starting to fester under my eyelashes. When I finally glance back, Vienne is staring at me. I can't deny it.

"I didn't want to love him," I say. "I couldn't help it."

Vienne smiles, but the movement doesn't reach her eyes. "I know. And that's how you know it's the real thing."

I interject fast, "But I can't live without you, either!"

Vienne cocks her head. "You think you couldn't live without me or Griffin? You don't give yourself enough credit. Every time you've run into adversity, you bounce back. You find a way to counter it. You may not realize it, but you could get by on your own if you had to."

"Is this what you were trained for?" I'm starting to understand Tomlin's most important lesson for Vienne. "Were you trained to bolster up my confidence?"

Vienne looks away.

"That's it, isn't it? Because he thought I'd need that, right?" I continue, starting to understand the extent of Vienne's psychology lessons. "You were trained to be the perfect counterbalance for me. And he thought I'd need some bolstering."

"We all need that. All of us need affirmation of some kind. I was just given extra information on how to administer it. None of what I tell you is untrue."

"Psychology lessons. Just for you. No one else gets those." It dawns on me slowly. "Because they thought I would be a special kind of crazy."

"Well, it's got to be rough having to pretend you're something you're not."

"Yes. Were you taught to make sure I didn't falter and somehow show my feminine side? Was that part of the...?" Before I can finish my sentence, we're already at the mouth of the prison, and the doors are being held open for us.

I'm resolute we'll find a way to protect Griffin from the harsh punishments outlined in the Technology Accord. Vienne and I can save him like we did Margareath. But this time it feels so different; I cannot bear to send Griffin away.

As we walk through the tight hallway, I feel bile rising in my throat again. Can I be getting a virus? I promise myself I'll take my temperature on a chemical strip when I get home. But for now, I push through the dizziness, only thinking of getting to Griffin. There are more guards than usual standing along the corridor. I wonder if any of them are also secretly part of the Technology Faction. I never thought my own security system would be penetrated, but since the Faction is so widespread, the idea doesn't sound so absurd anymore. The only question is: are they for Griffin or against him? Now that the Faction has splintered, it's more confusing than ever to determine people's motivations.

"Why the extra guards?" I ask Tomlin quietly enough not to attract the attention of the men closest to us.

"Griffin is a bit of a celebrity. There are many who'd like to break him out of here. And..." He pauses. "There are likewise many who now seem to want his head on a spike."

"Ugh," Vienne groans. I realize this is the first time she's been inside these walls. She's glancing around with wide eyes. "So the guards are for extra precaution?"

"Most of them," says Tomlin.

We enter Griffin's side of the cell. He's hunched over on the cot, but when he hears the door open, he jumps up. When I see his face, I'm reminded what a toll the last few days have taken. Griffin's usually spry features are clouded in gray. His lips are turned down. He tries to manage a smile when he sees us, but it's faint like the sun trying to shine after a horrific acid rain storm.

"Is this the same room...?" Griffin's voice trails off, but he looks at me imploringly.

Vienne darts over to him, grasping his elbow. "I'm sure this isn't the same room your father was in," she says.

I'd completely forgotten that Griffin's imprisonment in these walls might bring up other feelings beside the worry over his own self. I can't help but stare at the armor glass in the cell to make sure Vienne's words are true. Could any of Maran's blood still be left on the glass, spelling out that ancient word?

"It's not the same room," I reassure them. "It was farther down the corridor." I can hardly remember for sure but decide to go with this white lie anyway. I've told so many lately, one more doesn't seem to matter.

"You'll be ok, Griffin," Vienne says. "Aloy will figure out a way to fix this."

"I don't have too much time before people start demanding I drink the hemlock," he says.

"Well, it's your choice when to drink it," says Vienne. Her hand is resting on her hip in defiance.

"Even though prisoners are allowed to choose when they drink the poison, it's considered honorable not to wait too long," I explain to Vienne.

"She's right," Griffin continues, the stiffness in his voice moving to a more urgent tone. "I don't have that much time before a mob starts to riot. Watch for Grobe, Electeds. He'll take over the Technology Faction now. And next he'll go after the Elected role. His means of displacement will be more subtle, yet even more damaging than my father's were."

I suck in breath, trying to imagine an action that could hurt me more than an assassination attempt from Maran. I watch Griffin's gaze as it lingers on Vienne and then moves to her pregnant stomach. My insides cringe as I fully realize the extent of Grobe's intentions.

Vienne realizes it too and instinctively puts both hands around her stomach.

"We won't let that happen," I say, and Griffin nods.

"We can put security detail on Madame Elected twenty-four hours a day," Tomlin says. I sigh, realizing this is wise but that it'll derail our urgent need for privacy, as Vienne is an integral part of my escape plans for Griffin.

Vienne is about to assuage Griffin with some other explanation of how we'll negotiate his release, but I know her words are futile. She and I won't be able to use our designed method of extracting prisoners. She'll

219

be too heavily guarded to prepare the body in private, watch the prisoner wake up from his drink of sleeping potion instead of hemlock, and then ride out to the hills to deposit the accused in Mid Country as one of our spies. We'll have to think of another way.

I'm about to interject, offer to do something drastic like publicly deny the Technology Accord or rewrite it for the purposes of our country, when another guard bursts into the room. "Excuse me, Electeds, but there's been a theft."

We all turn our heads to the man in the door. He's out of breath from running to see us, one hand resting on his chest as he heaves big gulps of air. He's one of our younger guards, but I can't remember his name. For some reason, my brain feels cloudy, covered over with a filminess I can't seem to shake. It gives me a slight headache, but I shake it off to process everything the guard's saying.

"It's all gone. Just disappeared overnight, but with the town hall preparations, no one realized it until now. People are worried, Elected. This much has never disappeared all at once before. We can't figure out who could have removed it undetected."

I put my hand up to stop him. "Slow down, please. It's gone? What's all gone?"

The guard comes to stand in front of me, taking off his hat to hold it in both of his shaking hands. "The final store that the chemists were guarding. The nirogene. It's all gone."

"ALL OF IT'S MISSING?" My voice is bold, the anger bubbling over like lava from an active volcano. If there's no more nirogene, we won't be able to manufacture armor glass. "Search the whole country! Use all of the guards."

"Yes, Elected." The young man quickly follow my orders.

I turn to the other two guards who are standing in the doorway. "Take a team on bikes to the hills. Ensure harvesting is still in process." They nod and turn to go. We'll have to harvest a lot more before we can create any of the armor glass.

Then I look toward Griffin. "Is there anyone among your group who would steal this? Grobe?"

Griffin shakes his head, the muscles in his face and neck tight with tension. "No, I can't think who. Grobe wouldn't be interested in it. He wants widespread technology use, so he'd be the last person to take it away from others, especially when they were so close to using it for something other than just prevention of rust."

I nod in agreement. We spend a few minutes trying to work out different scenarios, but we can't think who in our own country would be motivated and able to steal that much of the chemical without detection.

"So it was stolen by Mid?" I ask.

"That theory makes the most sense," says Tomlin. "Our armor glass would have stopped anything flying over the border. It's strange how just when we decide to put up the glass, the whole nirogene store is stolen. As if Mid knew this would be their last opportunity."

Armor glass, besides being incredibly hard and able to stave off rust also has a unique property affecting mechanical sensors. The

221

undetectable vapors emitted at all times from the glass substance, render airrides and any other overhead mechanical objects unusable or unstable, at best.

"Like they could hear us talking about it over the last few days," Vienne says.

We go on like this for a few minutes more, but an intense pain overtakes my stomach. I grimace, trying to go unnoticed. They're so caught up in conversation no one sees me becoming more and more uncomfortable. Finally, I can't take the cramping anymore. I'm sure I must have a fever now because my forehead is perspiring in sheets.

Through clenched teeth, I say "I'm going to the hills. We'll figure out your situation, Griffin. Don't worry. We won't let the execution sentence stand."

I don't give them much time to respond as I fear I'll cry out in pain if I don't have a moment to myself. I hurry out of the prison into the fresh air and jog home with my hand on my abdomen. I do intend to visit the hills, but first I have to change clothes, as I feel like I'm perspiring through my armpits and down my arms. I also need to grab my horse, as I don't intend to walk miles to the hills right now.

When I reach the front doors, I pull them open fast and breathe a sigh of relief as the cooler air inside the house hits my face. I walk toward my bedroom, passing by a couple of maids without acknowledgement. Inside the room, I stumble over to a set of drawers and pull out a fresh pair of pants. Glancing at myself in the mirror above the wash basin, I'm surprised to see my skin is white and taut, like linens freshly bleached and left out too long in the sun to dry. There truly are droplets of water running from my scalp down my cheeks. I gather my discarded clothes into a pile and pull on the new ones.

However, the linen pants that have always fit so well are falling around my frame. I pull the drawstrings taut, but there are still gaps at the waist. I'm losing weight fast. I know I haven't had the stomach for eating recently, but the weight loss is too much, too aggressive. I look at myself in the mirror, and a cramp overtakes my stomach again. This time, I'm directly over the washbasin when I heave a sickeningly green puddle of vomit out of my stomach. The gush smacks into the bucket of water with a slurp, and the feeling of sickness overtakes me again. I retch a total of three times before I can raise my head again.

I stare at my red eyes in the mirror and grab a piece of cloth nearby to wipe off my face. I need to be strong to lead my people through this latest crisis. I need to take a pill already.

I pull a thin shirt over my head and leave the room again, the precious vault key on a cord, flapping against the bindings around my chest. I want to conserve the purple pills, but I don't think I can wait out this sickness. Whatever it is, I don't seem to be getting better. In fact, as the last few days have gone by, I seem to be feeling worse. Losing weight, throwing up, my face growing more pallid, not to mention the constant pain in my chest. This last symptom grows more noticeable as my sweaty bindings feel like they're constricting my lungs. The cloth around my breasts was the one thing I didn't change just now. It would take too long to undo myself from the linen to waste the time. Now that I'm resolved to take a pill, I can't get to it fast enough.

I look forward to the smooth feeling it will have going into my system. Everything inside me that is hurting will dissipate within moments. I pass our main foyer and the kitchen and then take two flights of stairs down into the bowels of the house, a section rarely used. I'm in front of the heavy iron door in moments. Already the key is out and in my hand. I plunge it into the ancient door and turn it to the right as I'd watched my mother do countless times. When I hear a faint click, I push on the door. It moans under my weight but scratches open, metal scraping the concrete floor.

Inside the small vault is a set of white shelves. It's dark in here since the room has no windows and, of course, I don't have Griffin's fireflies or electricity to show me the way. But I feel along the shelves until a glass bottle connects with my hand. I unscrew the lid without even having to see the vial and drop one small pill into my palm. Then I turn, feeling along the wall to make sure I don't stumble as I exit the vault.

And I run smack into something hard and fleshy.

A hand reaches around me to cover my mouth. Before I can scream, the figure turns with me so we're staring face-to-face. Even in the dark, I can make out my assailant's features. A sense of shock envelops me.

Our cook, Dorine, looks back at me with a large grin on her face.

"I've been biding my time. Waiting for you to come down here to get a pill for yourself," she says. "You'd think with the traces of poison I've been gradually depositing in your food, you'd have ventured down here well before now."

I mumble, trying to get out some words of protest, but Dorine's hand stays clenched over my mouth and right now I'm too weak to push her off.

"Not that I don't like you well enough, Elected, but you can't keep hoarding all these pills just for yourself. My son..." Her voice cracks. "My son is so thin now. It's just a matter of time. I need these pills!" Dorine puts a knife up to my throat. "I don't want to hurt you, Elected, but don't make me do anything rash." She reaches around me for the door and pushes it back wide open. Then she turns with me in her grasp, pushing me forward. "Now, don't make a peep." She lets go of my mouth but still holds the knife to my neck. Her other hand rakes across the shelves and clasps a few glass bottles. She reaches back up to the shelves again and again. Quickly, she empties all the pills into a pouch on her apron.

"You don't need all of those. If your son has cancer, two or three pills will do the trick." I breathe shallowly, aware that Dorine's knife draws droplets of my blood from my neck as I speak. Her hand shakes.

"I can't take that chance, Elected."

"You won't get away with this."

"We'll see." Then she backs up slowly, easing the knife away from my neck. I immediately put a hand to my throat to stave off the bleeding.

Dorine heads for the stairs in front of us. As soon as she's a few steps up and away from me, I call out with all the force I can muster. She looks back with an angry scowl and then launches herself faster up the stairs. I keep yelling for the guards, screaming "Thief" and "Dorine, get Dorine!"

I run after her but find I'm having a hard time getting back up the stairs for all the cramping in my stomach. I swallow the one pill I managed to keep hidden in my hand. I hardly have time to savor the feel of the drugs shooting into my system before I'm running up the stairs after Dorine at top speed.

Already there's chaos on the first floor of the house in response to my shouts. People are running around, trying to find Dorine as I continue to yell out her crime. Most of the guards are already gone, complying with my earlier request to look for the nirogene. There are only three guards who come to my aid now, running with me in the direction I think Dorine has gone.

"The stable!" I cry, thinking she'll know to get away on more than her own two feet to outrun my pursuit. We run out to the horses but find Dorine has already grabbed one and is galloping away, the stable door open and banging against the wall in the breeze.

"Grab some horses. We're going after her!"

There's a flurry of action as the few guards follow my orders.

"Ya!" I yell to my horse. I pump its bridle and begin our hot pursuit of Dorine. I think we'll easily catch up to her, as she's obviously never ridden a horse before. The terrain ahead is the flat wasteland on the way to the border hills, easy to traverse on a horse and easy on which to keep Dorine in view. I see the horse bucking her, as if it too realizes its rider is up to no good and wants her dismounted.

After twenty minutes of galloping hard, we're closing in on her. Our entire party is almost to the hills. Dirt billows up in back of us in large clouds, but I don't see it. I'm focused on the scene in front of me. I don't take my eyes off Dorine's figure.

She's at the base of the hills now, at the entrance to the nirogene mines. She slides off the horse and runs into the mines, her apron, holding all of the pills, still with her.

"She's in the mines!" I yell, although the guards can clearly see her escape path too. No matter, we're close now. She won't get away. The three guards leap off their horses and run into the mine behind Dorine.

I grab onto my horse's mane, ready to jump down and run in after the four of them, but at that second, a fiery explosion bursts from within the mine's entrance sending me and my horse flying backward in a tumult of arms, legs, and spraying dirt.

32

FIRE BELCHES FROM THE air all around me, so hot I can feel it searing my throat. I'm thrown from my horse, landing hard on the ground. The horse stumbles back onto its feet, screams in a pitch I've never heard from an animal before, and then gallops in the opposite direction of the explosion. From the ground I see people scurrying in all directions. Some try to get into the mouth of the mine. Others run along the hill away from the scene. Dust and black ash are everywhere.

I get up on my hands and knees, assessing myself for anything broken. There doesn't seem to be damage, but I'm sure I'll ache later. A miner runs to my side, holding onto my elbow to help me stand.

"I'm ok," I gasp. "Help others." The words come out as large coughs, black ash mixed with my own spit.

I cautiously move closer to the mouth of the mine. Large boulders obstruct the entrance.

"Can we get these moved out of the way?" I call out to the small group of miners gathered around the cave's opening.

The head miner steps forward. "Elected, the entrance is completely blocked. We'll start trying to move the stones, but we'll need more manpower."

"How many people do you think were inside the cave?"

"Maybe thirty. Half our miners were inside, gathering more nirogene, and the other half was carting more supply to the chemists to get it locked away and safe."

I try to pull out some of the smaller rocks. They're wedged in hard. "Okay, have three men go back to the village and gather reinforcements.

Then start a headcount of the miners. Find out who exactly is missing! And everyone else, grab hold of these stones with any tools you have available!" My words ring out louder than the flurry of activity surrounding us.

Work on my commands starts immediately. In an hour's time, the miners who left on bikes to gather help are back, reinforcements arriving on horses to facilitate as fast a return as possible. Everyone is heaving with the effort to move the rocks and get any survivors out of the caves.

I doubt Dorine or my three guards are alive. They were all too close to the entrance when the explosion occurred. I think of the pills as well. East Country's entire store has now been destroyed, and my mother's threats about the safety of the Elected family reverberate inside my mind. I wonder who set the explosion and what their motivation was. Perhaps Dorine or her son manufactured it to bar the entrance and buy some time to administer the pills. But if so, their timing was remarkably wrong. Dorine surely killed herself in the process and destroyed all of the pills at the same time. Or maybe whoever stole the chemists' nirogene earlier today set the explosion so we'd be unable to harvest anything more.

Tomlin rides up on a horse behind me, and I have a chance to explore both theories more fully. I fill him in on status of the miners still inside the cave, Dorine's deceit, and what the lack of pills means for the Elected family's health going forward.

"I knew you weren't feeling well," he says, raising an eyebrow when we've talked through all the other issues. Tomlin looks me over from head to toe.

"Yes, but don't worry. I got one pill in my system before Dorine ran." I take a moment to assess myself now that I have a break. I feel a little better. I don't think I'll throw up, and I'm not perspiring. But my chest still hurts, and the dizziness hasn't dissipated. I refrain from telling Tomlin about either affliction but am inwardly confused. The pill should have taken care of everything. Did it not work on me? Or do I need more than one pill for the particular poison Dorine gave me?

Tomlin interrupts my thoughts. "Tell me your theories on the nirogene again?"

I turn toward him, forgetting about my pain. "Someone doesn't want us using nirogene at all. They've taken our stores and we're conveniently blocked from harvesting more, at least for the time being. It'll be maybe three or four days until we can begin harvesting again."

"We need that armor glass up as soon as possible." Tomlin puts a hand on his forehead in consternation.

"We could take down the glass from the prison—use it to cover as much of the border as possible."

Tomlin nods, his hand rubbing his chin as he thinks. "At least that would be a start."

We create a party of guards to begin tearing through the prison glass. It won't be enough glass to cover the length of the border hill, but its unique properties could at least block some of Mid's airrides from entering East Country. If that's truly what's happening.

"And Vienne?" I ask Tomlin. "She's all right? There are guards protecting her?"

"Yes, she's staying close to Griffin in the prison." Tomlin's face is sad at the mention of our latest accused. "I know his execution will pain you and Madame Elected immensely." He shakes his head.

I don't say anything for fear I'll blurt out my true intentions to ensure the execution doesn't happen. I just nod and look down. I remember I need to ask Tomlin about the helmet, so I take the opportunity to ask my question and change the subject at the same time.

"Tomlin, there's something else. I used the Mind Multiplier a second time. I originally questioned the validity of what I saw, but there was an airride in my vision."

"An airride? So it's true then? We're being infiltrated by another country?"

"I think so. Based on my vision and what's happened since then, all I can think is Mid stole our nirogene and then blew up the mine so we couldn't harvest more. Somehow they knew we were about to build more armor glass and they've taken both actions to deter us. Perhaps they're even clearing out what's left of the mine's nirogene harvest from their side of the hills as we speak."

"Why didn't you tell me, Elected?"

"I didn't think what I saw was true, and my head hurt so much from using the Multiplier, I didn't understand how everything fit together. You told me yourself—sometimes the Multiplier shows real images, and sometimes it just shows you versions of the truth in symbols. It was hard to interpret."

Tomlin nods.

"But there's one more issue too. I don't know where the helmet went. I used it the night under the tree. It fell from my head, but when all of you woke me up, the Multiplier was gone. Did you take it? Do you know where it is?"

Tomlin is aghast. "No, I haven't seen it since you asked me to leave it with Vienne."

"Whatever happens, will you try hard to find it? If I'm not here, it'll be your responsibility to retrieve the helmet."

Tomlin looks at me oddly, his knuckles white as he knots both of his hands together. "Yes, but what do you mean by 'if I'm not here'? What are you planning?"

"Just... will you find it?"

As I start to piece together specific plans in my head, I turn to Tomlin again. "And Vienne."

"Yes, what about her?" His eyes squint as he looks at me.

"Will you watch her closely too? Make sure she's safe?"

"Yes, but she'll have many people watching over her, surely." His words come out slow and deliberate. "You for one, correct?" He stares into my eyes like he can decipher my plans.

I cough and look down. "Mmm-hmm." I don't want to lie to Tomlin, so I don't say anymore. When I look up at him, he's still staring at me oddly.

"You know your people need you here, right, Elected?" His eyes bore into mine.

I meet his eyes for an instant but then look away into the distance. "My people need me to keep them safe. That's what they really expect from me. Not my presence as a figurehead. I need to go see Griffin and Vienne. Will you oversee things at the hills?"

He nods but continues to stare after me. I'm about to walk away—to take one of the guard's horses for the ride back to town—but I turn back to look at Tomlin.

"You've been my best advisor, Tomlin. My best teacher. I won't forget that."

He puts a hand over his eyes to block out the sun and gazes in my direction. Assessing my plans, he loses the formality of our relationship, calling me by my given name.

"And you, Aloy, were my best student. Remember to use what you know, wherever you are. Trust in yourself."

He's all I have left of my parents. In fact, for all my life, he's acted like my guardian. Saying goodbye to him is like losing a father all over again. I nod at him, unable to speak for the emotion bubbling near the surface. Then I jump up onto the horse and ride away, refusing to look back.

33

IT TAKES ME MUCH longer to reach town than earlier, when I was pushing hard to catch Dorine. In fact, it's my sickness, now back again in full swing, which really slows me down. I have to stop once along the way to throw up. I thought I was getting better, but now I have no doubt what's happening to me. Dorine thought her slight doses of poison would inflict sickness, but she's only partially right.

It happens to all of our people at some point. I just didn't think radiation poisoning would catch up to me so young or that I'd be unable to use more of the pills to cure myself.

Weight loss, vomiting, dizziness, and chest pains. They're all symptoms of the affliction.

Now that I recognize what I have, I vow to use the remainder of my time wisely. I need to help Griffin escape and find a way to defend against Mid Country. And if I can find my parents and bring them back to East Country, they'll be able to unite the people in ways I haven't managed to do. My father's strong fist could silence the dangerous sections of the Technology Faction better than I've been able to do. I can accomplish all three agendas, if I just time my plans correctly.

The horse and I are both panting as we reach the prison. I hand the reigns over to a guard at the prison door. "Make sure he gets some water."

"Yes, Elected," the guard says and then immediately leads the horse to a bucket nearby.

I run into the prison and find a team of volunteers already hauling heavy sections of armor glass into the lobby. There's thudding and scraping coming from all over the building as they tear out the glass for use on the hill. I dodge past the guards and the glass to get to Griffin's room. It's the only one where the armor glass hasn't yet been taken.

"Are you both all right?" I ask upon entering.

"We're fine. But how many people were hurt at the mines?" asks Vienne immediately, her hand pressed against her mouth. She and Griffin have obviously already been told about the explosion. Vienne is pacing around the prison room, while Griffin sits quietly on the cot.

"We're not sure yet. Maybe ten were mining near the blast."

"A travesty!" exclaims Vienne.

"It's a good idea to use the prison's armor glass until you can make more," says Griffin. He points out the door toward men carrying thick sections of glass out to the lobby. His color's returned, and a little part of me is jealous Vienne was able to comfort him while I was out dealing with the worst aspects of my position. I want so much to have time alone with Griffin, my heart aches. But instead I say, "Griffin, do you mind if I pull Vienne away from you for a moment?" I'm breathless with my requests. I can't talk quickly enough.

"Of course." He looks at me confused, his head cocked to one side. We lock eyes for a moment, but that's all the time we have.

I think of his marriage proposal back at the abandoned house. The idea is just a wisp of smoke now. I won't be around long enough to see my nineteenth birthday, let alone my child's. So Griffin and I will never have a chance to legitimize our feelings for one another. I can't help sighing, letting my lungs expel everything they have.

Vienne follows me, pursing her lips. "What's going on, Aloy? You seem strange."

At this, I cough so hard I have to place a hand on a nearby wall to steady myself. The dizziness is overwhelming.

Vienne exclaims, "You're not well!"

"Shhh! I'm okay. Well, not okay. But we need to go somewhere private to talk."

We duck into one of the rooms already disassembled of its armor glass. It's empty and relatively quiet. As soon as we're inside, I pull Vienne over to the wooden bench to sit with me.

"Mid Country is stealing our resources. They somehow stole the last supply of nirogene. And now they've bombed the hill's entrance so we can't harvest more, at least until we re-clear a path. I'm sure Mid was behind both events. Tonight is the scheduled time you were going to meet Margareath on the border, right? Once every two weeks?"

Vienne nods her head.

"I need her to lead me into Mid Country so I can see for myself what's going on and perhaps negotiate a deal with their Elected."

"It's too dangerous!" Vienne gasps. "You can't go!"

"I have to." My voice grows lower. "I can take Griffin away too. We need to get him out of here."

"Yes, I agree he needs to escape, but then leave him there with Margareath and return to East Country." She leans forward, hands clamped together in a plea. Vienne's face is knotted with worry. I hate to have to burden her further, but I proceed with the final explanation.

"Vienne, I'm not well." To show this to her firsthand, I stand up, teetering a bit and find a corner of the room. Involuntarily, I spit up bile onto the floor.

I turn back to her, wiping my arm across my mouth. Vienne is aghast as she stares at me.

"I have radiation poisoning. Cancer. And the one pill I swallowed before Dorine took the rest wasn't enough to cure me."

Vienne stares at me for a long time, both of us letting the news takes its effect. I give her a moment to take it all in.

"I don't have much time. The best thing I can do for East Country is—" I start, but Vienne puts up a hand to shush me.

"No, stop a moment," she says. She looks me up and down.

"What? What is it? I've got cancer. I don't have long. I need to help the country in the best way I can before I'm no longer—"

Vienne cuts me off again. "Aloy, stop. There's something you're not telling me." Her voice is calm. Much calmer than I'd expect given the news of my impending death.

I'm a tad annoyed at her lack of response. "Not telling you something? I'm telling you everything. Right now."

"No, Aloy, you don't have cancer."

"Yes, I do." I'm exasperated. Now I see what is going on. She's in denial. She doesn't want to think about this news and its implications. That I'll die before the baby is eighteen. That East will have to hold another Election and she and our baby will no longer be part of the Elected family. I can't help any of it now. I just need to serve my country as best I can before I fall too ill.

Vienne stands. She puts both of her hands on my shoulders. "Listen to me. You don't have cancer. Do you know how I can tell?"

I roll my eyes now, frustrated she just won't accept the truth. "Sure.

How?"

"Because you and Griffin had sex."

I blanch at her words. They're true, but I don't see how they have anything to do with the current situation.

"He told you?" I ask, incredulous.

"No, he didn't."

I just stare at her, uncomprehending.

"You've just told me, Aloy."

I still don't get her meaning. I told her no such thing. I'm sick. I've told her I'm dying of cancer. Not that I had relations with Griffin.

"Vienne... no, I..."

She stops me again.

For the third time she says, "You don't have cancer."

Vienne pauses again and looks me hard in the eyes so I'll settle down and grasp her next words.

"You're pregnant."

34

FOR A FEW SECONDS I just stare at her, blinking.

"What did you say you felt? Dizziness? Vomiting? Those are symptoms of pregnancy too."

I still look at her in disbelief. "It can't be. Vienne, I was only intimate with Griffin once, I swear. I... I... don't even know how to get..." I'm finally admitting my indiscretion to her, and it tumbles out of my mouth too fast.

She stops me. "Apparently, he's a very fertile man. You're pregnant, Aloy." She pulls out a thin stack of filmy litmus paper, replicas of the one she used to show me she was pregnant. "I carry these around to ensure that I haven't miscarried."

Vienne holds out one of the small papers in front of me and I obediently spit on its center. Instantly, the film turns neon green.

Vienne doesn't comment further on my disloyalty to our marriage or my infidelity. But I stammer back a response to her about my symptoms. "Vienne, you're pregnant, and you aren't vomiting. You're eating just fine. Better than fine, in fact. You've seemed ravenous lately. And I can't eat a thing." I think of Dorine's poisoned meals, but it's not only her food I haven't wanted. I've turned away almost all food since a few weeks after that night with Griffin.

Vienne sits back down on the bench to my right and gives a short laugh. "Pregnancy affects women in different ways. You're right, I don't have dizziness or morning sickness, but many women do."

I breathe in again. "But my chest hurts. It feels like the cancer is eating away right there." I point to my torso.

Now Vienne really does laugh. It's not cruel. If anything, it's a sound

237

of relief. She takes my hands in hers and touches one of my breasts. "Don't worry. Your body is getting ready for milk production. Your chest is expanding. It has nothing to do with your heart whatsoever!"

Milk production? That's why my chest hurts? I'll be nursing like the rest of the women of my country? I think back to the milk bottles on the doorsteps and my jealousy over the female right to reproduce. I'll have this opportunity now too? Me?

I don't have cancer? I'll live?

I lean into Vienne, the tension draining out of my body. I feel tears of relief welling in my eyes.

"And you'll be more emotional," she says, still holding one of my hands in a warm embrace. With her other hand she reaches up and brushes away a stray tear from my eye. "It's the hormones."

I think back to when I've wanted to cry over the last few weeks. So it wasn't just me being weak-minded, after all.

I don't say anything, just lean into Vienne more heavily, letting the worry I've carried with me over the last few days melt out of my body. At once the pain in my chest feels lighter. I'll have a baby. My own to run the nation. Between my and Vienne's baby, there will surely be a child who can take the reins.

"But I see you're right, Aloy." She speaks quietly, breaking my reverie. "You'll have to leave." I look up at her, not contemplating her meaning. "If you want this family to hold onto the Elected position you must leave now. No one must know you're pregnant. You must maintain your image as a man. If you rip apart the Technology and Fertility Accords simultaneously, there will be hysteria. It's too much change all at once. The people won't accept it."

She's right. "In my absence, you'll have to run the country." I take her face in my hands and she lets me. "I promise I'll be back after the baby is born, but you have to take charge now."

She thinks about it for a moment. "No, I must focus on the pregnancy, as the Fertility Accord states. What about Tomlin? He can take office."

"Vienne, it has to be you, otherwise people will see it's too easy for someone outside the Elected family to take over. You just have to say you're making a few decisions until I return shortly. By the time people realize I've been gone for many months—that my time away isn't short—they'll already be accustomed to your authority. If Tomlin took office, we wouldn't be able to hold off a coup. The Technology Faction

238

is splintering into two groups. One that is more mild in their actions and one that will take any opportunity for power. You have to hold them off long enough for me to have the baby and bring home my parents."

"But I... I never..." Now it is Vienne's turn to look anxious.

"You can. You've been trained for this role, better than anyone else. You have all the qualities of an excellent leader. Empathy, resolve, intelligence." For once, I'm bolstering up Vienne, turning the tables on our roles. "I have to go, Vienne. I'll find out what Mid Country intends to do. If they plan to take us over or wipe us out."

My words hang in the air, like a dreadful omen.

"And I'll get Griffin away from here," I say at last.

Vienne stares hard at me for this last part. I can't determine whether she's mad at me or if she agrees with all the reasons for my plan. Then she softens and brings her cheek against mine.

"You love him, Aloy. I know you wish you could have married him instead of me."

I can't deny her claim. "You'll find someone you wish you could marry one day too. When the country is in a more stable position—when we're free to be our true selves—you'll also be free to find someone to love. Someone you love as more than just a duty."

Vienne is quiet for a moment but then says, "I never thought of the Madame Elected role as just a duty. I wanted it. When I was alone and Tomlin took me in to be your intended mate, that's when my life got its purpose. I cherished my duty. It was never a burden to me."

"But it was never a *choice*," I say, realizing I'm talking about my situation. "Your love was decided for you. It may be different when you finally get the option of choosing your mate. Once you get a taste of real love, you'll feel what a burden it's been catering to my every desire just because of who I was."

"Maybe..." She breathes. "But Aloy, don't you know? I wasn't forced to take the Madame Elected role. Tomlin told me I could walk away anytime over the many years I prepared for the position—if I didn't want it, they'd find you another wife. But I wanted to be with you. You looked at your arranged marriage as a burden, but I never did. I thought I was the luckiest girl in all of East Country."

I stare at her with wide eyes. All this time I suspected Vienne had more conviction for this role than me, and now I know I was right. On top of that she truly loved me.

"Vienne, I'm the one who's been lucky to have you as my wife.

Please, just do this last thing for me. Stay and be East Country's Elected, at least until I return with my parents."

She reaches toward me and hugs me hard, the soft locks of her hair falling around my cheek. "I will do what you ask." A moment later Vienne releases me and asks, "How will you break Griffin out of prison and rescue him without getting yourself caught? We can't rely on me to wake him up while I perform the ritual dressing of the body, as we've done in the past. I'm being watched too closely now. There will be guards around me."

"We'll need to move him fast so the guards don't realize he's still alive. And we need to get him out in time for the meeting with Margareath." I tell her the plan I've been hatching in my head for the past few hours. "We have to do it now."

VIENNE LOOKS DOWN AT the concrete floor, absorbing everything I've said. "He won't ever be able to come back," she says, her voice flat.

I know that. He's too controversial. And if I truly love Griffin, how can I return without him? The question nags at my brain, but I push the thought away. I just have to deal with the immediate threats. Rescuing Griffin. Returning with my parents. Saving the country. I'll have to deal with the consequences later.

I look over again at Vienne, determined to hash out as many aspects of my plan as I can before I need to meet Margareath at midnight. Our plan to free prisoners has always been risky. Letting them free, on the condition they'll spy on Mid Country for a period of time before I allow them back into the country, is dangerous. Vienne and I are relying on a criminal to help our cause. The person who broke our rules is now our main source of intelligence.

"What can you tell me about Margareath's situation over in Mid?" I ask.

"Margareath was helpful, but I've only met her once so far. Tonight was going to be our second rendezvous. But she'll be able to lead you and Griffin into the city."

"City?"

"Yes, she's managed to penetrate their inner society."

"And she carries no anger against me or East Country? Will she be any threat to us?"

"I'm not sure. She wants to get back to her family, so she's trying her best to gather enough information so we'll let her return. She wants to see her children."

"So she has strong motivation to cooperate?" I calculate Margareath as a resource.

"Yes, but be careful with her. She's desperate to return. In some ways that's just as dangerous."

I nod, taking Vienne's psychology lesson to heart. She looks down, seemingly disheartened.

"It'll be ok, Vienne."

"You'll both be gone when I give birth," she murmurs. "I know it is a small thing in light of everything. But I just thought... I imagined..."

"Maybe I can sneak back in at the right time. Still be here. We'll meet every two weeks like you were going to do with Margareath. I'll be able to see you when your time is near."

"You can meet me for a little while, but when we start nirogene collection again, we'll put up armor glass along the entire border. We won't be able to talk after that. And by the time I'm ready to give birth, you'll be very pregnant too. It won't be safe for you to keep traveling back to the border."

"Take heart. I won't leave you destitute. We'll find a way."

She shakes her head. "I'm sorry. Here you've granted me ruling power over the country, something a woman hasn't done in over almost a hundred years, and I'm thinking about myself, not the country."

I'm still for a moment. "A woman did watch over this country in the last hundred years. Me." I reach out and hold her hand within mine. "When they find out it was a pair of women saving us, everyone will have to admit the Fertility Accord is ridiculous."

Vienne gives a slight laugh. Then she grows serious again. "If you can't cross the border or meet me at the armor glass, it's okay. Promise me you'll be careful. You're carrying a baby now too. Don't take unnecessary risks."

Her warning is almost laughable as the risks I'm taking just by crossing into Mid Country are huge. But I don't negate her words. "I'll be as careful as possible."

"You come back to take the Elected position. You hear me? Promise me!" Vienne's voice is urgent.

"I will. I promise."

She stares at me, unwavering as her eyes are locked on mine. "All right." She stands and fixes her skirt back around her legs. "Then let's tell Griffin our plan."

We walk back into his side of the prison. Again he's sitting on the cot with his head in his hands, but he stands when the door opens.

"What's going on?" he asks, seeing our serious faces.

We request the guards to give us some privacy and then walk close to Griffin. No one must hear our plans.

"We have to go, Griffin," I say.

He looks down. "Yes, I agree. You and Vienne, you shouldn't be here. Shouldn't be seen with me."

"No! That's not what I mean."

"She means you and she need to leave," says Vienne. She puts a hand on Griffin's arm. I can't tell if it's to steady him or to give herself something to lean on as she utters these words. "We won't let the execution happen, and Aloy... she wants to see for herself what Mid Country is planning."

We tell him the details of our plan and what we'll need from him. Griffin is quiet, listening to everything. I tell him my reasons for needing to leave. All of them except the pregnancy. For some reason, that's the one thing I don't reveal. It doesn't seem right to tell him in prison like this. Vienne looks at me, but my eyes beg her to let the secret go untold for now.

I tell Griffin how the executions work. How it's up to the prisoner to decide when to drink the hemlock. How when he or she is ready, the drink is brought in, and I'm called to watch. How there's a window into his room from which guards will watch him drink the poison, so he'll have to put on the act. We give him the details of how we plan to break him out of prison. How we don't have time to say goodbye to anyone, including Brinn or Tomlin. Griffin nods, taking it all in. When we finish a few minutes later, we both get up to leave. Me to gather provisions for our trip and Vienne to procure the items she'll need for the break-out.

"Around seven, tell the guards you're ready for the hemlock," I say. "Then they'll come get me. That should give us enough time to run to the hills by midnight."

Griffin stands again as we both exit the room.

"Don't you dare drink anything before we come back," Vienne says.

Griffin manages a small smile. "I promise, I won't take a sip."

"Good," Vienne says, her voice breaking in her throat. She walks up near to him again, standing at his side. She grips his arm with one hand and her stomach with the other. "Griffin, thank you for this baby. Whatever happens after this, I'll always have this from both of you." She looks from Griffin to me and back again. "You both take care of each other. Griffin, I'm relying on you to get Aloy home again. Do you understand?"

Griffin says, "I'll do everything in my power. You take care of that baby. Give it the best life, all right?" He talks like he'll never see it.

Griffin bends down and gives Vienne a long hug. When Vienne turns she has tears in her eyes. She walks steadily out of the room without looking back. I proceed after her but then glance once more at Griffin. He stares out after me, his eyes firm. When we lock eyes, I know we're thinking the same things.

We both know there's a chance neither of us will be back to see Vienne's baby or East Country ever again.

Then I turn and follow Vienne out to the lobby.

✦

By seven that night, when there's a tap on our door and the guards come to get me, we're both ready. No one questions that for this particular prisoner, both Vienne and I go to watch the suicide. We each take a horse and follow the guards who walk in front of us on foot. It's a slow pace, and I can't help my heart from beating hard in my chest.

Vienne and I leave the horses as close to the prison doors as possible. Then we walk in through the lobby. I take a long look around, knowing I won't see this gruesome building again for a long time. We get to Griffin's cell and are escorted to the viewing section.

The crystal cup of hemlock sits on Griffin's side of the floor, halfway between the cot and the armor glass. Griffin is standing next to it. The door to his side of the room is locked. I shut the door to our room softly. There's no window on our side, so Vienne and I will be free to express ourselves without anyone watching. I see a guard peering in through the window on Griffin's side, but he steps back out of view when our eyes meet, giving us a slight bit of privacy. So now it is just me, Vienne, and Griffin staring at each other.

Vienne walks to the glass and puts a hand up to it. Griffin follows suit, bowing his head to each of us. He puts his hand up to the glass to match Vienne's. And then he beckons me forward with his other hand. I oblige him and Vienne, flattening my palm against the glass too. The three of us stand in a triangle, our hands across from each other through the clear material.

After a moment, Griffin nods his head resolutely and backs up.

Vienne and I do the same, moving to sit on the wooden bench away from the glass. Griffin picks up the crystal cup and puts it to his lips. I close my eyes for a second, asking the heavens for help to ensure not a drop happens to touch his lips in the ensuing process. I know what the cup holds. Pure, unadulterated, hemlock. As was our plan, Vienne did not sneak to the guards to replace the clear fluid with sleeping draught as she did for Margareath. What Griffin holds in front of him is the real thing.

I open my eyes again and see Griffin clutching the glass close to his face. His eyes look strange—far away, like he's thinking of something else. I have a creepy feeling like spiders walking across the inner walls of my stomach. At that moment, I beg the heavens for something else. That Griffin will truly follow our predetermined plan. That he won't take it upon himself now to change tactics and remove himself from the complicated situation, thinking it would be better for us.

I stare at him, willing Griffin to do what we decided. Not to take matters into his own hands. Suddenly, I'm not sure why I didn't consider Griffin's intentions more closely when hatching my plan. Drinking the hemlock would be just like him—careless for his own life if he thought his actions would protect me. Like when he got between me and the long arrows at the town hall. He never actually said he'd follow our plan. He only listened to us. If he took himself out of the equation now, then I might not cross into Mid Country. I would still be here to watch over Vienne and fulfill my Elected duties. I'm sure he thinks it would be safer for me to stay. As he lingers over the cup, I'm tempted to run out of the room and smash open the door on his side, flinging the hemlock out of his hand.

Vienne grips my hand hard, cutting off all the blood from the area. She must be worried about the same thing, but she refuses to take her eyes off Griffin to look at me.

I won't be fast enough. If I bolt out of this room into Griffin's, he'll still be able to finish drinking some of the liquid. So I stare at him too, just shaking my head back and forth, tears already starting to stream from my eyes. *Don't you dare do it*, I think. *Don't you dare. You wouldn't. You wouldn't dare!*

What he doesn't realize is his death won't protect me. It will kill me.

Griffin moves the cup away from his face so we can see his lips. He mouths one last word to us and then lifts the cup back up to his mouth. "Goodbye."

I jump up, banging my hands against the armor glass. "Nooooo!" I'm screaming. Tears gush down my face. I'm sure the guards outside the doors can hear me yell, but I don't care. All I can think of is stopping Griffin.

Then abruptly, he tilts his head back. The liquid travels past his face, and the glass crashes in back of him onto the floor. Immediately, blood bubbles out of his lips. He falls to the floor, thrashing, his arms rigid but moving in spasms at his sides. He gasps and his whole body shakes.

I'm still screaming, holding on to Vienne hard with my fingers digging into her shoulders. I see tears falling from her eyes too, but she utters no sound. I can barely look across the glass to Griffin's body. After a few more excruciating moments, he's finally still. I rub my arms across my face, trying to rid my eyes of the tears that refuse to stop flowing.

I have to see him. Now! I burst open the door to our side of the room, Vienne close behind. We get to the door leading into Griffin's side where two guards are standing outside.

"Let us in, please." Vienne says, her voice resonating with calmness I can't muster at the moment.

"Are you sure, Electeds?" the man asks. "The process might not yet be complete."

"Let us in," says Vienne softly. Her voice is quiet but still holds immense authority.

"Yes, Madame."

"Would you mind closing the shutter?" she asks. "We'd like a few minutes of privacy with Griffin's body."

"Of course," says the guard, his eyes deferential, set on the floor. He avoids my red face. I realize he's one of the same guards who presided over Maran's death. I wonder if he's still thinking about what the term "lesbian" means. But before I can wonder if he's deciphered the word, the guard complies with our wishes and unlocks the door to Griffin's room.

I run in and fall to the floor next to his body. Vienne follows but watches the door in back of us until it clicks closed and the shutter indeed moves across the window, blocking the guards' view of us.

Then she turns to us both on the floor. "Griffin, it's okay now," she says. "Get up."

36.

I WATCH INTENSELY AS Griffin's head moves. Then his arm comes up. He grips me around the wrist. Finally, his eyes open and his mouth turns into a rueful grin.

"Jerk!" I yell.

"What?" he asks, smiling wickedly. "You wanted it to look convincing." He licks the blood from his lips where he bit himself to create the effect. The cup of hemlock is strewn across the concrete.

"It was a little too real," I say. "There was... the blood and all. I don't think I told you about that part."

"Vienne told me."

Vienne turns to me. "I'm sorry, Aloy. But we needed it look authentic. The guards specifically looked for your reaction when we walked out of the viewing room." I glance at my wife with surprise. She's calculating when she needs to be. Not a wilting flower at all.

"Be careful," says Vienne to Griffin and me. "Make sure not to touch any of it." She points to the hemlock droplets strewn over the floor. "If it gets onto your hands and then you happen to touch your face later, the stuff might still be potent."

"She's right," I say, getting up gingerly, and pulling Griffin's arm to lift him. I'm still dazed from my concern over Griffin, but I realize the need to move fast. We only have minutes to pull off the next phase of our plan.

Vienne stands guard by the door to make sure no one intrudes and the shutter stays closed. She pulls a cloak out from underneath her own. Griffin catches it across the room and pulls it around himself. He and Vienne both take off their shoes as we planned. Vienne wraps the laces of Griffin's boots up her calves, stuffing socks into the toes. Griffin pinches her dainty slippers onto his feet and pulls her cape down so it's covering most of the footwear. His heels stick out the back of her shoes.

Next, Griffin lifts the hood of his cape up over his head. Vienne takes off her own cape and lies down on the floor, ensuring none of her exposed skin touches the stream of hemlock. With their identical capes both on, it'll be hard to tell them apart in the dark. The hardest part will still be getting them through the lit building, though.

We spread Vienne's cape across her, so no parts of her body show, except for the tips of Griffin's boots. When we think we're ready, we knock on the door for the guards to let us out.

"Thank you," I say to them when they open it. I try to act like I'm still composing myself. I don't look them in the eyes and neither does Griffin who stands next to me, bent over, clutching his stomach. We need him to look shorter so he can match Vienne's height. Her pregnancy is something we can use.

"Are you all right, Madame Elected?" one of the guards asks toward Griffin's stooped frame.

"She's all right," I say, interjecting so Griffin doesn't have to speak. "Just overtaken by the events tonight. With this and the pregnancy, it's a lot for her to take in. If you'll excuse us."

"Of course," says one of the guards. He steps aside so we have ample room to pass.

I lift Vienne's body, covered in the cape, off the floor. I act like it's Griffin's body, heavy and muscular. I pretend to strain my knees under the supposed weight of it. And, in fact, feeling so sick with my pregnancy, even lifting Vienne's slender body is hard for me. I want to retch as I stand up, my head spinning, but I push on.

"Do you need help, Elected?" asks a guard.

"No, thank you. I can manage." But I'm sweating, holding Vienne across my arms. Even Griffin looks over at me from under the hood, his eyebrows raised. I see his confusion at my hardship, but I can't very well explain my pregnancy to him right here, so I disregard his look.

We walk as quickly as we can out of the corridor into the lobby. My eyes open wide as I see at least a hundred guards milling around the lobby. As soon as they see us, they stop in their tracks, making a pathway for us toward the front door. They grow quiet and then their hands move up into the traditional symbol of respect. They hold both of their arms outward at forty five degree angles toward each other. First I think it's to show compassion for me and Vienne, but then I realize it's also a sign of respect for Griffin's supposedly dead body. He was one of their peers. A guard like them.

I nod at the large group, not quite catching their eyes.

The three of us exit the building, Griffin still bent over. We walk down the front steps with most of the guards all watching our backs. The young guard who told us about the explosion waits at the bottom of the stairs, holding our horses' reins.

I think we're home free now that we're out here in the dark, but a gust of wind gives us the biggest threat of the night. I feel the blowing air in my face. Before I can warn Griffin, a current rushes by, whisking up the bottom of his cloak. A few inches of Vienne's shoe shows through, displaying how Griffin's heel sticks out the back of it.

The guard looks down, and I see his eyes widen at the sight of Griffin's foot. He's too stunned to say anything, so I just propel us forward as fast as I can. I catch Griffin's eye and we both know we only have a second before the kid regains his voice and says something that'll ruin our getaway. Griffin climbs up onto one horse. I climb onto the other, still holding Vienne's limp body. She's doing her best to stay still.

We gallop at as fast a pace as I can manage without letting go of Vienne's body spread out across my lap.

"Go!" I command the horses when we're out of earshot of the kid. "He saw your foot! He'll be telling someone for sure, and it'll only take the guards a matter of minutes to mobilize."

"If they believe him," says Vienne from across my lap. The cloak has come off her face, and she's holding onto my waist with both arms.

"We'll know for sure in a moment," Griffin says. And then he leans forward, reaching out a hand to slap my horse's rump. "Ya!" he shouts, and in an instant both of our horses pick up their pace.

We reach the stables in a matter of seconds and lead the horses around to the empty stall. Vienne deftly slides off the horse, letting the cape drop around her. Griffin and I dismount as well, and the three of us stand in a tight circle.

"You take care," I say to Vienne. I don't know what other advice to tell my best friend in these last moments. I don't want to leave her. Walking away from the one person who completely accepts me as I am, feels like something heavy pressing against my heart. I want to pull Vienne back onto the horse and take her with us, but I remind myself she's strong and East Country needs her to lead in my absence. Suddenly,

I look at her with wide eyes. "You were the person who whistled at the Ellipse, distracting the Technologist five years ago. The one hiding in the pavilion the night I snuck out, weren't you?"

Vienne looks up into my eyes and nods, surprised I've deduced this. I realize she never meant to reveal that fact. Never wanted me to know she was responsible for saving my life. Always trying to bolster my self-confidence instead of having me think I needed support from others.

Griffin doesn't understand this exchange. He watches as Vienne and I look at each other. I try to say with my eyes what we can't say now that our time is so rushed. How much I'll miss her. How good of a wife she's been.

We hear horses' hoof beats in the distance, coming closer, and Griffin breaks in. "We've got to hurry."

"I'll take care of them," Vienne assures us, gesturing toward the group of guards rushing to the White House front doors.

We nod. Then Vienne says the only thing that seems appropriate—the prisoners' burial words that by ritual are her task to say over the deceased. It's what she would have said if Griffin had gone through with his suicide tonight. Her voice is rushed, but it still sounds like velvet. "May the heavens watch over your souls. May you find peace and happiness in this world and all others. I bless you." She presses a hand to her mouth and kisses it.

I reach out to hug her hard. Griffin does the same, the three of us locked in a tight embrace.

"Now go!" Vienne commands. "May the new day be good to you!"

I grab the satchels I've packed for the trip and toss one to Griffin. He's already put his shoes back on. I look once more at Vienne as we start running out of the stable. The moonlight illuminates her golden hair, making her look ethereal.

"Go!" she mouths quietly to me.

I lock eyes with her one last time, blink hard to capture this fleeting picture, and then lean forward into a run. Even though I've promised to meet Vienne in two weeks, I don't truly know when we'll see each other again. Leaving her now feels too final.

In the darkness, Griffin and I stay side-by-side. Years of play fighting come in use now as I push my lungs to exhaustion. Griffin keeps pace with me. We don't talk because we can't afford to waste breath and energy. But he's watching me like a hawk as I'm obviously straining my body with this run.

Griffin looks over to me. "Are you all right? You look pale."

"I'm fine," I say, taking a deep breath. It's still not the right time to tell him I'm pregnant.

After three hours, we see the hills looming in front of us. I spy the figures of two townspeople walking back and forth along the border. Since it is dark now, the group moving the rocks at the mouth of the cave has stopped its work and gone home. Without light, people dislodging the boulders can't be safe.

I walk up to one of the guards. "Elected!" he says in surprise. He's so astonished to see me he doesn't look closely at Griffin's cloaked figure.

"Hello," I say. "Have you found more survivors?"

"Yes! Twelve men crawled out of the mine with just minor injuries. We'll still be looking for more people as soon as dawn breaks tomorrow."

"Good," I say. "And the guards who ran in after Dorine?"

The guard looks down. "They're gone, Elected."

I swallow, feeling nausea creep up my throat again, but I keep a stoic face. "And Dorine?"

"She's gone as well. Not much remains of her or her son's body. We excavated them earlier this evening."

"All right." Vienne will ensure everyone receives a proper burial, even Dorine. I'd like to offer more consoling words right now, but the urgency of our timing forces me to stay mission-focused.

"Madame Elected and I've brought you a meal. It must be tiresome out here at this late hour, especially after the explosion earlier today," I say. "Will you bring this food to your comrade? You can eat together. We'll watch the border for a moment."

"Thank you very much, Electeds," he says, bowing multiple times as he backs up. After a moment he's met up with his friend, and they sit together, already tucking into the bread and apples Vienne prepared.

Griffin and I walk farther down the border and then glance back to see if they're watching us. Convinced the two men are focused on their dinner, we start to climb the border. We're supposed to meet Margareath at the hill's peak, a place I and none of my people have ever been before. Part of me is excited to see past the borders of East, but another part feels the danger of so callously disregarding another whole Accord.

The climb itself takes about twenty minutes. When we arrive at the crest, my eyes focus on something in the distance on Mid Country's side of the border. We're up high enough to see for miles now.

"What is that, Griffin?" The views from here are so staggering, my voice quivers.

"They're not just tinkering with electricity like I was." Hundreds, if not thousands, of lights dance on the horizon inside Mid's territory.

"Doesn't look like it. I wonder how else Mid's breaking the Technology Accord."

Griffin just shakes his head, but his eyes are wide, like mine.

I think I know the answer. If they have lights, I was probably right about airrides too. And who knows what other machines they've resurrected.

We wait in the darkness, glancing around to see if Margareath is near.

After we've stared at the lights for a few minutes in silence, Griffin looks over at me. "Aloy, I have to ask."

"Yes?" I'm alone with him again for the first time in a long while. I know what I'd like him to ask. I blush just thinking about the things bold enough to pass through my head now. How could I ever have thought I didn't want someone to touch me? Now it's all I can think about.

But he's not on the same wavelength at the exact moment. Instead he asks, "You and Vienne broke the law to let the prisoners go? You wouldn't put them to death?"

I look over at Griffin slowly. "Yes, we broke the Technology Accord. We didn't think it was moral to continue killing our people for creating technology."

"That's exactly why you make the best leader of East Country. You say you're going to bring back your parents to rule. But why can't you keep the position? You're the leader I always hoped for. And as for getting information on Mid, I can do that for you. As much as I want us to be together, it's safer for you to stay here."

I look down at the ground, my cheeks growing red. This is the moment I need to tell him about my pregnancy. How the search for my parents and for information on Mid aren't the only reasons pressing me to leave East Country. We're alone. This is the right time.

I start to shake my head and explain, "Griffin... I..."

"I love you, Aloy. But you can't leave East because of me. I'll find a way back to you eventually, no matter what." He takes a final step toward me and holds my cheek in his palm. Unlike the last time we were this close, I am the one to start kissing him first. I feel the muscles in his arms as I hold him close.

For the first time, I realize it's easy for me to return Griffin's words. "I love you too."

We pull back from each other and look once more toward the blinking lights on the horizon. Then I take a deep breath, about to explain our predicament in detailed terms—give him the explanation of why I must leave East, at least for the time being. That I want to go with him, but there are other reasons I'm leaving too. Again, though, he's too fast.

I can't utter anything before he says, "My father... will we see him on the other side?"

My shoulders slump, realizing what Griffin is asking. "You want to know if we saved him too?"

"Yes," Griffin's voice is low. "Will he meet us in Mid Country?"

I look at Griffin whose face is now cast down. Finally, the truth is out. He wants his father to be alive. I answer him quietly. "No, we didn't save him."

Griffin continues to look down and nods.

"His crime was violence," I say, hating to mouth the explanation. "He was too dangerous to save."

"I understand." Griffin is resolute, picking his head back up and looking at me.

My biggest fear is that Maran's prophesy will come true—that Griffin will turn against me and Vienne, ultimately agreeing with his father's rash beliefs. But for now, at least, I know we're united. I reach out to squeeze his hand, about to proceed with my big revelation.

And that's when I see a figure walking toward us, crouched low.

"Margareath?" I whisper into the darkness.

"Madame Elected?"

I breathe a sigh of relief. It's her.

"Margareath, it's me, the Elected. And Griffin. Madame Elected isn't here."

She looks toward us, her eyes fearful.

"Don't worry," Griffin says. "We aren't here to hurt you."

Margareath doesn't ask us if we're here to take her back into East Country, as I'd suspected she might. Instead she asks, "What do you want?"

"We need you to take me across the border," says Griffin. "I need to stay with you for a while. See for myself what's going on in Mid Country."

"Take both of us," I say, ignoring Griffin's look. Then I stare out in front of me at the pervasive technology alight on Mid's horizon. More quietly I say, "Yes, I need to come too."

"Ohhh," says Margareath. Her eyes are suddenly bright with excitement. "You won't believe what they have over there. It's amazing. I can't wait to show you!"

I look at her, cocking my head to one side. "Amazing?"

"Yes, it's simply unbelievable!" She's excited now, happy to be able to take us with her. She starts walking forward, and Griffin and I begin following her.

Maybe she just yearns for company. So I give in a little, thinking of Vienne's warning about Margareath's desperation to see her family.

"Margareath," I say from behind her. "Your family is doing well. They're coping. They'll see you soon. After we finish this mission, I'll let you go back to them. I promise."

Margareath stops and turns. She looks at me, an odd expression dancing across her brow. She lifts a hand to her forehead, one word escaping her mouth. "Who?"

I stop midstride and stare at her. "Margareath, your family? Your kids? Your three kids?"

Again Margareath looks at us, her eyes darting back and forth between me and Griffin. Then she shrugs and raises her hand. "Come on!" she says. "I have so much to show you!"

Griffin and I lock eyes behind Margareath's back, exchanging a sharp glance. I lift my eyebrows in alarm and he does the same, shaking his head. She doesn't remember her family?

Griffin grabs my hand, and then we both walk forward. Whatever Margareath has to show us, now we have to see. With Griffin's hand firm in mine, I look behind me as the crest of the hill begins to disappear behind us. I stand on my tiptoes, looking back one last time at my country.

"Don't worry," I say silently toward my home. "I'll come back for you. I won't leave you neglected for long."

Then we begin our descent into Mid Country.

THE END

Acknowledgements

There were so many people who made it possible for me to write and publish The Elected Series. Thank you from the bottom of my heart for all of your support, expertise, and enthusiasm. Thank you to:

Mom and Dad for reading every word as I wrote them and for your unfailing interest that kept me going. You instilled a love of storytelling by reading to me every night as a child and writing down the stories I "dictated" before I could scribble them myself. Jason for having one hundred percent confidence that I would write books and publish them. Your belief in me makes unbelievable things seem possible. I appreciate the many car rides spent discussing plot and character development. My oldest daughter who tells me "Mama's writing" anytime I sit at my laptop and for allowing me to write ELECTED on maternity leave with her. My youngest daughter who enabled me to write the next book while on maternity leave the second time around. Both of the main female characters in this book get pieces of their personalities (spunk, bravery, adventurousness, and compassion) from the two of you precious girls.

My agent, Sara D'Emic and the team at Talcott Notch, for believing in the story of ELECTED and taking a chance on me. Sara, I knew the second you talked to me on the phone about ELECTED and discussed Aloy, Griffin, and Vienne like they were real people, you understood and could nurture the book. May there be many writing years ahead where we gush about our mutual love of Halloween!

Silence in the Library Publishing, who saw ELECTED's potential and brought me onto the team. Janine Spendlove, Ron Garner, Tanya Spackman, Kelli Neier, Bryan Young, Maggie Allen, and Amberley Young, thank you for your dedication to making ELECTED happen. My editors: Diana Bocco, Kara Leigh Miller, Julie Wingfield, Tricia Kristufek, Eden Plantz, Kelly Coffey, and Emily Ward for guiding ELECTED through multiple iterations to ensure it flowed and sounded like life-on-pages. My cover artist Suzannah Safi. You worked with such grace and efficiency as we determined what feelings ELECTED's cover should evoke. Misty Williams and Suzanne van Rooyen, my publicists, for tirelessly working to promote ELECTED and answering coordination messages so fast. I barely press send on a note before you respond with the much-appreciated information.

Ron Romanski from Preactive Marketing for making my website and giving me advice on social media.

My current writing critique group members: Clifton Tibbetts, Jon Sourbeer, and Vivian Bloomberg for your unfailing enthusiasm and the detailed analysis you've given the book. Every time I'm on the phone with you, your dedication to write inspires me. To my earliest writing critique group members: Kellye, Stephanie, Mo, and Linda, for picking ELECTED when I asked you which of my novel ideas you'd want to read and for encouraging me to join the Society of Children's Book Writers and Illustrators (SCBWI).

My friendly legal team (literally made up of my friends) Leif and Heather. The time you took reviewing my various contracts was invaluable.

Beta readers who peeked at ELECTED when it was a very... very rough draft: Erin, Kat, Kim, Luke, Amy, Jon, Pina, Matt, Colleen, and Sara. You told me ELECTED seemed like a real book you couldn't get out of your head, and that made me feel like a real writer.

My writer friends: Diana Peterfreund, Nancy Grossman, and Debra Shigley for giving me advice on the industry early-on. The entire DC Mafia Writers group, made up of a welcoming bunch of literary gurus. The MD/DW/WVA SCBWI chapter that offers a breadth of writing information through their conferences and events.

To all of my long-time friends as well as the new ones from social media, for Tweeting, blogging, Facebooking, emailing, talking and, in general, sharing info about ELECTED. There is an army of "East Countrymen" that got this book into the hands of readers.

THANK YOU!

Excerpt from SUSPECTED

The second book in THE ELECTED SERIES

WE STAND IN FRONT of the double glass doors for a moment, looking at each other to bolster our resolve. "No going back after this," Griffin says.

"Nope."

"One more chance to turn back, Aloy. I'd walk back with you to East tonight, if you wanted."

"Nope," I say again and press firmly on the entrance door. Inside, cool filtered air hits our faces as we pass through into the sterile hallway. It's eerily quiet here, and for a moment I wonder if we misunderstood and stepped inside the wrong building. "Maybe we should turn back," I start to say before a voice in front of us interrupts me.

"Right this way." A man stands up from behind a high counter to our side. "Come to register?"

"Yes," says Griffin. He drops my hand and goes to shake the official's, but no hand is offered to Griffin. Finally, Griffin looks away, confused, and pulls his hand back. Maybe they don't have the same customs here. I watch to see if the official will bow to us or make some other kind of sign, but he just looks down on his desk, adjusting thick glasses.

"Where do you originate from?" asks the man. He still doesn't look up.

"West Country," I say without hesitation.

"You're late." He glances at us, pushing the rims of his black frames low on his nose.

I cough a little, thinking the jig is up. "Doesn't matter, though," says the man before I can even think what to say next. "We'll take you either way. Always good to increase our numbers. Don't know how you survived out there longer than most, though. Your brethren all mostly came a year ago. Just dribs and drabs of people now." The man seems to be talking to himself now, staring down at a book in front of him.

"What do we have to do to register?" asks Griffin. He's leaning forward just a bit, trying to see the big book behind the desk.

But the official doesn't try to hide it. At once, he grasps hold of both thick ends and grunts, pulling it up on top of the counter.

"You need to sign in. Do you know how to write?"

"Yes," I answer, surprised at his question. Were the people in West illiterate?

"Sorry, just have to ask. You're all pretty uncivilized over there."

I try not to seem offended. It's not even my country he's talking about, but the superior tone he uses when referring to West is unnerving.

"All right, sign your name here." He points to a blank line on one of the large, yellowed pages in front of us. Griffin grabs the offered writing implement first, scrawling something noncommittal for his name. All I can make out is a large G. The rest is purposefully indistinguishable.

The man twitches his nose at Griffin's scrawl but doesn't ask him to redo the signature. "Ok, your turn," he says, handing me another writing implement. It's not like the charcoal sticks we used in East Country. This stick is white and long with a blue tip on the end. I set it against a spot on the page and start to write an A-L-O, before thinking better of it and finishing my A-L with an I-C-E-N. Alicen. That'll be my name here. It could be either a boy's or girl's name, ambiguous. I like how the thin stick glides across the page, and I take an extra second letting the letter N slide off my hand into text.

"What do you call this?" I ask the man, holding the writing implement out in the middle of us.

"What? The pen?" he asks.

I nod.

"You've never seen one of these before? The rest of your people did."

I stop holding the pen in front of my face with interest, instead dropping it with a tiny clack onto the white desk in front of us. I need to be more careful. We don't know anything about West, and even this tiny question could show us for who we really are.

"We were poor," I respond, my voice low and quiet as if I'm ashamed. I don't have to fake the tone of my answer. I'm so scared, my voice cracks easily on its own.

This seems to pacify the official. "Many of you people from West were." He shakes his head in condemnation and turns the book back toward himself. "All right, I'm going to assign you places to stay. It'll just take a few moments. In the meantime, look through this listing of jobs. Everyone works here, so you'll need to pick something."

He thrusts a thinner book in front of us and turns it to the first page. After each job, there's a short description and two numbers in parentheses. Griffin immediately sees the listing for "Animal Caretaker" with the number "10" in back of it and another number "2."

"What do the numbers mean?" he asks.

"Oh," says the official looking up at us from behind another stack of papers. "The first number is the amount of openings we have in that area. The second is how long the earliest one's been available."

Griffin puts his finger on the page and silently traces the description next to the listing while glancing back up at me. I lean in, reading what he's pointing to.

"Animal Caretaker: Consists of generating clones of existing mammals, reptiles, insects, and birds. With more experience, creation of new species."

This is not what either of us were expecting, and we both scan down the page to see if there's anything else involving care of animals. But this is the only listing dealing with animals at all. Griffin sighs, and shakes his head in disgust. It's almost enough to catch the attention of the official, though, so I don't answer it back with any recognition. I just keep looking down the list for any job that I could do.

"I'll take this one," Griffin says, motioning to the official. The two of them start to talk about Griffin's experience, and the man is obviously satisfied. This time he's clicking keys on some type of machine, not using another pen to input Griffin's information.

"All right, this will just take a moment to go through the system and get accepted," the official explains, pointing to the small, square machine in front of him. "I'm sure you'll get the job, though. Don't worry."

I keep peering down the list. The jobs are listed in alphabetical order. I page through to the middle and see "*Engineer (20-1), Guard (80-4), Holder (90-3)*." I grimace at "Holder," redoubling my efforts to find something I'll be qualified for. On the same page as Holder, I see one interesting listing. It catches my eye because of the numbers in back of it. "*Historian (1-110)*." I squint at it closer. There's only one position? And it's been open for a hundred and ten months? That's a long time. I read the description, not quite understanding it even after the third review.

"Historian (1-110): Knows things forgotten."

261

"What's this one?" I ask the official. He's almost finished typing in Griffin's experience into his machine, but he stops to quickly look at the job I'm pointing to. Once he sees it, he stands up, leaving the machine altogether.

"I'm sure you don't want that one," he says, squinting at me. He looks at me harder than he's done before, this time removing his glasses completely. Maybe I've made some blunder. Requested something I shouldn't.

"I don't know. I might," I say. "What does this job entail?"

He doesn't answer me. Just states the obvious. "It's been open for a very long time. No one is qualified."

This makes me mad in a way I remember feeling years ago when I asked my parents if I could leave the White House and constantly got "no" for an answer. It makes me feel young and stubborn again. My fingers start twitching in my clasped hands.

"Well, maybe I am. How do you know?"

"Historian? You think you know things others don't?"

At this, I stare at the man without looking away or down at the floor in defeat. His thick brown hair leaves sweat marks on his forehead. He's not good-looking, and his face, all contorted, as he looks at me makes him look even more like a troll from my old fairy tales.

"I might," I say. "Try me."

The man *humphs*. "Fine. What is a turbine?"

"Any of various machines in which the kinetic energy of a moving fluid is converted to mechanical power by the impulse or reaction of the fluid with a series of buckets, paddles, or blades arrayed about the circumference of a wheel or cylinder," I blurt out without even giving it a second thought.

Both Griffin and the official stare back at me with wide eyes. I shut my mouth hard. What have I just done?

The official starts to stammer, still looking at me in amazement. "Umm... I suppose that answer is correct. I'm... I'm not too sure, actually. Let me just type it in here."

He bends down to thumb my answer into his machine, asking me to repeat parts of it a few times. We all wait in silence as the machine registers my response and pings back after just a few seconds. It gives a small, upbeat "ding."

The official looks up at me, eyes still wide. "Ok, answer this then. What kind of weapon did governments use back in two thousand thirty

262

for assassination?"

I look at the official like he's joking with me. But when he just stares back, completely serious, I answer, "Long arrows."

He types my answer in again, and it only takes a second for the machine to ding.

This time the official fumbles nervously with the keys in front of him, typing in something fast. He peers at the screen, pushing his glasses back on his face to see clearly. Finally, he looks back at me and says, "Ummm... all right. What year was the last Accord dictated and which one was it?"

I think back to my lesson with Tomlin the day I saw my first execution in East. I got the answer wrong back then, but this time I'll be right. "The Ship Accord. Twenty-one fifteen."

The official chokes loudly into his hand and immediately turns back to his machine to log my answer. The computer doesn't just beep once this time. It comes back with a fast "bing, bing bing." The official turns to me, his mouth open wide.

"You got the job," he says. He thumbs through the book again, looking once more at how long the position has been open. More than two years.

Griffin mouths "Way to go" at me while the troll-like man paws through the book. Griffin smiles big, proud that I've been able to knock the official down a peg or two.

"How... how... did you know those things?" the official stammers, looking up once again.

I shuffle my feet in front of me. I can't very well tell him I'm the Elected in my country and was raised on all this information. So I just look over his shoulder, letting my facial expression go flat and closed. "Books," I say. "My father collected books." It isn't a lie, so it comes off my lips easily.

"Well..." The official shakes his head in confusion, trying to comprehend how I've been able to answer questions that others haven't. "Report to building thirteen tomorrow morning at eight am sharp. You got the job. But," and at this he smiles slightly, feeling his own power leveling the playing field once again. "You'll be on probation for a few months. You'll probably have to come back here in a few weeks and pick a new job."

I just nod noncommittally, not wanting to fully acknowledge the official's warning. He starts talking to Griffin again, inputting the last bits of Griffin's answers into the machine. The two converse back and forth and it affords me a few seconds to flip through the big book of names on the official's desk again. I pretend that I'm just checking my signature, but it doesn't matter. The official is so caught up typing in Griffin's information that he doesn't pay me any attention.

I'm looking for just one thing in the book, and it's not my signature. I flip back ten pages to a date months in the past. My fingers fly across the names. I'm frustrated that I can't find what I need until my eyes finally rest on the hard scrawl that I've seen many times in my life. This signature's written on official documents. Birth certificates. Execution warrants. Speeches. I can't help smiling slightly, and I pull my finger along the small indentation the two signatures made into the pulpy paper.

"Claraleese and Soyer." My parents' names. They're here.

About the Author

Rori Shay is a member of the Society of Children's Book Writers and Illustrators (SCBWI). She lives with her husband, kids, and two proficient hair-shedders: Misch the cat and Gerry the 90-lb black lab. Rori studied public relations and marketing at the University of Maryland and received an MBA from George Washington University. She enjoys traveling, running, reading, pumpkin-picking, and snow-shoeing!

Email: rorishay@gmail.com
Website: www.rorishay.com
Twitter: @RoriShayWrites
Facebook: www.facebook.com/RoriShayWrites
Goodreads: www.goodreads.com/author/show/7266322.Rori_Shay

Pre-order now from Silence in the Library Publishing

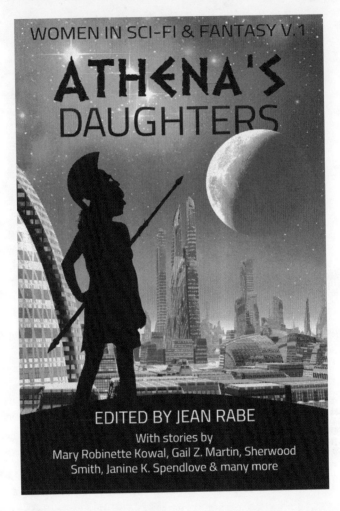

WOMEN IN SCI-FI & FANTASY V.1

ATHENA'S DAUGHTERS

EDITED BY JEAN RABE

With stories by
Mary Robinette Kowal, Gail Z. Martin, Sherwood
Smith, Janine K. Spendlove & many more

From a young girl facing a life-threatening crisis at Lunar Camp to a crew of elderly women graced with the power of Greek Gods, you'll find an engaging and diverse range of science fiction and fantasy stories by women, about women.

With an introduction by former NASA astronaut Pamela Melroy and illustrations by Autumn Frederickson and Betsy Waddell, this anthology is not to be missed.

Coming soon from Silence in the Library Publishing

All sixteen-year-old Jacob Evans wants is to win the heart of Emilia Gray, but with order in the magical world crumbling, war threatening, and Emilia's boyfriend living across the hall, he may never have the chance.

Jacob Evans loses everything he has ever known and is tossed into a world of magic. The Dragons, a group of rebel wizards, are threatening to expose the existence of magic to humans. Jacob is determined to find a way to fit into Emilia's family, but as his powers grow, so does the danger. With the death toll mounting, Jacob is accused of acts of rebel terrorism and must fight to stay in a world he's only just beginning to discover.

When Emilia's life is threatened, Jacob must risk everything to save her. Does he have the power to rescue her in time? And what could their survival cost?

Other books from Silence in the Library Publishing

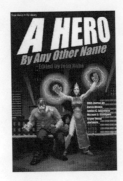

Founded in 2011 by a group of authors, Silence in the Library, LLC was established with the goal of creating an environment that allows authors, artists, editors, and other publishing professionals to work collaboratively to showcase their work. Our model keeps the creative decisions, throughout the publishing process, as close to the actual creators (i.e. authors and artists) as possible. Authors are deeply involved in their projects from start to finish. By closely controlling the quality of inputs to the process, we ensure a high level of quality in the final product while allowing space for imagination to flourish.

WWW.SILENCEINTHELIBRARYPUBLISHING.COM

Made in the USA
Lexington, KY
11 April 2014